A Very Large Consulate

By Howard R. Simpson

A Very Large Consulate

HOWARD R. SIMPSON

CRIME CLUB
Doubleday
NEW YORK   LONDON   TORONTO   SYDNEY   AUCKLAND

All of the characters in this book
are fictitious, and any resemblance
to actual persons, living or dead,
is purely coincidental.

A Crime Club Book
Published by Doubleday, a division of
Bantam Doubleday Dell Publishing Group, Inc.
666 Fifth Avenue, New York, New York 10103

Doubleday and the portrayal of
a man with a gun are trademarks of
Doubleday, a division of Bantam
Doubleday Dell Publishing Group, Inc.

Library of Congress Cataloging-in-Publication Data

Simpson, Howard R., 1925–
A very large consulate/Howard R. Simpson.—1st ed.
p.   cm.
I. Title.
PS3569.I49V4   1988
813'.54—dc19   88-3522
ISBN 0-385-24604-8

To Kate

A Very Large Consulate

I

The center of Marseille never sleeps. Only the residential districts become deserted after midnight. Lone vehicles speed through the streets in a brief flash of light, leaving darkness in their wake. Patrolling police vans make their slow rounds, radios spitting static while the bored voices of central operators catalogue break-ins, assaults and car thefts as if they were announcing football scores. Cats slink through the blind alleys in search of promising refuse and the occasional plump rat sprints from curb to gutter before disappearing down the grate-covered drains.

The rue Ambroise-Paré in the Perrier quarter was silent and empty. The windows of the walled villas and town houses were darkened, but bright security lights burned over the iron gate of No. 3 illuminating the large, tarpaulin-wrapped bundle lying in the driveway. A cab appeared on the Square Monticelli, its headlights throwing a temporary glow over the thick boles of the plane trees. The driver was on his way home. A game of belote had kept him out too late. Roland Fayoll was constructing a believable lie to avoid another painful scene with his wife. Swinging into the rue Ambroise-Paré he suddenly applied his brake.

"What's this?" he asked aloud, peering at the form in the driveway of the Soviet Consulate. Fayoll had a lively imagination. He guessed in seconds the probable contents of the bundle. "*Oh, la, la,* " he murmured, not liking what he saw. The rope-cinched black tarpaulin had the unmistakable proportions of a body. Fayoll scanned the street and glanced at his rearview mirror. No one in sight, only shadows. He eased his foot off the brake and pressed the accelerator. He knew any involvement would mean hours lost talking with the police. He slowed for a traffic light near the Avenue de Prado and took a cigarette from the packet on top of the dashboard. It was a stiff, no doubt about it. He frowned, nodding affirmatively. He had been right to drive on. A stiff in front of the Soviet Consulate? God knows what that could mean! The light changed and he turned right.

Fayoll cursed under his breath and drew deeply on the cigarette. He felt a pang of conscience. For a brief moment he considered going back but he thought of a better alternative. When he reached home he'd call the police without identifying himself. It was their business, not his.

Consul Viktor Popov's slumber was interrupted by the buzzing telephone. He rolled over, noted it was 5:22 A.M. and picked up the receiver. As duty officer for the consulate he expected off-hour calls. He guessed it could be a problem with some of the crew from the freighter *Zavotny*, which had arrived in the port of Marseille that morning.

"*Allo?*" Popov responded in French. "*Consulat Soviétique.*"

"Comrade Popov," an excited voice addressed him in Russian, "you must come to the office!"

"Who is this?" Popov demanded.

"It's Sheshin. We have a grave problem. You must come . . ."

"Calm yourself," Popov replied angrily. "Tell me what this is about."

"It would be better if I did not—on the telephone."

"Very well," Popov replied. "I'll be there soon."

He put down the phone and stared at it, trying to think. The call was most unusual. Sergeant Sheshin was a dependable man. He'd been detached from a Spetsnaz unit to serve in the consulate's communications section after being wounded in Afghanistan. He wasn't the type to panic in an emergency.

Popov groaned and pushed himself up off the bed. The two cognacs he'd had after Consul General Anisimov's dinner had disagreed with him. He stretched and walked groggily to the bathroom to throw some cold water on his face. Popov was a darkly handsome man of thirty-two. He was developing a belly from the food and drink consumed during his assignments to France. He'd made a resolution to cut down on his alcohol intake but it had proved impossible given the demands of his profession. His official assignment as press officer for the consulate meant he had to match glass for glass with the hard-drinking Marseille press corps. His prime task as contact with local Communist party leaders demanded an equally bibulous activity. He put two hands on the washbasin and looked at himself in the wall mirror: bloodshot eyes, mussed hair and a dark shadow of beard. He wasn't a pretty sight.

He reflected on Sheshin's call as he brushed his teeth. The more he thought about it the more angry he became. Surely Sheshin could have told him more. He should have demanded more details but he'd been too drugged by sleep. Maybe it was some stupid internal crisis: one of the code clerks arriving drunk on his shift, or Moscow demanding an overdue report on the activities of the oil refineries at Fos, or movements of the American 6th Fleet in French Mediterranean ports. He was sure it was something that could have waited until the consulate opened.

Popov decided not to shave. He was pulling on his shirt when the phone rang again. He hurried to the bedroom and picked up the receiver, primed to reprimand Sergeant Sheshin, but he remained silent. The authoritative voice of Anatole Zavorin, the consulate's cultural attaché, was cold and precise.

"Popov," Zavorin ordered, "get to the consulate immediately. Come in by the service entrance."

"Certainly," Popov responded, "I . . ." He didn't finish his sentence. Zavorin had already hung up. Popov buttoned his shirt and pulled on his socks. One did not argue with Comrade Zavorin's orders. His cultural duties were secondary to his role as KGB resident.

Inspecteur Principal Roger Bastide glanced at his watch as he drove up rue Paradis. It was almost 6 A.M. The police car he'd commandeered at headquarters had an electrical problem. Neither the red light nor the Klaxon worked. He had to take chances, speeding through waking streets and running traffic lights.

Bastide's salt and pepper hair was uncombed. Not fully awake, he blinked in the dawn light. He was wearing a heavy blue turtleneck sweater and he'd turned up the collar of his worn trench coat to protect him from the morning cold. The heavy holstered Manurhin .357 Magnum on his right hip pressed into his back. He eased it forward, wishing he'd had time for a cup of espresso before leaving his apartment. Homicide work, he thought ruefully, required night owls. Murderers could kill in daylight, but they usually dumped their handiwork in darkness. The call from the police switchboard had rousted him out of bed with the cryptic message that a corpse was lying in the driveway of the Soviet Consulate. He would have taken his time on a normal call. *Macchabées* usually stayed put and undue haste was unnecessary. He knew this would be different. Murder victims rarely appeared in consulate driveways. The fact that it had been discovered in front of the Soviet Consulate had already made it a special case.

He swung his car left on the Avenue Frédéric Mistral, crossed the Place Monticelli and braked to a stop in front of the consulate. A police van and an ambulance were already there. As he slammed the door he could hear shouting and recognized the voice of Inspector "Babar" Mattei, his Corsican assistant.

"Non et non," Mattei was bellowing. "He stays right here!"

Bastide pushed his way past some uniformed police and put his hand on Babar's shoulder.

"What the hell is going on?" he demanded.

Mattei spun around, purple-faced, and recognized his boss.

"Ah, *patron*," he said, a note of relief in his voice. "This idiot . . ." he explained, pointing to an unshaven man in a rumpled suit, "was trying to move the victim next door."

Bastide glanced at the corpse. Someone had untied the ropes over the upper part of the body and pulled back the tarpaulin. A shock of blond hair was showing.

"Monsieur," the man in the gate appealed to Bastide in perfect French, "my name is Viktor Popov. I am a Soviet consul. This man is being unreasonable."

"I am Inspector Bastide and this is Inspector Mattei," Bastide snapped, "and he is not being unreasonable. The body is not to be touched. This case is our responsibility."

Popov was mentally cursing Anatole Zavorin. It had been Zavorin's idea to shift the body from its place in front of the consulate. Popov knew he was in trouble. A cold sweat was prickling his neck. He guessed Zavorin was watching from one of the upper-floor windows of the consulate. The thought infuriated him.

Bastide had not dealt with foreign consular officials since the McCallister case. He knew the intricacies of diplomatic immunity were full of pitfalls for the unwary. He made an effort to reduce the tension. He asked Mattei to supervise the forensic technicians who were busy around the tarpaulin and addressed Popov in a calm, businesslike manner.

"Why," Bastide inquired, "were you moving the corpse?"

"I . . . was only clearing the driveway," Popov told him.

"He was trying to dump him in front of the next villa," Mattei interjected from a distance.

Bastide ignored Mattei's comment. Two cars had stopped across the street. Curious gawkers were inching closer to the group of policemen. Some local residents had joined them.

"Perhaps," Bastide suggested, nodding toward the consulate, "we could go inside to talk."

"That would be impossible," Popov said quickly, moving between Bastide and the consulate gate.

"As you wish," Bastide replied. "Why did you untie the rope?"

"I only wished to help this person," Popov replied. "I thought he might still be alive."

"Was he?"

"No, not at all."

"Do you know him?"

Popov covered his mouth with his hand and belched. He made a special effort to control his nerves. He had already said too much. Bastide's hazel eyes narrowed as he waited for a reply to his question.

"Well?" he finally asked.

"*Monsieur l'Inspecteur,*" Popov said, "I will answer no further questions until I've discussed this matter with the consul general."

Bastide sensed Mattei's heavy presence behind him. "Let's take the bastard in," Mattei suggested. "We're wasting time here."

"*Ferme ta gueule,*" Bastide ordered. "Take the cold meat to the morgue so Dr. Colona can go to work." He took the Russian's arm and led him a few paces away.

"*Monsieur le Consul,*" Bastide said, "I am sure you want to cooperate. We certainly don't want a diplomatic incident. It will only take an hour of your time, at the most."

"No," Popov said firmly, shaking his head. "I am a Soviet diplomat. You have no right to order or coerce me in any way.

You have my name. I shall remain here. Once I have spoken with my superiors I will be glad to assist you if I can."

Bastide stepped back, sizing up Popov. The Russian was nervous. He was pill-rolling with the thumb and forefinger of each hand. He'd obviously been pulled out of bed hurriedly with no time to shave or dress properly.

"I'd like to speak to your consul general," Bastide said.

"That is impossible," Popov told him. "I am going inside now. You have no right to detain me." He turned and walked toward the consulate's entrance.

"Laurent!" Bastide called to the police photographer working with the forensic experts, pointed to Popov and mimed taking a photo. The photographer hurried to his side.

"Monsieur Popov!" Bastide shouted.

Popov turned and the photographer's strobe flashed, freezing Popov's image with one hand on the iron gate. Bastide smiled, turned and walked to the ambulance, where Mattei was supervising the corpse's removal.

"What's it look like?" Bastide asked.

"Oh, can I talk now?" Mattei responded sarcastically. "Or are you afraid I might hurt the Russkov's feelings?"

"*Ça va,*" Bastide said. "Your elephant hide isn't that sensitive. Did you take a good look at the victim?"

"Blond, blue eyes, about thirty-five. I didn't want to unwrap the gift package till we got to the morgue. There's no visible blood or wound."

"How long's he been dead?"

"I'd say hours, not days."

The ambulance doors banged shut and the driver looked at Bastide, waiting for permission to leave.

"Babar," Bastide said, "ride in with the *macchabée.* I don't want any unauthorized person near it."

"You know something I don't?" Mattei asked.

"No, but this already smells of complications and trouble. Get back to the office as soon as Colona finishes his butchering and bring me the results."

"*À vos ordres, Chef!*" Mattei barked, flipping Bastide an exaggerated, openhanded salute. "How about my *bagnole?*"

"I'll have a uniform take it back to the motor pool."

Bastide watched the ambulance pull away from the curve. He could see Mattei sitting across from the litter through the pebbled glass of the rear windows. He turned toward the consulate. The blood-red flag with its gold hammer and sickle was billowing in the wind. He wasn't sure if it had been there all the time or if someone had just run it up the pole. He watched two uniformed policemen stretching a yellow plastic band from tree to tree, enclosing the area where the body had been found. It was obvious that any vehicle leaving or entering the consulate would have to wait for the band to be removed. He summoned a young detective assigned to remain at the scene.

"Get the plate number of all cars entering or leaving the consulate," he ordered. "Note how many people are in each car. Try to jot down their physical description. Did you see the Russian I was talking with?"

"I did."

"Good. Contact me by radio if you see him leave and follow him. I'll call in now and have Lenoir join you here. He can take over the tailing. Send Mattei's car to the Hôtel de Police. Understood?"

"Parfaitement, Monsieur l'Inspecteur Principal."

The bright lights of the police morgue were giving Mattei a headache. He'd turned his back on the stainless-steel dissecting table and Dr. Colona. The doctor would have to wait a statutory twenty-four hours before cutting while the police attempted to contact the deceased's family or friends. For the moment he was trying to winnow out any clues that might indicate the cause, time and circumstances of death. Mattei had no particular sensibilities when it came to the dead, but like Bastide, he'd not yet had his breakfast. The sight of the stocky, bald-headed doctor probing the gray corpse with his rubber-gloved fingers was too much for Mattei so early in the morning. Mattei could hear Colona's stentorious breathing broken occasionally by his deep-throated smoker's cough.

"The body has a surface integrity that indicates a lack of violence," Colona said. "I've scoured every inch of him: not a bruise, not a pinprick. The ears are sound, the eyes normal for a dead man; the anus unscarred and the penis okay; the mouth shows no abnormalities. All orifices are accounted for."

Mattei turned and walked over to the table. The dead man's mouth was partially open, showing even, white teeth. The thick blond hair was mussed from Colona's examination of the scalp. The open eyes were pale blue and dulled by a glaucous film. There were no rings, no watch, no tattoos, nothing to serve as a link to the outside world.

"Hold on," Colona said, bending over the corpse, sniffing at the mouth. "Here," he told Mattei, "smell this."

Mattei grimaced but did what the doctor asked. He sniffed and pulled back. "What the hell is that?" he asked.

"Bitter almond," Colona said triumphantly. "I'd say our friend has inhaled a lethal dose of hydrocyanic acid. He would have been lucky to live for two minutes. It's likely he said his adieu in one minute's time."

Colona inhaled again and nodded his head affirmatively. He snapped off his rubber gloves, poked a cigarette into his mouth and flicked his lighter.

"He didn't swallow the stuff?" Mattei asked.

"It's possible, but I doubt it. If you gulp cyanide, death comes more slowly. It can take up to several hours. That would have been inconvenient for his murderers."

"Now you're saying it's murder."

"In light of the evidence, yes."

"I've heard of cyanide suicides," Mattei argued.

"But few suicides package themselves for delivery," Colona replied.

"When can you confirm it?"

"I'll call you after I've gone inside," Colona told him, exhaling smoke from both nostrils. "Allow me to put this new arrival on ice and I'll buy you a *café crème* and a croissant."

"Sorry," Mattei replied, "I can't. Bastide's waiting for me."

"Tant pis," Colona said, preparing to roll the corpse onto a dolly. Mattei blew his nose as he left the morgue, but the odor of bitter almonds remained in his nostrils.

Roger Bastide stopped in the drafty police canteen before going to his office. He stood at the counter to gulp a scalding espresso and eat a flabby, cellophane-wrapped concoction full of seedy raisins labeled "cake." Since his promotion to Inspecteur Principal, he'd had a number of ordinary cases. It now seemed his luck had changed. He was intrigued with the tarpaulin-wrapped corpse. He ordered a second espresso. He knew he would have to report to Commissaire Aynard as soon as Aynard arrived at the Hôtel de Police. The commissaire was Bastide's *bête noire* but he had to be informed of what had happened before the Préfecture and the Ministry of the Interior in Paris got on the telephone.

The young girl who served his coffee smiled and took his fifty-franc note to make change. Bastide reminded her of Cary Grant, an actor she'd never heard of until her parents had brought home some videocassette films. There wasn't much substance to her romantic parallel. Bastide was shorter, huskier. His broken nose, the legacy of a brawl in Oran when he was serving in a parachute regiment, put him closer in appearance to Jean-Paul Belmondo. If his thick black mustache had not been well trimmed, he might have doubled as a gunfighter in a spaghetti Western.

"You're in early today," the waitress said, moistening her lips and smoothing her blouse to display her ample charms as she returned the change.

"What? Oh, yes," Bastide replied, noticing her for the first time. "A lot of work to do," he said, returning her smile before hurrying toward the wide, stained stairway of the Hôtel de Police.

The little coquette is making a play for me, he thought. Just what I don't need. He smiled, resolving to tell Janine when they met for dinner that evening. He forgot the waitress and Janine when he pushed open the door of his office and found Jacques Boniface of the Direction de la Surveillance du Territoire sitting on his desk.

Boniface was the counterespionage service's liaison with the Marseille police. He was always eager to pry information from his police contacts but it was usually a one-way street. The few times Bastide had requested help from Boniface he'd been served platitudes about sensitive material and state secrets.

"*Bonjour, ami!*" Boniface greeted Bastide effusively. "I'm glad to see someone in this country club gets to his office early."

Bastide slung his jacket over the back of a chair, took a Cuban Partago from a breast pocket, clipped the end with a cigar cutter and struck a match. He waited for Boniface to explain his visit. Boniface was a beefy man with hard, close-set eyes. They didn't go with his set smile.

"We're interested in what happened at 3 rue Ambroise-Paré," he told Bastide. "We may soon take the case off your hands."

"Oh?" Bastide replied, settling slowly behind his desk and drawing on the cigar.

"Do you have an identity yet?" Boniface asked.

"No. Nothing. Do you?"

Boniface laughed. "Let's stop sparring," he suggested. "Everything indicates a political motive . . ."

"Not at all," Bastide cut in. "The fact a body was found in front of the Soviet Consulate proves nothing."

Boniface's smile faded. "Listen, Bastide," he said, "we expect full cooperation from you. This could be of the highest priority and importance."

"Boniface," Bastide countered, "you've been around here long enough to know the proper procedures. If you have instructions from your boss in Paris, you should be talking to the Préfet de Police or the commissaire. That's the chain of command. They pass their orders on to me. You're starting at the wrong end of the pyramid."

"Voyons, " Boniface said, sitting back in his chair, his smile reappearing. "You and I are the people who do the real work. I only thought it would save time if we cooperated from the start."

"Tell me," Bastide asked, "how did you get on to this so fast?"

"Professionalism," Boniface replied.

"I see. Well, as we're talking priority, importance and professionalism, I suggest you begin at a higher level. It will make things easier for everyone."

"If that's what you want," Boniface said, getting up slowly, buttoning his wrinkled houndstooth jacket. "I'll be back."

"I'm sure you will," Bastide said, watching the DST man leave the office. "Con!" Bastide murmured as the door clicked shut. His experience told him that if the DST was already salivating over the case, the DGSE would not be far behind. Although the DST was charged with domestic investigations, he knew the Direction Générale de la Sécurité Extérieure would soon be involved. Their charter was supposedly limited to overseas operations but that was only a myth to feed prying politicians and the public. It was almost time to see Commissaire Aynard. Bastide walked to the window. Wisps of milky clouds drifted by high over the sea. Several trailer-trucks were lined up on the Quai de la Joliette waiting to board a ro-ro ferry. A Norwegian freighter was making its way slowly into the port, its bow cutting a creamy wave through the slack water. He expected it would rain before noon. It had been a strange spring.

Vasili Aleksandrovich Anisimov carefully put down his glass of strong tea on a cork coaster so it wouldn't make a ring on his highly polished desk. The consul general had summoned Anatole Zavorin and Viktor Popov to an emergency meeting. He removed his heavy-framed reading glasses and placed them on top of some official papers.

"We have a real problem," he said, isolating each word for emphasis. "There are television crews out on the street, photographers trying to sneak in our rear gate, and my telephone has been ringing all morning." He turned to Popov. "Have you drafted the message for Moscow?" he asked.

"Yes, Comrade Consul General, it is on your desk at the top of those papers."

"Excellent, Viktor, excellent. We'll send it the moment we're finished. I don't know what they'll suggest, but it's better to keep everyone informed, is that not right, Zavorin?"

"I agree," Zavorin replied.

"Of course, they will require answers," Anisimov continued, "answers that I don't think we can provide . . . or can we? Comrade Zavorin?"

"We have no way of knowing who the man might have been," Zavorin said, leaning forward in his chair. "We will have to wait now till the French authorities attempt to identify the body."

The consul general drank his tea and nodded. "Why would someone place him in front of our consulate?" he asked. "I take it neither of you has an idea or a suspicion?"

Zavorin and Popov shook their heads. Anisimov marveled at his own ability to remain calm. In eighteen months he was due for retirement, a pension, a dacha on the Black Sea and the gratitude of his government for a record of long and faithful service. His career had been unmarked by blemishes of any kind, and now this.

"Comrade Popov," he said in a more official tone, "can you tell me why you attempted to move the body?"

Popov cleared his throat and glanced sideways at Zavorin. The KGB resident's walleye was fixed on the colored photo of Gorbachev hanging on the wall behind the consul general's chair.

"It was a mistake," Popov said weakly, examining his shoe tops. "I wanted to avoid embarrassment for the consulate."

"You achieved just the opposite," Anisimov said dryly. "When one is on post, one must avoid involvement and suspicion. That is a cardinal rule. Have you never learned that?"

"Yes, Comrade Consul General," Popov replied, swallowing hard.

"Well," Anisimov said with an air of resignation, "spilled vodka won't go back in the bottle. But listen carefully. You are not to speak with the press. Have your secretary refer them to the French police. Remember, we know nothing. As a matter of fact, that is the absolute truth."

Anisimov read the message Popov had drafted and handed it back to him. "Take this," he said, "and send it quickly. Comrade Zavorin, I would like you to stay for a moment."

Anisimov waited for the door to close behind Popov before he spoke to Zavorin. He opened an embossed silver box and offered a cigarette of dark tobacco to the cultural attaché. Zavorin declined and watched the consul general light his own.

"Zavorin," Anisimov finally said, "we have been together here for over two years now. You have your work, I have mine. Our cooperation has been exemplary. Both my diplomatic superiors and your people on Dzerzhinsky Square are pleased. Comrade, I have a question to ask you and I expect you to answer it truthfully. Is this murder in any way involved with your activities and do you know anything at all about it?"

"Comrade Anisimov," Zavorin lied, "I assure you I have no knowledge of this affair."

André de Coursin stood at the rain-lashed window of his office at the headquarters of the Direction Générale de la Sécurité Extérieure on the Boulevard Mortier and thought about the disagreeable Paris weather. It was mid-May, but he hadn't seen a patch of blue sky for five days. The lowering, yellow-tinted grayness of the capital had a depressing effect. You could sense it in the way people moved, the way they spoke and the way they snapped at each other.

His office was on an upper floor of what the initiated called *"la crémerie"* or *"la boîte"* and what the press had baptized *"la piscine,"* because of the swimming pool across the street. As a senior officer de Coursin enjoyed certain privileges, including the right to superior furnishings. The imitation chairs looked almost real, the copy of a Louis XIV table had a certain majesty and the heavy crystal ashtrays were from a well-known company. The floor was carpeted and two colorful Dufy prints brightened the room. A heavy security safe had been placed against the inner wall, its exterior camouflaged by a formica door painted to resemble grained wood. It looked more like a bar cabinet than a safe. His desk was of African hardwood, a gift to some DGSE officer from an African Prime Minister. De Coursin's administrative assistant had found it in a basement storage room. Its polished surface was bare except for a clock, a calendar, a pen set and a small pile of classified dossiers. Except for the prints the beige walls were bare. No commissions, no awards, no photographs to link the room with its occupant or hide the peeling paint over the radiator or the water stains near the window.

De Coursin's silver hair was neatly cropped and his tailored gray suit was set off by a blue silk tie with thin red stripes and the red *tomate* of the Legion of Honor in his lapel. He was a tall man with a soldier's bearing. His dark eyes looked tired as he watched the comings and goings in the courtyard below. He thought of the plaque in that courtyard, a simple monument to the dead of the DGSE decorated with a few rain-soaked flowers. There were no names on the plaque. The dead of France's intelligence service were destined to remain anonymous. De Coursin allowed himself the luxury of remembrance for a few moments. A slow smile spread over his tanned face as he recalled some old friends, those of the Service Action who would never return.

De Coursin glanced at the wall clock. He'd called the meeting for 11 A.M. Only ten minutes to wait. He was expecting Giraud from the Ministry of the Interior, Delglade from the Direction de

Surveillance du Territoire and Morel from his own Service Action. De Coursin had made a special point of keeping the number of attendants to a minimum. He wanted the meeting to be short. Reaching for his reading glasses, he opened the gray dossier on his desk. It contained detailed information on the staff of the Soviet Consulate General in Marseille. Vasili Aleksandrovich Anisimov, the consul general, headed the list. A smiling mug shot revealed his stainless-steel incisor. De Coursin's forefinger ran over Anisimov's biography. He was not particularly interested in Anisimov. The man was a career consular officer. His wartime record had shielded him from political upheavals and purges within the Soviet diplomatic corps. According to the file, Anisimov was looking forward to a quiet retirement. He passed quickly over the listing on Viktor Popov, the consul. Popov's birth in Paris of Russian parents and his long service in France made him a good candidate for an eventual "turning" attempt, but that would be well in the future.

De Coursin was primarily interested in Anatole Zavorin, the consulate's cultural attaché. When he came to the details on Zavorin, he put both hands palm down on his desktop and leaned over the dossier. Zavorin was well known to de Coursin. His knowledge of the KGB resident in Marseille was based on innumerable verbal and written reports, wire and electronic taps, clandestine films and photographs. Zavorin's latest file photo had been taken recently by a DGSE stakeout in Marseille as the Russian was leaving a restaurant after lunch. The lab had enlarged the image and cropped the background to obtain a head shot. It was a little grainy but detailed enough to illustrate Zavorin's striking walleyed condition and reflect something of the man's intensity. He reminded de Coursin of Jean-Paul Sartre.

De Coursin noted the last entry on Zavorin. It referred to a recent intercept of a Zavorin telegram. He flipped several pages till he came to a reference tab and read a translated summary. The message to Moscow detailed the current state of the French Communist party in Marseille, enumerated its strengths and weaknesses, delved into the personal foibles of its leaders and ended with a brief prediction of the party's probable showing in an upcoming regional election. It was a precise, masterful job of analysis—one that de Coursin couldn't fault.

He flipped back to the biographic listings, turning the pages slowly. The Soviets had eight career officers assigned to the consulate in Marseille and double that number of "administrative personnel." The DST had many of them tagged as intelligence agents, some of them under surveillance. De Coursin knew the Soviets considered Marseille one of their most important listening posts on the Mediterranean, but they did tend to exaggerate things. It was definitely a very large consulate.

Antoine Morel was first to arrive in de Coursin's office. He was a broad-shouldered, solid man of fifty with short-cropped auburn hair. His muscular torso seemed to threaten the seams of his tight suit jacket. Morel looked out on the cloudy world of clandestine operations through amber-tinted glasses. He handled the nuts and bolts of the Service Action with the sure hand and the calm determination of one who'd earned his position in the field. He was carrying a classified file under his arm.

"I'm glad you came early," de Coursin said as they shook hands. "I want you to remain once we've finished. There are aspects of this Marseille business that our colleagues have no need to know. I'll explain later."

"Very well," Morel replied, sitting down in a straight-backed chair. He was a man of few words. The two minutes before Pierre Delglade's arrival passed in silence. Delglade was a small dark man with the air of someone holding the key to many secrets. He was known in intelligence circles as *le limier*, the bloodhound, for his expertise in successfully pursuing suspects. His relations with de Coursin were cool. Despite repeated lip service to cooperation between the DST and the DGSE, both organizations remained rivals. The de Coursin-Delglade relationship reflected this professional rivalry and fueled a long-standing personal antagonism. De Coursin eyed Delglade's obtrusive light suit with disapproval as the DST official exchanged pleasantries with Morel.

Yvon Giraud was eight minutes late. He made his apologies while hanging up his expensive camel hair coat and putting his leather briefcase on the conference table. He fell into an empty chair and began filling his pipe, his chubby fingers spilling strands of brown tobacco onto the gray carpeting. He had the plump face of a gourmand and his effusiveness tempered the seriousness of the meeting. De Coursin fitted a cigarette into his onyx holder, lit it and blew some smoke toward the ceiling.

"Gentlemen," he began, "thank you for coming. We are here to discuss the incident in Marseille, the body found in front of the Soviet Consulate. It could be a sick joke. It could be a deliberate attempt to embarrass the Soviets or our own government. Whatever it turns out to be, the act has an unfortunate political significance. Because of its possible intelligence links, the Élysées and the Matignon have asked me to coordinate things here—for the moment."

Pierre Delglade shifted in his chair and glanced in Giraud's direction. He was obviously not pleased with the situation. Normally, the DST would be charged with such an investigation as it had occurred on French soil. De Coursin sensed Delglade's displeasure.

"If," he continued, "subsequent information clarifies the motives and identity of those involved, I am to turn over the case to either the DST or the Ministry. In fact, Giraud, we would like the Police Judiciaire in Marseille to continue their work for the moment as if this were a simple homicide."

"Simple homicide?" Delglade exclaimed. "That won't wash for long. It stinks of a hit tied to espionage."

De Coursin pointed his cigarette holder at Delglade.

"Exactly," he agreed, "and that is why we don't want to rush in with unmarked vehicles full of your *barbouzes* until we have more definite information. Now, what can you tell me?"

Delglade cleared his throat. "The Soviet Consulate in Marseille is under our surveillance. . . ."

"Too bad you didn't have someone on the street this morning," Giraud commented.

"The KGB resident in Marseille, Anatole Zavorin, holds a high rank," Delglade continued. "The Marseille Consulate is an important post for them. . . ."

"Excuse me, Delglade," de Coursin interrupted, "but do you have anything on the dead man? Possible identification? Motive for the killing? The reason he was dumped where he was?"

"May I remind you," Delglade responded, "it has only been a few hours since the body was discovered. The DST is not officially involved in the murder investigation. We are not in the habit of pushing aside the police when they're still responsible for a case."

Giraud smiled and winked at Morel.

"I know, I know," de Coursin said, "but as your men watch the Soviets on a twenty-four-hour basis, I thought you might have some ideas. Is there any current activity that could be linked to the packaged corpse?"

"No," Delglade replied.

"Then why do you say it's an espionage matter?"

"Come now," Delglade said, "none of us are infants. We know a Soviet consul was first on the scene; that he tampered with the corpse and tried to move it. He obviously had no intention of calling the police. Why did he take such a risk if it wasn't important to them?"

"Perhaps he panicked?" Giraud suggested. "Was the person in question KGB?"

"Not according to our files," de Coursin replied.

"Nor ours," Delglade added.

"And the police?" de Coursin addressed Giraud. "What is new with them?"

"Commissaire Aynard called me just before I came over here," Giraud told them. "There is nothing new. They're waiting for the coroner's report."

"Who's heading the investigation?" de Coursin asked.

"Inspecteur Principal Bastide."

"Ah, Bastide," de Coursin said, "I remember him. I met him during the McCallister case. He's a good man. I'm glad to hear he's been promoted."

"He's a tough nut and a good *flic*," Giraud commented.

De Coursin tightened the knot of his tie. "Well," he said, "it appears none of us has much to contribute. I . . . ."

A knock interrupted him. The door opened and a young DGSE officer hesitated before stepping into de Coursin's office.

"What is it, Baur?" de Coursin asked.

"Urgent telephone message for Monsieur Giraud," he said, nodding at the phone on de Coursin's desk.

"Thank you," de Coursin said. "Would you prefer a private line?" he asked Giraud.

"No, I'll take it here."

De Coursin pushed the phone across the desk toward Giraud and busied himself dislodging the cigarette butt from its holder. Delglade took a notebook from his pocket and flicked through it. Morel sat calmly with both hands on his knees, his face without expression.

Giraud finished his conversation, replaced the receiver and returned the phone to its place. "The coroner's report cites cyanide inhalation as the cause of death. He estimated the time at three or four hours before the dump. The fingerprint and dental data will be on its way to us soon."

De Coursin rubbed his chin, thinking. Cyanide was a universal poison, but intelligence services now had other more practical, less traceable potions for elimination purposes.

"There is something else," Giraud said. "The Soviet embassy has contacted the Ministry to complain of our handling of the case in Marseille. It seems Bastide's assistant 'insulted' the consul, who specializes in moving corpses. The Quai d'Orsay is expecting a diplomatic protest. They're wetting their pants over there."

"It won't be the first time," de Coursin said wryly. "I don't think there's any more to discuss. Thank you for coming. We shall be in touch. The key word now is 'cooperation.' "

De Coursin saw Giraud and Delglade to the door and shut it after them. As he returned to his desk, lightning flashed in the sky, followed by a low rumbling and the crack of thunder.

"The gods are angry," de Coursin said, sitting down. "Very well, Morel, tell me a story."

Morel opened his file, adjusted his tinted glasses and began to speak in a slow, deliberate tone.

"We have every reason to believe that the dead man is Grigori Drankov, alias Jean LeCompte. He was a young GRU officer working in Addis Ababa in 1980 when he first came to our notice as a possible target. He was watched carefully for two and a half years. Léger's team turned him in Egypt in 1983. He worked for us in Egypt and later in Algiers. In early 1985 we had indications that both the KGB and the GRU had become suspicious. This was later confirmed. We got him out of Algiers and put him in isolation for six months at our 'farm' near Pau. In January '86, after the usual screening, he was put to work in Section D evaluating our dossiers on GRU officers and interviewing defectors. It seemed he was doing a competent job. Six months later we sent him to Lyon to mother hen a Ukrainian defector from a Soviet scientific delegation. Two months after that, we received a signal from one of our agents in Moscow warning that Drankov had done another flip. Close surveillance confirmed Moscow's warning. Drankov, alias Jean LeCompte, had turned triple agent. The bastard was being run by a KGB control out of Marseille. I think you know the rest."

"I do," de Coursin said, "but refresh my memory."

"A termination order was sent to my office," Morel continued. "A *trois zéro* team was charged with the mission on April 8, 1987."

"And?" de Coursin demanded, fitting another cigarette into his holder.

"And, as of today, we have this mess to contend with."

De Coursin shook his head slowly. "Who is responsible?" he demanded.

"As section chief I take full responsibility," Morel said calmly.

"*Bon Dieu!*" de Coursin exploded. "Don't use that official jargon with me. I want to know the name of the cretin who delivered the body to the consulate!"

"I am not yet sure," Morel replied solemnly.

"But you have a damn good idea?"

"It might be Léon Faubert. Up to now he's been solid and dependable. He was in charge of the team. But he may have psychological problems."

"May have?" de Coursin barked. "He is undoubtedly a 'nutter,' as our British colleagues would say. Are you in touch with this crazy man?"

"I've already ordered him to Paris."

"Amend the order. We don't want him in the capital. Send him and his team to the Pau farm and keep them under guard. This is a *bavure* of the first order. If any of this leaks, you and I can count on a reduced pension and plenty of time to grow our own beets. How many others are involved?"

"My deputy, Levallois, the section's armorer and my secretary."

"We can't lock up everyone in Pau," de Coursin said, getting up to pace the floor. "I depend on you to impose total and complete silence."

"They will say nothing, I promise."

"Make sure of that," de Coursin ordered. "I also want to know just what twisted logic prompted Faubert to act the idiot, and I want a full verbal report on your talk with him. From this moment on there are to be no internal papers on what you and I have just discussed."

"Understood," Morel replied.

"Now get out," de Coursin said, massaging his temple with one hand. "You've given me a headache."

Once alone, de Coursin walked to his safe, opened it and reached past the stacked dossiers and a 9-mm Browning automatic for the bottle of fine Champagne cognac he kept there for special occasions. He poured a generous measure into a Baccarat snifter and returned to his desk. Sipping the cognac, he made a quick analysis on the LeCompte case, breaking it down in numerical order. First of all, the dead man and everything about him must be buried. Secondly, the police should be allowed to handle the whole affair and no other intelligence agency should be involved. Third, a plausible "structure" for the murder would have to be devised and fed to the police through secondary contacts. Fourth, and most important, he must sell his plan to the director of the DGSE. If the patron agreed, it would then be his decision whether or not to inform the Minister of the Interior.

De Coursin snapped on his desk light and watched the light play on the crystal prisms of his glass. He thought about Léon Faubert. If Morel was correct and Faubert had been responsible for dumping LeCompte's body in front of the consulate, the man was a loose cannon on a slippery deck. He pondered the reasons behind such an irresponsible action. The exterminating angels of the Service Action had always been a problem. Their psychological makeup was an uncertain quantity—a taut, highly tuned mechanism prone to sudden burnouts. Strained nerves, repressed complexes and constant pressure sometimes broke the machinery. When this happened, the damage they could do was inestimable.

Janine Bourdet was sitting at a table on the glassed-in terrace of the New York on the Quai des Belges. She was nursing her Kir, watching the flow of hurrying pedestrians as she waited for Bastide. He was already twenty minutes late, but that wasn't unusual. Police business had no set hours. She'd read of the body found in front of the Soviet Consulate in *Le Soir*, the evening paper. She was certain Bastide was already deeply involved. The event had been bannered on the front page under the head "*Mort Mystérieuse Chez les Soviétiques.*" The few facts in the story had been embellished with sensational conjecture hinting at intrigue and speculating on the "possible" involvement of the KGB and "other" intelligence agencies.

Janine sipped her drink and sighed. Two well-dressed young men passing on the sidewalk slowed their pace. She could feel their eyes on her and she looked away. Sitting alone on a café terrace was always a hazard for an attractive woman. Janine Bourdet was particularly appealing. Her dark eyes, short, jet-black hair and large, sensuous mouth were enough to catch any man's attention, and her voluptuous, small-waisted figure was guaranteed to hold it. A waiter brought a small plate of green olives and she munched on them, hoping that Bastide wouldn't be too long.

He arrived ten minutes later, out of breath. They kissed and he caught the waiter's eye, ordering a *pastis*.

"Don't tell me," she said with a broad smile. "You've been with the Russians."

"This morning I was," he replied. "I've been at the office ever since."

"*Le Soir* says it's a great mystery."

"It is," Bastide replied as the waiter arrived with his drink.

She recognized a familiar symptom. Bastide was not really with her. This often happened when he was on a particularly difficult case. She decided to change the subject.

"Do you like my new dress?" she asked.

"What? Oh, yes, it's quite chic."

"You approve?"

"It's a good fit," he told her, "in all the right places."

"Théo insisted I go out and buy a dress," she said. "The older he gets, the more generous he is." Janine had been Théo Gautier's mistress. Now that the aged Marseille industrialist had become a semi-invalid, she'd become his companion and surrogate daughter. Gautier knew Bastide was Janine's lover and he didn't object. He was a practical man. He knew he'd lose her completely if he did. Bastide was also a realist. He'd never met Gautier, but listening to Janine describe his kindness to her he'd developed a certain sympathy for the old man.

Janine continued to make small talk, knowing that most of it was lost on Bastide. He was replaying the meeting with Aynard in his mind. The dyspeptic commissaire had blanched when Bastide reported on the events at the Soviet Consulate. He had reacted bureaucratically, listing the hazards involved, including the need for Bastide to consider the diplomatic side of the affair. He had warned Bastide not to offend any of the consulate staff and had expressed a fervent wish that the DST would take over the case. When Bastide told him that Boniface had paid him an early morning visit, the commissaire became particularly agitated, torn between relief that the DST was already showing interest and resentment that Boniface had not gone through the proper channels.

"Allo, allo!" Janine's voice cut into his thoughts. "You planning to solve the case here tonight?"

"I'm sorry," Bastide said, gulping his *pastis*. "Let's eat."

The New York had been an excellent but expensive restaurant frequented by businessmen on generous expense accounts, but recession had thinned the clientele to the point where there had been more waiters looking out at the Vieux Port than clients eating within. The patron had decided to adjust to the times. He'd turned his establishment into a *brasserie*, maintained the same quality and dropped his prices. His waiters were now busy and the New York was crowded.

They dined on a *salade niçoise* and an unctuous *brochette de moules* accompanied by a bottle of white Palette. Once they'd selected their cheese and ordered a small bottle of red Palette to go with it, Janine abandoned her attempts to distract Bastide.

"Soit," she announced, "so be it. You're interested in nothing but your case. Let's talk about it."

"Not with dinner," he grumbled.

"Don't make me laugh," she said irritably. "That's all I've had with my dinner. I could have had a livelier time at home with a poached egg. And don't tell me you're sorry again!"

He put down his knife and took her hand. "Let's go to my apartment now," he suggested.

She shook one long-nailed finger in front of his face like a metronome. "No, you don't," she chided him. "Eating with an absent man is bad enough. Making love to one is insupportable."

"You're not staying with me tonight?" he asked, surprised.

"No," she told him, rising to pull on her coat. "You obviously need to think." She bent over to kiss him. *"Bonsoir, chéri,"* she murmured before striding from the restaurant under the admiring but puzzled gaze of their waiter.

"Is everything all right?" the waiter asked.

"Fine," Bastide responded gruffly. "Just fine. Bring me an Armagnac, if you will."

The waiter hurried to the bar to fill his order. Bastide sat back in his chair and reached into his jacket pocket for a Partago. His frown faded as he thought about Janine's show of pique. He found himself chuckling. The case of the consulate body had hardly begun, and it had already cost him a night with Janine. But she was right. It would have been a waste of time for both of them. As he left the New York, it began to rain.

II

Inspector Mattei listened to Jean Lenoir with growing impatience. "You can find cyanide in fumigants and it's used in photo processing," the young detective was telling him. "It's also in silver polish. Only three hundred milligrams of potassium cyanide and it's goodbye." He opened his notebook and began reading. "The extreme toxicity of cyanide is due to its ready reaction with the trivalent iron of cytochrome oxidase. . . ."

"*Basta!*" Mattei demanded, holding up his hand. "Just tell me what you learned about outlets."

"Hydrogen cyanide is a bit different," Lenoir began.

"Would it be difficult to obtain?" Mattei asked.

"Not particularly," Lenoir replied.

"That's all I want to know," Mattei said, folding his husky arms and frowning. Lenoir seemed to be in a little world of his own, a modern Candide untouched by reality. "I'm going to the Soviet Consulate with Bastide," Mattei said. "You cover here. If any journalists call, refer them to the press office. Don't volunteer anything, particularly where we are. Got it?"

"Yes, Inspector," Lenoir replied, smoothing his sparse blond mustache.

"You can also call Montpellier, Toulon, Perpignan and Nice. Fill them in on the case. Check to see if they have anything in their working files on deaths from cyanide."

Mattei stood up, adjusted the Magnum on his right hip and pulled on his blazer. It needed a cleaning and one of the brass buttons was missing. He glanced at his reflection in the window and smoothed his wavy black hair. Even after a long, happy marriage and six children Mattei dreamed of new female conquests and worried about his weight. Lenoir picked up the telephone and began to dial the number of the Police Judiciaire in Perpignan. Mattei waved a quick goodbye from the doorway.

Bastide was waiting for Mattei outside the Préfecture on the Place Felix Baret. He'd been speaking with Patrice Lombard, the officer charged with the security of foreign consulates. Mattei pulled the police sedan to the curb. Bastide climbed in beside him and slammed the door.

"Well?" Mattei asked, heading into the traffic. "Any luck?"

"No," Bastide told him. "They're too busy worrying about the Armenian threat to the Turkish Consulate. Aside from an occasional demonstration or some crank calls the Soviets haven't had any trouble."

"Who do they deal with *chez les Russes?*"

"The vice consul in charge of administrative affairs. They say he's a nothing."

"Not a real security man?"

"Who knows?" Bastide said. "Lombard considers all of them KGB and waits for them to prove otherwise. I wonder what Consul Popov will have to say to us?"

"Better yet, what are you going to ask him?"

"I want to know what he was doing out on the street at six in the morning manhandling a stiff. That's hardly a consular chore. Lombard did tell me that Popov is a *picoleur;* he downs booze in great quantities. Lombard's people have spotted him drunk more than once."

"Here we are," Mattei announced, slowing to park in the Square Monticelli. Bastide got out and stood for a minute looking at the square and the stone villas. This had long been the chic quarter of Marseille. Lombard had told him it was fast becoming a Soviet diplomatic compound. The consul general and most of the seven officers figuring on the official consular list lived there. The moment a neighborhood villa went on sale, the Soviets put in a generous bid. Lombard had called it "little Moscow."

Bastide and Mattei crossed the street to the consulate's tall iron gate. Some former owner had named the villa "les Tuileries," and the name was still cut into the wall.

"We're on Russkov television," Mattei murmured, indicating the boxlike remote control, closed-circuit camera over their heads. Bastide pressed the bell. Fifteen seconds later a male voice asked what they wanted. Mattei activated the button on the intercom, identifying himself and Bastide.

After a short wait and the click of an observation slit being opened and closed, the gate was thrown wide by a well-dressed young Russian in a dark suit. He led them up a paved path to the consulate's entrance. He ushered them into a large circular waiting room and asked them to sit down. A color print of Gorbachev beamed down on them, his birthmark removed by an airbrush artist. They could hear a typewriter clacking nearby. An unidentifiable, sweet odor permeated the waiting room as if someone had just sprayed it with deodorant.

"Inspector Bastide and Inspector Mattei!" Consul General Anisimov appeared from a side door with a broad smile, his bulk propelled by short, hurried steps. "Welcome, welcome," Anisimov said, shaking their hands. "It is not often we receive the police here. I trust the next time you come it will not be on business." He chuckled at his own joke, indicating the two detectives should precede him through a set of wide, mirrored doors.

Both Bastide and Mattei recognized Viktor Popov when they stepped into the consul general's office. Popov shook hands solemnly and said nothing. They were then introduced to Anatole Zavorin.

"Monsieur Zavorin is our cultural attaché," Anisimov explained. "As we do not have our own legal officer I have asked him to sit in on our meeting. Before losing himself in art and ballet Consul Zavorin was a law student."

There was one other man in the room. "Allow me to present Maître Regnier," Anisimov said. "He represents the consulate in matters of local law. Perhaps you know each other?"

"No," Bastide replied, shaking the French lawyer's hand. "I don't think we've ever met."

"It's a pleasure," Maître Regnier said, returning Bastide's firm handshake.

Patrice Lombard had mentioned Regnier. He was known in Marseille law circles as "the shark." He had the reputation of a young man in a hurry. He was also a member of France-USSR, the Franco-Soviet friendship society, and he had made three trips to the Soviet Union linked with the Marseille-Odessa sister city twinning.

"Come," the consul general suggested, indicating a small conference table and chairs. "Let us sit."

Bastide examined the office as they took their places. It was high-ceilinged and spacious, and the overhead chandelier was lit. Heavy drapes covered the windows. The consul general's desk was dominated by a large family photo. A vase full of yellow tulips was displayed in a stand near the window and an ornate porcelain clock ticked on the marble mantelpiece. A smaller facsimile of the Gorbachev portrait hung over the consul general's desk and a large bird's-eye view of Odessa in dull oils dominated the fireplace.

"Allow me to open our little meeting with a few words," Anisimov said. "First of all, I want you to know that we will do all we can to help in this unfortunate affair. We are guests in your country and we respect its laws. We also know the difficulty of your work. My brother was a policeman. It is not an easy job in Russia or in France."

"Thank you," Bastide replied. He and Mattei had left their arms in safekeeping at the office. One didn't enter a foreign consulate carrying weapons.

"Now," the consul general continued. "Please tell us how we can help."

"*Monsieur le Consul,*" Bastide began, "thank you again for your obvious understanding of the problems we face. As you must know, our presence here is a routine part of this investigation."

Mattei produced a small pad and began to take notes. Between scribbles he observed the others. The consul general was nodding his head in agreement with what was being said. Popov, the corpse mover, was examining his shirt cuffs. The skinny, walleyed cultural attaché had his head thrust forward as if he had a hearing problem. Maître Regnier was slouched in his chair with a quizzical look on his face.

". . . and I would like to direct some questions to Consul Popov," Bastide was saying.

His first questions established where Popov lived, how he had been notified of the body's presence, why he had been called and how long it had taken him to arrive at the consulate. Popov explained that he'd been called as the consulate's duty officer. No mention of a body had been made on the telephone. He had arrived at the consulate at approximately 5:50 A.M., about twenty-seven minutes after he'd received the call.

"Can you tell me what you did on your arrival?" Bastide asked.

"Excuse me, Inspector," Maître Regnier interrupted. "But I find this questioning more apt for a suspect than a cooperative witness. Perhaps it would be easier if you just let him tell his story in his own way."

"Very well," Bastide replied, keeping his voice neutral.

Maître Regnier nodded toward Popov. "Tell us what happened," he said.

"I was told of the . . . package in the consulate driveway by one of the consulate chauffeurs who lodges on the premises," Popov explained. "I went out to look and immediately knew it was a person . . ."

"How did you know?" Bastide asked.

"Please, Inspector," Regnier said, "let Consul Popov continue. Then you can ask your questions."

"I knew it was a person by the outline, by the shape," Popov said. "Is this person alive, I asked myself. Quickly, I untied the ropes and pulled away the covering. To help the person . . . if I could. But no, the man was dead. It was upsetting. I became very nervous. I felt ill. He was lying there, blocking the driveway. I decided to move him out of the way. That was when the police came and Inspector . . ."

"Mattei," Bastide prompted.

"Inspector Mattei arrived. I regret to say it, but the inspector was very rude. This increased my nervousness. It was then that you arrived, Inspector Bastide."

Bastide turned to Regnier with exaggerated deference. "May I ask my questions now, Maître?"

"Please do," Regnier replied.

"Why did you decide to move the corpse?" Bastide asked.

"As I explained, he was blocking the driveway," Popov explained. "I feared he . . . it . . . might be run over."

"Run over at six in the morning? Surely you don't have that much traffic at the consulate. Were you expecting a vehicle to arrive or leave immediately?"

"No, but I was nervous. It seemed necessary."

"Inspector Mattei," Bastide addressed his assistant, "will you read your notes from that morning?"

"Certainly," Mattei said, flicking the pages of his notebook.

"Here it is: 'The subject, Consul Popov, was attempting to drag the corpse onto the verge of the neighboring villa. When challenged, he continued his efforts. He desisted only when physically restrained.' "

"That is not true," Popov countered, his voice rising. "I was distracted and upset. I didn't know who Inspector Mattei was. He frightened me."

"Consul General Anisimov," Bastide said, "would you not describe Consul Popov's behavior as strange?"

"Inspector," Maître Regnier cut in, "I must caution you that this is not an interrogation. Remember that the consul general and his staff are protected by diplomatic immunity. You are only here because of their willingness to cooperate."

"Allow me to respond," Anisimov said, opening his hands in a placating gesture. "It is true Popov should not have touched the body, but he is inexperienced in matters of this nature. You and I, Inspector, are unfortunately familiar with corpses. You, because of your profession. Myself, because of my wartime experience. When one sees violent death for the first time, the reactions are unpredictable. Popov's desire to learn if the man was still alive was normal. I am sure his attempt to move the corpse was an emotional reaction. I don't see how the shifting of the corpse can have any particular significance."

"I understand that you were unable to identify the corpse," Bastide said to Popov. "Is that correct?"

"That is correct," Popov replied.

"Did anyone else in the consulate see the man's face?"

"No, no one else came outside."

"Do you think the dead man might have been Russian?"

"Really, Inspector," Regnier said with an edge of sarcasm. "Consul Popov is not an expert on the physical characteristics of national types. I find that question absurd."

"That, Maître, is your privilege," Bastide responded, "but I would like the consul to answer if he will."

"He could have been any nationality," Popov said, looking to the consul general for support. "French, English, Norwegian, American—I don't know."

"Russian?" Bastide prompted.

"Perhaps," Popov said, flustered. "Who knows?"

"Is that all, Inspector?" Regnier asked, making a show of looking at his watch.

"One other point," Bastide said. "I would like to ask the consul general and his staff if they would come to the police morgue to look at the corpse. We have no leads on identification yet. There is always a possibility that the dead man may be a Soviet citizen. I'm sure the murder of a Soviet citizen would be of great concern to the consulate."

"This is unheard of," Maître Regnier protested. "I would certainly not advise the consul general to do such a thing."

Anisimov leaned forward over his clasped hands, looked at both Bastide and Regnier and chuckled. *"Voyons, Inspecteur,"* he finally said, "we have promised to help. For once I will disregard the legal advice of my friend. We will come look at this fellow for you. But not together. We will come singly and over a period of time. I would not want a photo of our staff taken in front of the morgue as if we were on an outing. Now," Anisimov said, "enough of this grim business." He went to his desk and pressed a button. "I will ask you to take a glass of vodka with us."

The door swung open and two aproned women appeared carrying a tray of open-faced sandwiches and a bottle of chilled vodka and glasses. The consul general filled the glasses and distributed them while the women passed the food.

"Eat before you drink," Anisimov told his guests with a grin, "or you will tell us all your secrets." He raised his vodka in a toast. "May you soon find your murderer."

Antoine Morel's Citroën CX rolled to a stop on the graveled drive of Le Refuge, an isolated, discreetly guarded country house near Saint-Germain-en-Laye just outside Paris. It was late afternoon and the weak sun had already dropped behind the tall oaks surrounding the property. Morel buttoned his overcoat and climbed the marble stairs. He rang the bell and turned to watch his chauffeur drive the car into the peaked-roof garage. Although Morel maintained an official office in *la crémerie*, this was his operational office. The only feature that distinguished it from the other homes and villas in the area was the elaborate TV antenna rising above the tall chimney. In reality, it was a radio mast for a powerful, high-frequency radio installation. Pierre Levallois, Morel's deputy, opened the door for him.

"Anything new?" Morel asked, as he strode through the empty corridor to his office.

"I'm afraid there is," Levallois replied, limping behind Morel, his cane tapping the tiles. "Faubert did not arrive in Pau as ordered."

Morel said nothing until they'd entered his office and shut the door. He calmly hung his coat on a rack and went to sit at his desk. "Let's have it," he said quietly, lifting his tinted glasses and rubbing his eyes. Levallois let himself down gently into a chair and put his cane between his knees.

"Faubert and the two members of his team were on their way from Toulouse to Pau by road. They stopped for petrol in Tarbes and Faubert went to piss. He didn't come back."

"Did they look for him?" Morel asked.

"Thoroughly. They scoured the neighborhood and doubled back as far as Saint Gaudens. There was no sign of him."

"Merde, merde et merde!" Morel said slowly, without emotion. "What's the prognosis?"

"I've grilled both men. There are indications that Faubert has cracked. It was his idea to dump the *cadeau* in front of the Soviet Consulate. He evidently wanted the KGB to get a message about triple agents. His team argued with him, but he pulled rank. When they persisted, he threatened their lives."

"We work with complex people," Morel murmured, almost to himself.

"What's that?" Levallois asked.

"Nothing," Morel replied. "Where do we stand now?"

"I've sent two teams after him. I thought of concocting a story for the Gendarmerie and asking them to help but . . ."

"Thank God you didn't. We don't want anyone else involved. Where do you suppose he's gone?"

"He could be over the border into Spain. He could be drinking in some café, in bed with a whore or praying at Lourdes."

"What were your orders to the teams?"

"To bring him to the farm at Pau."

Morel nodded and looked down at the documents and telegrams on his desk. "Anything else pressing?" he asked.

"A Libyan agent arrived last night in Djibouti traveling on an Algerian passport. We have him under surveillance. We've had to pull Coussac out of Chad . . . hepatitis. I'm arranging a replacement. Run-of-the-mill stuff."

"Let me get through these," Morel said, "and we'll talk some more about Faubert."

He waited for Levallois to leave before picking up his secure phone and dialing de Coursin's personal number. He would need de Coursin's clearance for his plan to deal with Faubert. Until he did there was no reason to discuss the matter with his deputy.

Bastide was puzzled by the sudden summons to the Préfecture. He was surprised that the call had not come through Commissaire Aynard. He'd planned to check a sample of the tarpaulin that had covered the body with some ship chandler and warehouse suppliers, but the trip to the Préfecture took priority. Entering the Préfecture's wide portals at twelve noon, he automatically headed for the office of the Préfet of Police. A young man in a well-cut suit stopped him before he could enter.

"Inspector Bastide?" he asked.

"Yes." Bastide paused, puzzled.

"Would you please come with me?" The young man motioned toward the inner parking area.

"I don't understand," Bastide said, following reluctantly. He didn't know who his guide was, but he had the stamp of officialdom.

"Here we are," the man said, indicating a black Citroën with tinted windows. He opened the rear door for Bastide.

Bastide bent over to look inside and saw de Coursin's extended hand.

"Good to see you, Inspector," de Coursin greeted him as they shook hands. "Do sit down. Excuse all this mystery, but I'm not supposed to be in Marseille, and the fewer people I see the better. Let's go," he said as the young man took his place beside the driver.

"I'll fill you in quickly so you can relax," de Coursin said as they rolled out of the drive. "We are going to Puyloubier for a quiet lunch. There are things I must discuss with you. The commander of the Foreign Legion is an old friend. He has arranged for us to dine in private at the Legion's retirement home. It is not the Ritz, but they set a good table and our meeting won't be the talk of Marseille."

Bastide looked quizzically at de Coursin. He began to speak but thought better of it. De Coursin understood immediately. He closed the glass partition with a well-manicured hand, shutting them off from the men in the front seats.

"Go ahead, Inspector," de Coursin prompted.

"This is about the consulate case, isn't it?"

"Bravo!" de Coursin replied. "I wish some of my people were half as quick. But I'd rather wait till we get settled for lunch before going into it. Congratulations on your recent promotion. It was long overdue. Tell me, how is Commissaire Aynard?" De Coursin was in a good mood. The director had approved his plan. His visit to Marseille was the first step in its implementation.

"He's fine," Bastide replied. Bastide wasn't sure about de Coursin. He had no real loyalty to Aynard, but the hint of derision in de Coursin's voice when he'd mentioned the commissaire made Bastide cautious. He'd had a little experience with intelligence officers in Algeria. He'd worked with them as a para during the battle of Algiers, and he didn't trust them. De Coursin couldn't be compared with the rough *barbouzes* he'd seen in action, but there was a similarity in their detachment. They existed in a special world, and everyone outside their intimate professional circle was expendable. The environment of secrecy in which they worked gave them a special advantage. Bastide reflected that his ride with de Coursin bordered on a semiofficial kidnapping. He didn't know who might actually have been told of his whereabouts, whether his superiors had approved of this meeting or on what grounds he was to cooperate. The cards were stacked and de Coursin had the best hand. The driver put a heavy foot on the accelerator when they reached the *autoroute*, flicked on his warning lights and began to pass all vehicles in their path.

"I know Marseille fairly well," de Coursin remarked, lighting a cigarette. "When you were chasing the FLN in the Casbah, I was hunting the OAS bombers here. It was a busy time."

De Coursin continued to talk as they sped toward Aix. A bright sun had emerged from the gray cloud cover. The fields looked particularly green. The trees were full of spring buds. They turned off the *autoroute* and slowed to negotiate the narrow country road leading to the Legion's rest home.

"The Legion is both a phenomenon and an anachronism," de Coursin was saying. "Who would have thought it would still exist in our modern world? Of course, the Legion is useful to all our governments, regardless of who may be in power. They're professionals who can be sent anywhere without a public outcry. The politicians and the public don't complain when they take casualties, and their traditions and color appeal to the Napoleonic streak hidden in all of us."

They pulled up beside a complex of stucco buildings surrounded by vineyards. A *sergent-chef* of the Legion came down the steps to meet them, saluted de Coursin and led them inside. They walked along a well-scrubbed hallway and were ushered into a small room with tall windows looking out on a fertile valley. A table for two was set near the windows. The walls were hung with brightly colored recruiting posters. A sideboard contained everything needed for a cold meal: meat, cheese, salad, bread and wine. A young legionnaire appeared with an aperitif tray. Bastide took a *pastis*. De Coursin selected a small whiskey and nodded to his young assistant, who withdrew and shut the door, taking the *sergent-chef* with him.

"A beautiful day," de Coursin remarked, looking out of the window. "They make their own wine, you know. We'll have some at lunch. It's not bad at all."

Bastide was becoming tired of de Coursin's chatter. He was used to direct dealing. He had neither the time nor the stomach for polite conversation.

"Monsieur," Bastide said, "I am not sure why you feel our meeting is necessary, but I'd like to know what it is you want. To begin with, I'd like to know if the commissaire or anyone else at the Hôtel de Police knows I'm here."

"Your préfet knows you're here," de Coursin told him, finishing his Scotch. "The commissaire does not. Let me reassure you, our meeting has been approved by the highest authority. Shall we help ourselves?"

They filled their plates with slices of saucisson, mortadella and ham, portions of the green salad and hunks of freshly cut bread. De Coursin brought unlabeled bottles of red and white wine to the table. They unfolded their napkins and de Coursin began to speak.

"The murder case you're working on is not like the others," he said. "I'm sure you're aware of that. The discovery of the corpse outside the Soviet Consulate has opened a Pandora's box of possibilities and complications. We are all asking why the body was dumped where it was. As of this moment, however, we see no espionage or intelligence involvement in the case."

Bastide raised his eyebrows but continued to butter his bread.

"I know it sounds unlikely," de Coursin continued, "but to us, this looks like pure police work and we have no intention of interfering."

"Why are you telling me this?" Bastide asked.

"Because we've had echoes that your commissaire and others would like to turn the matter over to the DST. Such a move would be disastrous. It would fuel all the wild rumors the media has already spread. It would turn the murder into an international incident of the type we do not want."

Bastide chewed thoughtfully and poured himself some red wine. De Coursin's words had done little to clarify the situation. He was well aware of the old DGSE-DST rivalry and he didn't want to get involved. He drank the wine and was surprised at its body.

"Inspector," de Coursin said, "you are obviously an intelligent man . . ."

Beware intelligence officers bearing compliments, Bastide told himself.

". . . I wanted to tell you personally that we have confidence in your work and that you needn't worry about having any of my people hiding behind doors during your investigation."

"Go on," Bastide suggested, knowing there was more to come.

"Very well. I would also like your word that you'll contact me directly if anything unforeseen comes up. Any new twist in the case that could be of interest to us."

"How am I to judge what might be of interest to you?"

De Coursin smiled, his mouth full of saucisson. He chewed and swallowed before speaking. "Don't play innocent with me, Inspector," de Coursin said. "I'm sure you know what I mean. If not, let me make it clear so we have no misunderstanding. At the slightest hint of any intelligence involvement: KGB, GRU, CIA, MI6, DST, even DGSE, you will contact me directly."

"You've just said there was no such involvement."

"Nothing in life is certain," de Coursin countered, spearing a piece of lettuce with his fork. "We must always think of contingencies. We may never see or speak to each other again. Or you may find yourself calling me within the next few days. I could have had the préfet pass on these instructions to you, but I believe in personal contact. I wanted you to understand or to ask questions if you don't."

"In fact," Bastide said, "you're giving me an order."

"In a certain sense," de Coursin replied, "but it's an order that has been cleared on a high level."

"It seems very complicated," Bastide said. "I'll be deceiving the commissaire. Why doesn't the préfet inform him what's going on?"

"I can see that you're streetwise and intrigue-foolish," de Coursin chuckled. "I also sense that you don't quite trust me. When you get back to Marseille, you can check with the préfet. He won't keep you long. He'll confirm what I've told you. Please don't read more into this than there really is."

"Naturally," Bastide replied. "There will be nothing in writing?"

"Naturally. Would you like some cheese? Or a slice of that apple tart?"

Bastide shook his head and filled his wineglass. He'd guessed that the case would be unique. Now de Coursin had thickened the mystery. "If I do call you with the information you seek, does it mean that it is no longer my case?"

"Not necessarily. It depends on the circumstances." De Coursin smiled again. "I understand if my conversation troubles you. We tend to talk in riddles at *la crémerie*, a malady of the business. But I think you understand the basics?"

"Yes," Bastide said. "I do."

"Perfect," de Coursin sighed. "When we're finished, I suggest we help ourselves to a glass of the Legion's excellent cognac and a cigar. I understand you're a connoisseur of cheroots."

Two hours later Bastide stood in front of the Préfet of Police's desk. The préfet had just returned from an official luncheon. His uniform coat was unbuttoned, his cap trimmed with gold leaves was on a nearby bookshelf. His cheeks were flushed from too much food and wine. He did not ask Bastide to sit down.

"Yes, Inspector?" the préfet demanded, making it clear he had little time to devote to their conversation.

"I just had lunch at Puyloubier," Bastide said.

"I know," the préfet replied. "You are to do what you were told."

"Yes, sir."

"Not a word to anyone, do you understand?"

"Yes, sir."

"Very well," the préfet said. "Good day, Inspector."

The Minister of Foreign Affairs was normally a calm, courteous man, but his patience had its limits. The ornate chandelier in his large office at the Quai d'Orsay seemed to vibrate as he shouted at his press secretary.

"What is this idiocy?" he demanded, thumping a stack of the morning papers with his fist. "No one in this government seems to know what's going on and the press is free to concoct fairy tales! Well, I know what's going on in my ministry. We are being crucified, made to look like fools by everyone. The Soviets have just canceled an important diplomatic visit to France; our Prime Minister is furious; the Soviet ambassador has asked to see me this afternoon; and the Élysées has just passed the word for us to keep our mouths shut! Meanwhile, our so-called colleagues in intelligence can tell us nothing."

The minister took a deep breath, glaring at the press secretary. "What was the last word from the Ministry of the Interior?" he demanded.

"They say it appears to be a simple police case," the press secretary replied. "They've found no links to the Soviet Consulate."

"Tell me," the minister asked. "Do you believe that?"

The press secretary shrugged.

"If Interior had their way," the minister continued, "it would be a crime of passion or some narcotics murder. That might get them off the hook. But jealous lovers and Marseille thugs don't take the trouble to drive their victims to the Soviet Consulate and dump them there. Have you read all these stories? They've dredged up every ex-agent in France to quote as an expert. Look at this." He shook one of the newspapers. " 'Exterminators Strike in Marseille.' And this one, 'KGB Involvement Possible.' "

"*Figaro* called," the press secretary told the minister. "They'd like an interview."

"I'm sure they would. The answer is no. Refer them to Interior." The minister was winding down. He took a deep breath and shook his head. "I don't know where the DGSE and the DST fit in all this, but they are being very quiet," he said.

"They seem to agree with the Ministry of the Interior," the press secretary ventured. "Perhaps they know more about it than we do?"

"Everyone does!" the minister said bitterly. "Here, take these scandal sheets back to your office. Respond to all queries with the statement we used yesterday. 'The police investigation proceeds etc. . . . .' Ask my Cabinet secretary to come in as you leave. I've got to decide what I'm going to tell the Soviet ambassador."

Bastide was flat on his back with his eyes closed. Janine's head lay on his chest and each breath he took filled his nostrils with the pleasant odor of her perfume. They were nude under the linen sheet. Bastide could feel the rhythm of her breathing and the pressure of her body. It had happened spontaneously. Janine had arrived at his apartment at 6:30 P.M. while he was preparing dinner. He'd kissed her at the door. That casual greeting had struck a spark that neither of them anticipated. They'd clung to each other, exchanging caresses, until a mutual wave of desire led them into the bedroom. They'd discarded their clothes on the floor, a bookshelf, a chair and the foot of the bed. Their usual, practiced exchange of pleasure had been abandoned in a unique frenzy of erotic sharing that had surprised them both.

Janine ran her hand slowly over Bastide's chest, her large eyes watching him. "That was very nice," she said softly, "and very strange."

"Hmmn," Bastide murmured in agreement. He was enjoying the silence and had no desire to talk.

"You'd think we were two adolescents," Janine said.

His only answer was a smile.

She lay silent awhile, her eyes blinking as she thought about Bastide. They had become even closer in the past year. She wasn't sure of Bastide's love but three months earlier she'd analyzed her own feelings. She'd decided she was in love with him. Janine Bourdet had seldom been frightened of anything, but this personal revelation troubled her. She didn't know where it might lead and she was afraid to meet the problem head-on. She couldn't imagine being married to Bastide. She couldn't imagine living without him. The specter of Théo Gautier's death haunted her thoughts. She knew her aged protector had been a convenient buffer, preventing her from facing the realities of the future.

Bastide stirred and raised himself on both elbows. He looked out the bedroom at the terrace. "This is the first time we've made love with the terrace door open since last October," he said.

"How romantic," she replied, pulling herself up till her full breasts rested on his chest. She kissed him. "Maybe spring is really here."

"I've got to get back to the kitchen," Bastide said, sitting up.

"Wait a minute, Inspector!" Janine cautioned. "You're not leaving this bed until you explain how this happened."

"How what happened?"

"Why we jumped into bed like two overheated rabbits."

"Chemistry," Bastide said, smiling down at her. "The first day of spring. Your perfume. The sway of your bottom. Take your pick."

"You're never serious," she reproached him. "Something unusual happened and you don't want to talk about it."

"We can try to find out after a good dinner," he said lightly, swinging his legs over the side of the bed.

"It won't be the same," she said, running a fingernail along the small of his back.

"If Madame will permit me," he told her, "I must return to work. My *écrevisses à la provençale* need attention or you'll think you're eating thinly sauced rubber."

He put on his robe and walked into the bathroom, shutting the door.

The DGSE officer charged with producing a plausible structure for the LeCompte-Drankov murder rubbed his chin with the blunt end of his pen and examined the paper on his desk. It was a labyrinth of lines, arrows and labeled blocks. A few dates were scribbled on the right border. He'd done this type of work many times before, but this particular situation presented a special challenge. There was more to it than pleasing his superiors. He had to remember that his scenario was meant to convince the Marseille police, a group he knew to be highly skeptical. He was a desk-bound officer, someone who did all his work within the DGSE's walls. He reached for a dossier, opened it and read the brief de Coursin had written on Bastide for the third time.

His mind focused on the key words. Bastide was "clever," "painstaking" and "determined." De Coursin had also underlined the word "suspicious." Normally, the officer had a low opinion of the police. He considered most of them fatheads who could be led by the nose. He knew he couldn't disguise the LeCompte-Drankov corpse as the result of any local gangland killing or narcotics feud. No one in Marseille would buy that. It had to be the work of someone from the outside, a situation involving persons unknown in the south. But who and for what reason? It was almost 8 P.M. and he'd been working all day on the project.

"The motive," he murmured to himself. "What is the motive?"

It was too late, he'd worked too long, his eyes hurt and he was hungry. He gathered his papers and the file and locked them in his safe. He was putting his Hermès scarf around his neck when it came to him. Jewels! The dead man had been a jewel smuggler! He sat for a moment on the edge of his desk, thinking hard. He'd thought of arms smuggling earlier, but that was too close to politics. Jewels were perfect. The scenario took shape in his mind. The dead man had tried to betray his boss. He'd been caught and killed. But why Marseille? He was . . . he was on the run. Trying to get out of the country by sea. But what possible logic could there be in dropping him in front of the Soviet Consulate? The DGSE officer rubbed his head with both hands and groaned. It wasn't easy. He put on his coat and hat and walked to the door. He flicked off the light and suddenly slapped his hands together. "That's it!" he said aloud. The dead man would be a

Soviet Jew . . . whose departure from the U.S.S.R. had been facilitated by a man he'd worked for in the diamond business. When he'd betrayed his vengeful employer, he'd been given a lungful of cyanide and symbolically returned to the Soviets. The scenario was a bit rough, but it gave him a foundation to work with.

Anatole Zavorin arrived at the Palais de Pharos for the Consular Corps reception after the official speeches had begun. He accepted a glass of champagne from a white-coated waiter and surveyed the crowd as the député-maire wove a tissue of clichés designed to please the foreign diplomats on post in Marseille. The Palais, built by Napoléon III for his empress, was an ornate pile of Second Empire construction. The ballroom, with its tall windows, looked out on the port. The light from the chandeliers played on the gold trim and dark wood of the walls. The wide parquet floor creaked under the feet of the guests.

Zavorin hated official functions, but they were an integral part of his cover. He identified the various members of the Consular Corps as they stood listening to the député-maire's speech. The tall American consul general was easy to spot. He and his wife were standing next to the plump British consul general. The Americans and the British always seemed to drift together at these affairs. Zavorin wondered if it was friendship, the ease of a common language or a political gesture of some kind. The aristocratic Spanish consul general stood aloof like a bored grandee in a Velázquez painting. The Italians were bunched together around their senior officer, eyeing the food and whispering among themselves. The gray-haired Dutch consul general was reaching for his second glass of gin. A flurry of polite applause followed the député-maire's speech. Then the Swiss consul general, the dean of the corps, began his reply. Zavorin moved several feet for a better view of the proceedings and saw Consul General Anisimov and his wife Natalie beaming at the speaker from the inner circle of diplomats. Zavorin considered Natalie Anisimov a harridan and the real power behind her husband. Her reign of economy at the consulate had alienated the staff. She reminded him of a thin vulture. Her voice matched the image.

The dean's speech was mercifully short. There was a sudden

rush for the buffet and the bars. A long serving table in the center of the floor was filled with *hors-d'oeuvres:* tiny hot sausages and meatballs; small slices of pizza; finger sandwiches of ham, cheese, egg and beef; and tiered crystal plates of *petits fours.* Champagne, whiskey, gin, *pastis* and fruit juice were being served at the bars. The volume of conversation increased as the guests formed into small groups greeting each other, talking, drinking and eating.

Zavorin found whom he was looking for. Viktor Popov had gone to the bar for another drink. Zavorin watched Popov accept a good three fingers of whiskey from the barman.

"Good evening, Comrade," Zavorin said in Russian. "Enjoying yourself?"

"Yes, thank you," Popov replied, putting his glass to his lips.

"I did not have time to thank you the other day," Zavorin said quietly, guiding Popov away from the crush at the bar. "I appreciated your cooperation."

Popov looked blank.

"It was wise of you to say nothing," Zavorin said, watching Popov carefully, "during our meeting with the consul general."

"I still think I should have told him that you ordered me to move the body," Popov said, rotating his whiskey glass with both hands.

"I suggest you don't, Comrade Popov," Zavorin cautioned, one eye fixing the consul, the other seemingly examining the far wall. "It would only cause complications and upset Comrade Anisimov."

"But why should I take the blame?" Popov complained. "I only followed your orders."

"I like you, Popov," Zavorin replied. "Your career has only begun. A good future lies ahead of you. Believe me, we were both acting in the higher interest of the state."

"But . . ." Popov didn't finish his sentence. An obese French woman, her short blond hair plastered to her head like a cap, appeared beside them and put her stubby fingers on Zavorin's arm. Her heavy, spangled dress hung from her like a sagging tent, and her ample bosom was covered with varicolored bead necklaces.

"Monsieur Zavorin," she purred, "how lucky I am to have found you. I must insist that you come to our *vernissage* next week.

We're showing the work of the Austrian painter Bischoff. He lives near Avignon. A true genius."

Zavorin avoided a response by introducing Popov to the gallery owner. She gave Popov several seconds of her time before pursuing her conversation with Zavorin. "All of Marseille will be there, including the Americans," she told him. "I will be truly hurt if you don't come."

"Madame," Zavorin said, "I look forward to your *vernissage.*"

"Good. I'm counting on you," she replied. "Oh, bring your friend," she added, turning toward Popov, but he had already left them for the bar.

Popov watched the amber whiskey gurgle into his glass and smiled. He knew the KGB resident was enduring a purgatory in the role of cultural attaché. The two stiff Scotches he'd already consumed had eased his nerves. He knew the third would provide the level of euphoria he sought. He moved away from the bar laterally. He wanted to avoid further conversation with Zavorin. He joined a mixed group of French and American officials standing by the window.

Zavorin had freed himself from the gallery owner but turned to find himself face to face with an effusive honorary consul from a West African nation. Honorary consuls were usually French businessmen who had been appointed because of their commercial or trade connections. This particular honorary consul was a Marseille shipping agent with an affinity for Chekhov. He launched into a description of his experiences acting in a Chekhov play as a student. Zavorin had heard the story before, but he pretended to listen. He'd also noticed Popov's return to the bar and his obvious desire to end their conversation. Zavorin decided Popov was drinking too much and would have to be watched.

When Zavorin left the Palais de Pharos a half hour later, the night sky was studded with stars. Miniature dust swirls in the parking area presaged an imminent mistral. He drove his consulate sedan to the Quai de Rive Neuve and turned onto the rue de Paradis. The evening traffic was heavy. It took him twenty minutes to reach the consulate. By the time he'd settled behind his desk, it was almost 9 P.M. He took a writing pad from a drawer and began to compose a message, printing the Russian characters with a heavy hand.

Zavorin's small office was on the top floor of the consulate. Exposed roof beams slanted down over his desk. The walls were decorated with posters of Soviet cultural events and expositions that had been held in France. An entire wall was occupied by a full shelf featuring French translations of Soviet books: novels, scientific works, histories, biographies and volumes on the art holdings of Russian museums. This was where he received official visitors: the artists, gallery owners, writers, opera directors, university professors and specialists of Russian language and culture that were his legitimate local contacts. His real working office was an even smaller room on the same floor next to the consulate message center. Behind its double steel doors was a state-of-the-art installation of secure communications equipment. Zavorin had access to the incoming and outgoing messages of the consulate, but no one other than he and his two assistants were cleared to read the traffic from KGB headquarters on Dzerzhinsky Square.

Zavorin removed his heavy-rimmed spectacles and wiped them with his handkerchief. He bent over to read the text he'd written. The message was slugged for the 5th Department of the KGB's First Chief Directorate with information copies to the 12th Department and Department V (Victor). The 5th Department handled operations in Western Europe; the 12th arranged agents' cover assignments. Department V, the Executive Action Department, handled *mokrie dela,* or "wet affairs," the ultrasecret elimination of enemies of the Soviet Union. Department V was not yet involved in the death of Drankov, but Zavorin had decided it was wise to keep them informed. He used a soft pencil to edit his handiwork, dropping some superfluous words, and read on. In one short paragraph he related the current state of the case, tying it to his previous message on the police visit to the consulate. The second paragraph reiterated Zavorin's suspicion that Drankov had been killed by the DGSE. He explained that the Police Judiciaire of Marseille seemed to be the only official body responsible for the investigation and stressed the crucial importance of developments in the case. The third paragraph requested the services of Comrade Larissa Kedrov on an urgent basis, suggesting she be sent to Marseille on a temporary diplomatic assignment with cover as a temporary assistant in the Cultural

Section. He concluded the message by naming Larissa Kedrov's target and promised a separate telegram on the man's background.

Zavorin completed his task. He would send the message on a priority basis. Before leaving his office he turned and looked out of a dormer window. The leaves of the plane tree were already dancing in the freshening wind. He thought for a moment about Larissa Kedrov. He hadn't seen her in four years, since she'd gone to work for the 8th Department and been sent to the Middle East. As one of the KGB's top "swallows," a professional seductress of foreign targets, Larissa Kedrov was much in demand. He was not sure she'd be free for the assignment. He remembered her long, shapely legs and husky voice. He knew her large dark eyes and striking high cheekbones had come from her Uzbek mother. Zavorin gathered the pages of his message. A rare smile spread over his face. He was savoring the fact that Inspector Bastide had no idea what was in store for him.

III

Babar Mattei sensed he was being tailed as he climbed the steep stairs of the rue de Beauregard. He paused momentarily, as if to get his breath, and glanced over his right shoulder. A man in a tan topcoat had suddenly taken a great interest in the tires displayed in a garage window. The cold mistral lashed through the wind tunnel of the covered stone stairway, tossing bits of plastic and paper into the air. Mattei pulled his wool cap down on his forehead and continued his climb. If the tire fancier started up the stairs his suspicion would be confirmed. He reached the Montée des Accoules and crossed to the Place des Moulins, walking with his head down.

Mattei was on his way back to the Hôtel de Police after a talk with "Nénesse la Guitare," a senior member of Marseille's leading Corsican gang. He'd grilled Nénesse without success on a possible underworld link with the consulate corpse. Nénesse had received him in his luxurious apartment overlooking the Vieux Port, offered him coffee and sworn on his family's honor that he had no information to share. Mattei's long experience, and the fact that he too was a Corsican, had made it easier to believe his compatriot. He'd known Nénesse to lie before, but this time there'd been little doubt he'd been telling the truth. Mattei didn't need a polygraph. For him it was all in the eyes and the tone of the voice. He'd extracted a promise that Nénesse would tell his people to keep their ears open and left him, his gaudy furniture and bad breath to return to the office.

The vendors of the small open-air vegetable market in the Place des Moulins were packing their wares and folding their collapsible stands, capitulating to the fierce wind. Mattei paused, feigning interest in a box of carrots. The man in the topcoat had appeared at the top of the stairs. Mattei continued up the paved incline of the deserted Place till he came to the large kiosk on the corner. He turned abruptly to his left and put his back against the kiosk, massaging both hands. He didn't have long to wait. The tan topcoat appeared to his right. He stepped from behind the kiosk, grabbed the coat by the collar and pulled it down over the wearer's shoulders, immobilizing his arms. With a coordinated swing of his powerful shoulders, he propelled the man forward, smashing his head against the kiosk. The man staggered and tried to recover his balance, but Mattei pulled him close and delivered a solid head butt that drove him down into a sitting position. Then Mattei was on top of him, one knee on the man's groin and his right thumb pressing hard just below his Adam's apple.

"*Alors, petit père,*" Mattei growled, "you want to talk?"

The man made a gesture of surrender, swallowed hard and spit some blood onto the pavement. "My identity . . ." he rasped, nodding to the inner pocket of his jacket.

Mattei eased his knee out of the man's groin and relaxed the pressure on his throat. He worked the wallet out of the pocket and flipped it open. There was a diagonal red, white and blue slash across the identity card. Mattei compared the photo with his bloody-nosed victim. He had butted Norbert Travers of the DST.

"*Espèce de con,*" Mattei said gruffly, lifting the DST agent to his feet. "I could have killed you, you asshole! What's your game?"

Norbert Travers unfolded a handkerchief and applied it to his scarlet nose. The owner of the kiosk appeared. "*Eh, là!*" he shouted. "What the hell's going on here? You almost demolished my stand!"

"Get back into your pulpit," Mattei told him, "or I'll run you in on a pornography charge."

The vendor withdrew grudgingly and Mattei concentrated on Norbert. "I'm waiting for an answer," Mattei said, clenching his right fist.

"*Bon Dieu,*" Travers sniffed, "I was just following orders!"

"Really? Well, *mon ami,* you can tell your boss Boniface that it would be easier to call Inspecteur Principal Bastide for an update on our activities than waste shoe leather and manpower following me. You see, *we* don't have time for childish games. We work in the real world. You're damn lucky I didn't put a few holes in you.

When someone follows us it's usually a question of life or death. Now, get the hell out of here . . . and fast."

Norbert Travers hurried downhill, crossed the Place and disappeared from sight. Mattei sighed and continued on his way to the Hôtel de Police.

Antoine Morel met with de Coursin two hours after de Coursin's return from Marseille. Their rendezvous point was a small, noisy café on the Boulevard Latour-Maubourg about three blocks from de Coursin's apartment. They'd taken a booth in the rear of the establishment and ordered coffee. Morel had broken the news about Faubert's disappearance. De Coursin, already dressed for a dinner that evening, had not lost his composure.

"Is there anything else that could possibly go wrong?" he'd asked. Morel knew he wasn't expected to answer the rhetorical question. Instead he outlined his plan for coping with Faubert.

"The man is obviously deranged," he reasoned. "Even if we put him in an asylum he'll be a potential threat."

"So?" de Coursin asked.

"He must be neutralized," Morel said. "I hate to recommend such action when it comes to one of my own men but it is necessary."

De Coursin pushed his coffee cup aside and looked directly at Morel. "I am not sure," he said. "There are moral questions involved. Perhaps we should sleep on it."

Morel took a deep breath and shook his head. "Every minute he's free is a minute of high risk. I don't know what he might do next but I do know what he's capable of doing. He could walk into the Soviet embassy tomorrow with plastic explosives strapped to his body. He could call a press conference to explain his role in the Drankov business. He might telephone the President of the Republic for a revealing chat. He could fall into the hands of the police. No matter how you look at it, he's a bomb waiting to go off. If our teams pick him up and we salt him away he'll probably sing like a canary. Every ward attendant and *toubib* that takes care of him will hear the story. Then there's always the chance he'll escape. He's well trained, clever and tough. At this point, if our estimate of his mental condition is correct, he probably doesn't give a damn what happens to him. I'm afraid his neutralization is essential."

"If we did make such a decision," de Coursin asked, "how would you go about it?"

"I would handle it myself," Morel replied in a flat, unemotional tone.

"I don't like it," de Coursin said. "I'd need higher authority for such an order."

"If you go higher, we'll never get a decision," Morel said. "Each tick of the clock takes us closer to disaster. I've never seen such an urgent need for someone to disappear."

Morel stood up, put some money on the table and buttoned his jacket. "You know where to reach me," he said, extending his hand. "I hope you call soon."

When Morel had left, de Coursin stared for a few moments at the clock on the far wall, watching the second hand jerk its way around the clock face. The coffee he'd drunk tasted bitter in his throat. He automatically drew a cigarette from its pack and twisted it into his holder. Morel was right. Faubert had become a dangerous liability. Something had to be done. But a death sentence? He wasn't a judge. He'd left the café and walked a hundred yards before he realized he'd forgotten to light his cigarette.

Roger Bastide's mind was bubbling with contradictory thoughts and vague premonitions. The Russians were a puzzle. The consul general with his exuberant good-fellow façade, Popov, the nervous body mover, and the cultural attaché, Zavorin of the distracting gaze. Bastide knew there was a link with the murder there somewhere, but it was still a Byzantine mystery. Then there was de Coursin. Since their luncheon and Bastide's brief meeting with the préfet, he'd been bothered by his new allegiance to de Coursin. This unease had now turned to irritation. As the senior police officer charged with the murder investigation, he should not be burdened with an "unofficial" responsibility to a high-ranking officer of the DGSE. God knows, he thought, with their budget and resources they shouldn't seek additional help. He understood the need for absolute discretion when it came to intelligence matters, but there was something about de Coursin's sudden dependence on him that didn't ring true.

Bastide was alone in the office. He'd turned his chair around and was sitting with both feet braced on the windowsill, his arms folded, a cigar clenched between his teeth. He found it impossible to forget the cloak-and-dagger aspects of the killing, to think of it as a simple homicide. He reflected that the de Coursins of this world didn't make sudden side trips to Puyloubier to invite undistinguished *flics* to lunch. The Préfet of Police didn't ordinarily allow his men to be used by other agencies unless there was a very good reason or an order from on high. Bastide had seldom been so frustrated.

He tapped his cigar on a heavy glass ashtray and checked the time. Mattei was at the morgue, receiving members of the Soviet Consulate according to a carefully paced schedule. Lenoir was winding up his questioning of residents along the rue Ambroise-Paré, and Bastide was supposed to be brainstorming the big picture, bringing into preliminary focus all the details, possibilities, suspects and motives until they began to form a coherent whole. The only product of his ruminations had been the certainty that he was in an untenable position with no one to turn to, not even Commissaire Aynard.

"*Merde,*" he muttered, swinging his feet off the windowsill and leaving his chair. "What a mess!"

At exactly that moment, Jacques Boniface of the DST appeared at the door. "Talking to yourself now?" Boniface asked, smiling. "They say it happens to all of us." He was wearing a gray Tyrolian hat with a brush of boar bristle in its leather band. If there was one man Bastide did not want to see, it was Boniface. He quickly made it obvious.

"I take it you're following a Nazi war criminal," Bastide said, indicating Boniface's hat, "and trying to look inconspicuous?"

"Most amusing," Boniface replied, "but I'm not here to listen to your doubtful humor. I come bearing a gift."

Bastide raised his eyebrows, exhaled a cloud of cigar smoke and waited.

"First, let me tell you that we're asking the préfet's office for your full cooperation. Commissaire Aynard will be so informed. I wanted you to know."

"*Merci,*" Bastide said. "And the gift?"

Boniface shut the door behind him, pulled a chair close to Bastide's desk and sat down. Bastide remained standing.

"Have you identified your stiff?" Boniface asked.

"No."

"I thought not," Boniface said with obvious relish. "While you've been cloistered here carrying on your personal dialogue, we've been busy. We've made a tentative identification, thanks to the fingerprints you distributed and to one of our sleepers with the Algerian police. It appears your blond cyanide sniffer is a certain Grigori Drankov, a GRU officer who worked Algiers about 1984 to '85. The Algerians have a devious habit of picking up fingerprints from diplomats' passports when they apply for Algerian diplomatic cards and *laissez-passer* documents. It's been useful to us before and we decided to try it again. Not only do we have a match, but our sleeper, who is far from asleep, recognized Drankov after we got back to him with a physical description."

Bastide sat down.

"That's all right," Boniface grinned, "you can thank me later."

"A Soviet military intelligence officer dumped at the door of the Soviet Consulate?" Bastide said, frowning. "It doesn't make sense."

"That depends," Boniface replied. "It might be most logical, depending on who did it. I have a feeling you will soon be turning this case over to us. It appears to have moved well beyond your area of responsibility."

"It's still my case," Bastide warned. "Until I receive orders to pull out I don't want your people underfoot!"

"Don't worry. You won't even know we're around. Look what we've accomplished so far with the little you've given us. Perhaps when your commissaire orders you to cooperate fully we'll be able to roll this thing up. Or maybe there isn't anything to pass on?"

Bastide walked to the coatrack by the door and pulled on his jacket. "I have an appointment," he told Boniface, "and I'd like to lock up. Do you mind taking yourself and that ridiculous hat out of here?"

"Not at all, but I expect to return soon to pick up the case file . . . for what it's worth. *Au revoir.*"

Bastide turned his back on Boniface and locked the door. He

made his way to the garage, signed out an unmarked Peugeot, drove it around the Vieux Port and up the rue de Paradis to the Préfecture. He left the car in a metered parking slot and entered the Préfecture by a side entrance. He followed de Coursin's instructions: walk down two short flights to the basement, turn right and follow a long, cool corridor laced with overhead pipes. He came to a barred gate with a code key lock. He punched in the required numbers, pushed open the gate, shut it firmly and walked about thirty feet to a heavy iron door surmounted by a closed-circuit camera. He pressed the bell button twice and waited, glancing up at the camera to make sure his face appeared clearly on the interior monitor.

There was a muffled click and the door swung open. He stepped into a brightly lit anteroom. There were two young men there. One sat behind the closed-circuit monitor; the other came forward to check Bastide's identity and search him. He obviously knew his business. He sought the blind spots where weapons might be hidden: deep in the crotch, in the crease of the buttocks, at the wrists, the armpits and the ankles. He even checked Bastide's mouth.

"Through there," he finally said, indicating another steel door on the other side of the small room.

Bastide stepped into a compact office with two desks and a wall full of electronics equipment—a telex, coding machines and taping gear. A hanging metal basket of grape ivy caught Bastide's eye before he realized someone was watching him intently.

"Welcome to DGSE South, Inspector," the man said, putting down his coffee cup and extending his hand. "Monsieur de Coursin told us we might expect your visit, but I didn't think it would be this soon."

Bastide shook hands, examining his host. He was an athletic, tanned man of forty with light blue eyes and thick blond hair. He reminded Bastide of a tennis pro he'd once questioned in Cavalaire.

"I've come here to use one of your secure telephones," Bastide said.

"I'd guessed as much. Take that one on the other desk with the red decal on it."

Bastide approached the desk and paused.

"Don't worry about me," the DGSE officer told him. "I know the music. Monsieur de Coursin has filled me in." He sat down and returned to reading a thick report.

Bastide was surprised at the rapidity of his connection. Only one intermediary spoke to him before de Coursin was on the line. Bastide described the Boniface visit. He didn't miss de Coursin's sharp intake of breath when he mentioned Drankov's name.

"Inspector," de Coursin said, "thank you for this information. I deeply appreciate it. Please notify me immediately of anything Boniface says or does. Meanwhile, I would ask you to forget the name Drankov. Do you understand?"

"Certainly."

"Good. Is there anything else?"

Bastide hesitated, trying to think. "This is putting me in an awkward position," he said. "It's easy to forget Drankov, but if Boniface already knows he'll spread it around. He might even pass it on to Commissaire Aynard. If so, I'll look like an idiot."

"No, no," de Coursin said. "I don't believe you have anything to worry about. I'm sure the DST has made a mistake. Allow me to handle it from here. Just continue your normal investigation."

Bastide was getting nowhere. He decided to end the conversation. It sounded as if he were interested solely in his own reputation. "Very well; until next time."

"*Au revoir,*" de Coursin replied, "and thanks again."

Bastide replaced the receiver. He glanced at the DGSE officer behind the desk. "I didn't get your name," Bastide said.

"Let's keep it that way," the man replied, smiling.

André de Coursin sat for several minutes with his hand still on the telephone. If the DST already knew about Drankov, he didn't have much time left. There was no use calling Delglade. *Le limier* would like nothing better than to rip the cover off the Drankov case at a high level as a demonstration of DGSE incompetence. Someone would have to come down hard on the DST and warn them off. The order would have to come straight from the Élysées. Before calling his contact in the President's office, de Coursin would have to get in touch with Morel. Considering the latest developments, he had no choice. Léon Faubert was already a dead man.

Léon Faubert wasn't in Tarbes, Saint-Gaudens, Lourdes or Spain, but he had fallen within the parameters of Levallois' predictions in two respects. He was drunk and in bed with a prostitute. He'd doubled back on his tracks in the direction of Marseille and gone to ground in the port city of Sète. He'd registered in the Hôtel du Soleil Levant on the Quai de Bosc, where they never asked to see identity papers. He'd used the name Pierre Monet. He'd then used an automatic teller to draw a sizable amount from his account with the Banque Nationale de Paris. Money in hand, he'd found a café facing the Canal de Sète and revived himself with several cognacs. He'd picked up the *poule* in the café, selecting her from a lounging trio of prostitutes at the bar. Her gypsy looks, long dark hair and overblown figure appealed to him. They'd dined together on garlicky terrines and grilled *rouget* before retiring to his room with a newly purchased bottle of Courvoisier. She'd proved good at her work. They'd fallen asleep, exhausted, at 3 A.M.

He'd been awakened by the chugging of boat engines from the canal. The *poule* was sleeping with her mouth open, her large-nippled breasts exposed. The bed and the room were permeated with the fragrance of her cheap perfume. Faubert needed black coffee and fresh air. He slipped out from under the heavy sheet and began to dress. He put on his tan slacks, pulled a blue cotton turtleneck over his head and checked the 9-mm Beretta in the pocket of his brown windbreaker.

De Coursin had been wrong about Faubert. He hadn't cracked or suffered a nervous breakdown. He had simply had enough. Too many risky, clandestine assignments; too many unexplained orders; too many unavenged friends lost in dubious operations. The Drankov liquidation had put the last feathery weight on an already overloaded scale. Faubert's revolt had been instantaneous and unplanned. His superiors might believe his actions were those of a madman, but to him delivering Drankov to the Soviet Consulate had been pure logic. He wanted the KGB resident in Marseille to know what had happened to his triple agent. He wanted de Coursin and Morel to know that Action agents had a limit of tolerance beyond which they shouldn't be pushed.

Faubert found an outside table at another café, ordered a large black coffee and watched the waterborne traffic on the turgid canal. He looked more like a garage mechanic than a DGSE agent. His dark hair was thinning, his tanned face was prematurely lined and his soft brown eyes had a permanent air of sadness. Sète was known as the Venice of Provence. It was bisected by canals and dotted with stone docks. Fishing boats and barges moved slowly through the drawbridges, old men fished from the quais and a bustling outdoor market under brightly colored parasols drew the housewives for their morning shopping.

The coffee helped to clear his head. He knew he would have to move on. They'd soon trace his bank withdrawal. He estimated that he had a maximum of twenty-four hours in which to move. He didn't know what had happened since he'd slipped away from his team in Tarbes, but he could imagine the reaction at *la crémerie*. He had done the unthinkable and the unforgivable. He wasn't worried about the KGB. Triple agents were expendable and the Russians were practical people. For them revenge was a dangerous luxury. Faubert would have to look out for his own colleagues. He yawned and stretched his arms in the warm sunlight. He would have to leave France, but he'd not yet decided on a destination or a method of departure. He recognized the fact that he might not elude his pursuers. Strangely enough, it didn't seem to bother him. He had cracked a fresh deck in a completely new card game. Somehow the idea pleased him.

Babar Mattei was standing with a glass of *pastis* in his hand looking out of Bastide's kitchen window. Bastide worked over the stove, manipulating a casserole, spreading the hot oil evenly. He'd invited Mattei for a light lunch rather than eating again in a restaurant. Pieces of a young rabbit were on the chopping board, ready for cooking. Bastide left the stove and began to chop a shallot. He paused and drank from his glass of Gigondas.

"We'll have a salad with the rabbit," he said, "and there's some Brie for later."

"No potatoes?" Mattei asked, glancing over his shoulder. "A rabbit without potatoes . . ."

Bastide chuckled. "This is supposed to be a light lunch," he said. "We can both stand to lose a few kilos."

Mattei shrugged and turned back to the window.

"What's so interesting out there?" Bastide asked.

"Not much. I was just thinking about the consulate case. We are getting absolutely nowhere. None of the Russians could identify the *macchabée;* there's no gangland link; we've had no feedback from other departments; the cyanide trail seems to have dissolved; and here we are with you cooking a damn rabbit and talking about light lunches like a dietitian. *Bon sang,* it's frustrating!"

"*Doucement,*" Bastide replied, throwing some parsley onto the board and attacking it with his sharp knife. "We're bound to come up with something soon."

"You know what I think?" Mattei asked.

"No, what?"

"I think the whole damn thing stinks of an intelligence operation."

Bastide glanced up sharply but continued his chopping.

"Why do you say that?" he asked.

"Because it's the only possibility that makes sense. We're being blocked. Someone's making us look foolish. I think it's the DST."

Bastide tossed the chunks of rabbit into the casserole, where they hissed and spit in the hot oil. "There," he said, shaking the casserole, then wiping his hands on a cloth. "We'll let it brown."

"Roger!" Mattei erupted. "Are you listening to me? That *salaud* Boniface is involved in the case somehow. I can feel it in my bones."

"You may be right," Bastide agreed, "but what can we do? Complain to Aynard. You know what that will get us. A half-hour lecture on keeping our noses clean and staying on the job. Relax, have another *pastis.*"

Mattei, frowning, finished the dregs in his glass and moved to the sideboard. He paused with the *pastis* bottle in his hand and sniffed.

"That does smell good," he said, his hunger winning over his professional misgivings. "I haven't had rabbit for a long time."

"This is a little beauty, tender and fresh," Bastide explained. "I got it from Dominique yesterday. She'd had a delivery from her supplier in Manosque. It's been feeding on mountain grass and herbs."

Mattei took a slice of *baguette* from the bread basket and bit into it. "This afternoon I'm checking the last possibility on the tarpaulin that was covering the body," he said. "It's a firm that supplies the Port of the Chambre de Commerce. I'm going to see him at three-thirty."

Bastide turned the golden brown hunks of fleshy rabbit, sprinkled them with salt and pepper, added the chopped shallots and shook the casserole again. He squeezed a lemon half over the rabbit and let it steam off before removing the meat to warm the plates. He put a tablespoon of bouillon into the casserole, deglazing it with a wooden spoon, and poured the juice over the rabbit, sprinkling it with chopped parsley.

"Let's eat," he announced, untying his butcher's apron and handing Mattei his plate. "I've set the table on the terrace. I'll take the Gigondas, you take the bread. The salad's already on the table."

They sat down in the sun and began to eat, breaking their bread into pieces and dipping it into the dark sauce.

"*Alors?*" Bastide asked. "What do you think?"

"Delicious," Mattei replied, his mouth full. "But a few small potatoes wouldn't have hurt."

Bastide laughed, filling Mattei's glass with wine. "You're impossible," he said, "I don't see how your wife puts up with you."

"How's your mother?" Mattei asked, changing the subject.

"She's fine, but since she's met Janine she's decided we should marry. She won't let it go."

"Maybe she's right," Mattei said, pausing to look directly at Bastide. "Have you considered it?"

"Oh, not much," Bastide mumbled, his eyes on his plate.

"You could do a lot worse," Mattei said. "Janine is a terrific woman."

"I know that," Bastide said sharply. He was a private man and he didn't like being reminded of his own indecision.

Mattei shrugged and concentrated on his meal. He knew the signals. There was no use pursuing the matter.

"I'm going to see Dinh Le Thong after lunch," Bastide said. "His contacts may have picked up a useful echo."

"I doubt it," Mattei said. "He'd have been in touch. Besides, the consulate case is a little out of his league."

"I think you're wrong. He's still on the DST payroll. He may have heard something interesting. I'd like to sound him out on Boniface. That bastard bears watching."

"I agree," Mattei replied. "I'm sure Boniface knows a lot more than we do about the Russkovs. I'd like to know which one of them is KGB. It's the least Boniface could tell us. I'd guess it was Popov."

Bastide served himself some salad and looked out over the Vieux Port.

"No," Bastide mused, "he's too young, too nervous. I'd pick Zavorin."

"The type with one eye that says *merde* to the other? But he's a cultural attaché."

"Didn't you find it strange that he sat in on our meeting with the consul general?" Bastide asked. "All that garbage about him having been a law student didn't hold up. I'd say he was their KGB resident."

"So you agree with me. It is more than a simple murder?"

"It could be," Bastide replied. He was tempted to tell Mattei about the Boniface visit, but he remembered his promise to de Coursin. The normal deceits of espionage were already influencing his working methods.

Larissa Kedrov arrived at Marseille-Marignane on an evening Air Inter flight from Paris. She took a taxi to the Hôtel des Calanques in Endoume, unpacked her bags and changed her clothes. At 9 P.M. she met Anatole Zavorin at a small restaurant two blocks from her hotel. Her entrance created a sensation. The waiters were immobilized, like a freeze-frame in a film; male customers paused with their forks halfway to their mouths. Women stopped talking as she walked to Zavorin's table.

Larissa Kedrov had chosen a flowing, low-cut gray-green dress of light silk. Her black hair was pulled back and thickly braided. She'd spent a lot of time on her makeup, accenting her doelike eyes and the clean lines of her beautifully sculpted face. Zavorin noted with approval that her figure hadn't changed. Her long legs were as he'd remembered them. They greeted each other formally and the *maître d'hôtel* helped her into her seat.

"Welcome to Marseille," Zavorin said. "I am pleased you're here."

"You have saved me from a boring week in Berlin," she replied.

"I've taken the liberty of ordering for you," he told her. "It saves time and avoids hovering waiters. You still eat lightly?"

"I do." She surveyed her surroundings, examining the customers and noting that Zavorin had asked for the most isolated table in the restaurant. A waiter brought them their drinks. A Scotch for Zavorin and a split of champagne for her. He poured water into his whiskey and raised his glass.

"To a profitable collaboration," he toasted.

"I have read the background," she said, speaking precisely. "It appears to be a difficult assignment. This policeman doesn't sound like a likely target. I am concerned with my cover. If I am to be your temporary assistant in the cultural section, how will I get close to him?"

Zavorin's walleye seemed to be fascinated with a silver duck press on a nearby table, but his good eye remained fixed on Larissa Kedrov. "It will be arranged," he told her. "Don't worry about Inspector Bastide. On paper he appears all business. But he's potentially a hot-blooded Marseillais, a prototype of the macho Latin. If you can strike the match that lights that fire, we should have no trouble. The important thing to remember is that we aren't after secrets, nor do we seek to compromise the inspector. We want to know what is happening in this case as it develops. We need forewarning if there is any need to act."

She raised her glass and Zavorin noticed the ruby ring she was wearing.

"That is most beautiful," he remarked.

"It's a gift," she said, smiling, "from an admirer. A lieutenant colonel of the West German Army who, unfortunately, is now in jail for passing secrets to a foreign power."

"A pity," Zavorin said, clearing his throat as the waiter arrived with their first course. Her cucumber salad was arranged on the plate like a green and white castle. His seafood pâté was a rainbow of colors.

"Do you have any questions?" he asked when the waiter had left.

"What of the consulate?" she asked. "How do I fit in? Who shall I be working with?"

"Vasili Aleksandrovich Anisimov, our consul general, is a useless, overweight career man interested only in his imminent retirement. His big moment came in the Great Patriotic War and he won't let you forget it. He is nothing to worry about. His wife, Natalie, is impossible. She's forever poking her long nose into consulate affairs and checking expenses in the hope of finding someone guilty of extravagance. If she had lived in Stalin's time, she'd have supervised his purges. Do your best to keep out of her path. Viktor Popov, the consul, is a good-looking fool who drinks too much. He was born in France of Russian parents. An unstable officer who needs watching. The rest of the staff are mediocre. We have some military under cover as administrative personnel. They help with communications and security. One of them is a former Spetsnaz sergeant detached from the GRU. He handles visits from the GRU office at our Paris embassy. You will meet my two assistants, Yegerov and Boldin. Both solid and dependable . . . if unimaginative."

"You have sent for me to assist in an important exhibit. Is that correct?"

"Yes. We have a shipment of icons coming from Odessa. They will be exhibited at the Palais Longchamp as part of the celebrations marking the long-standing twinning of Odessa with Marseille. Helping me arrange for this event will give you a good excuse to be out of the consulate often, moving around the city."

"Excuse me, Comrade Zavorin," she said, "but I see no link at all with this Inspector Bastide."

"There will be," he told her. "I am arranging that. I've already planted the seed with Consul General Anisimov, telling him that my sources have warned that members of the consulate may be in danger because of the incident. I've hinted we have information that some radical anti-Soviet group was behind the man's death, and warned that they may try something further to embarrass us or harm our personnel. Yesterday I recommended that he ask Inspector Bastide for increased protection."

"I am no expert on French police methods," she said, putting down her fork, "but would that not be the work of another section?"

"Normally, yes. But I have convinced Anisimov it would be unseemly and awkward to have various police visitors. He called the Préfet of Police this afternoon to explain and the préfet agreed. Inspector Bastide is to be our sole police contact."

"Efficient as always," Larissa Kedrov complimented Zavorin.

"That is my job," he said. The waiter came to clear their plates.

"Would you like white wine with your sole?" Zavorin asked.

"No, thank you," she replied. "I still have some champagne."

"I hope to introduce you to Bastide tomorrow. I'll be interested in your first impression. We have no time to waste, but we must be cautious."

"Your description of him was complimentary. I take it he is not a typical thick policeman?"

"No. He isn't what you'd call an intellectual either. But he has a brain and he uses it. He is also a nonconformist in his methods. Incidentally, there's one thing I did not mention: he does like to eat and he himself is an accomplished cook."

Her husky laugh surprised Zavorin, who saw nothing amusing in what he'd just told her.

"I am trying to preserve my figure and you introduce me to a confirmed gourmet," she said. "I'll have to invite him to share grilled Uzbek lamb and yogurt."

"I would not presume to tell you your business," Zavorin replied, distracted by her levity, "but I expect you to keep his mind on more important things than eating."

Antoine Morel had wasted no time. One hour after receiving the report on Faubert's bank withdrawal, his Citroën CX was speeding toward Orly Airport. Morel was studying the personnel dossier of Léon Faubert. The teams searching for Faubert had been called off. Morel had taken on the responsibility. He was sunk in the soft rear seat, swaying with the vehicle's movement as his driver wove in and out of the evening traffic. He'd planned his trip carefully. He was taking a commercial flight to Montpellier-Frejorques—not the small DGSE jet normally at his disposal. His assistant thought he was visiting an important academic at the University of Montpellier on a research project. Morel's wife didn't know where he was going. She'd helped him pack, but she'd been with him long enough not to ask questions. De Coursin was the only person who knew where he was going and why. If anything went wrong, he too would know nothing.

Morel read one of Faubert's citations before flicking back to the mug shots stapled to the folder. The full-face portrait told him nothing. Faubert faced the camera with a slight smirk. Why was it that official photographers always asked you to smile like puppeteers demanding a performance? The profile shot revealed a bit more. Faubert resembled a tired falcon, older than his years. It crossed Morel's mind that DGSE psychiatrists should learn to read personnel photos as a physician reads an X ray. It might save a lot of breakage. He went back to the citations.

There was one from the director's office dated May 19, 1986. In Chad, Faubert had led a team of two DGSE agents and three *chasseurs parachutistes* on a heliborne raid to Tombé in rebel territory. The document provided few details, but Morel knew the results of the hunt—two dead Libyan intelligence officers, including a major implicated in the assassination of a DGSE officer in Abéché. More dry official verbiage spoke of Faubert's role in tracking and retrieving funds stolen from a DGSE courier. The report hadn't mentioned the capture, torture and death of the courier, or Faubert's initiative in stalking and eliminating the killers one by one in Khartoum, Tunis and Bastia. Morel watched the headlights flash by and forced himself to think about Sète. DGSE had run an operation in Sète three years ago. It had involved scraping paint samples off the hull of a Soviet cruiser in port for a goodwill visit. It was a question of chemical analysis. Something to do with antisubmarine measures. His people hadn't been involved directly. He tried to recall who'd been in charge and finally gave up. He picked up his car telephone, dialed a number at headquarters, gave his coded identification number and hung up. His phone rang within thirty seconds and he asked for the name of the hotel in Sète used by the DGSE team who'd done the job.

By the time his driver pulled to a stop in front of the departure terminal he had the answer; the Hôtel du Soleil Levant on the Quai de Bosc. It was a long shot, but agents tended to share information on hotels and restaurants just like anyone else.

Larissa Kedrov sat on the rug of her hotel room in her underwear doing stretching exercises. Her lithe body responded easily to the effort as she touched her toes repeatedly. She breathed like an athlete, inhaling and exhaling with a controlled rhythm. When she'd finished on the floor she stood in front of the armoire mirror pushing her palms together, flexing her pectoral muscles and examining herself critically. Her body was essential to her profession and she kept it in perfect condition. She was pleased with her breasts. She'd taken particular care to see that they maintained their firmness. She was not as pleased with her hips. Despite diets and exercise the centimeters crept on without warning. She paused for a moment and turned so she could see the curve of her buttocks in the mirror. Everything appeared in order. There wasn't the sudden swelling of flesh she'd experienced a few years ago in Vienna when her target had insisted on feeding her cakes and cream-topped chocolate in the coffeehouses.

She went to the bed and sat down, stretching her arms. She began to unbraid her hair but paused for a moment to admire the ruby ring. Colonel Kurt Dietz of the Bundeswehr had actually fallen in love with her. That had been unusual. Most men were primarily interested in her body and the promise of her professional talents. She shook her dark braids free, remembering the colonel with cool detachment. He was a nice fool and an easy mark. When he'd been confronted with the videotape of their lascivious lovemaking, he'd disintegrated before her eyes. He'd appealed to her as a woman, citing the trauma such revelations would cause his wife and family. He'd offered large sums of money for the tape. When the KGB officer she'd been working for decided it was time to contact Dietz, he was ripe for the plucking. He'd leaped at the chance to lift some secret NATO documents on the new armor of the West German Leopard tank. Larissa Kedrov had taken a certain pleasure in calling the Criminal Investigation Section of the Bundeswehr with an anonymous tip that the colonel was involved in espionage. She didn't like weak men.

She walked to the window and looked out at the Mediterranean. A bright moon hung over the water and lit the stony offshore islands. She breathed the air and made a mental note to ask Zavorin where she could take advantage of the sun. She was determined to leave Marseille with a tan, but her free time would depend on her progress. She wondered what type of man Bastide was and how long it would take to attract him. She'd had few failures in her career. She saw the French detective as an interesting challenge.

IV

Antoine Morel was under no illusion about the difficulty of his task. Normally it would have been a job for a three-man team, but the director and de Coursin had agreed that knowledge of the operation was not to be shared beyond their limited circle. Morel had helped train Léon Faubert. He knew how good he was. He could not allow Faubert to see him first. Morel had taken a room in the Hôtel Orangers on the Boulevard Danielle Casanova at some distance from the Canal de Sète. The dark corridors smelled of acid disinfectant and there were plastic roses in the lobby.

Morel left his room at nightfall and walked toward the canal. A chopped and bobbed Colt .45 was nestled in a shoulder holster under Morel's left arm, and the leather sheath of an assault knife with a six-inch surgical steel blade was strapped to his right thigh, the knife's haft readily available through the cutaway pocket of his trousers. He could see the lights of the city reflecting from the water like tiny, dancing candles. Accordion music spilled out of an open third-story window as he passed below. He stepped carefully over some refuse in the gutter and paused, allowing his whole body to relax. It was something he'd learned in the Far East; the ability to turn his physical clock back, loosening the muscles, voiding the brain, cleansing the senses, concentrating on nothing. After a minute of physical suspension and mental void, the rewind began. His brain was prodded into a slow examination of the body's resources; the muscles tightened, were tested, and the mind was forced to reject superfluous distractions and concentrate on the immediate objective. With more time and someone to assist him he could have assured Faubert's complete disappearance. As it was, he could only make certain that any identification of the body was impossible. Morel took a deep breath, stepped out onto the cobblestones bordering the canal and walked toward the Hôtel du Soleil Levant.

Commissaire Aynard reached Bastide at La Mère Pascal as he was preparing to order his dinner. Dominique, the voluptuous proprietor, watched Bastide return to the bar after the phone call and automatically poured him a new *pastis.*

"*Oh, la, la,*" she said, "you look like a rain cloud about to piss on the world. It can't be that bad."

He shrugged. "It looks like I'm doomed to a sandwich for dinner," he told her. "Someone needs my services."

"What's her name?" Dominique chided him.

"For the *patronne* of a respectable restaurant," Bastide replied, "you have a very rustic humor."

"Don't blame me if you've chosen the wrong profession," Dominique countered. "You'd probably be much happier selling fish."

He paid for his drinks. "You're probably right," he admitted. "*Ciao!*"

Aynard had received a call from the préfet. The Soviet consul general was worried about the safety of his personnel. The consul general had requested increased police protection and insisted that Inspecteur Principal Bastide arrange it. He'd explained that they already knew Bastide, had confidence in him and expected the matter to be handled with discretion. The commissaire had told Bastide that the consul general was waiting for him at the consulate and instructed him to go there immediately.

By the time Bastide parked his police sedan on the rue Ambroise-Paré, his stomach was growling and he regretted not having eaten something before leaving La Mère Pascal. He was duly ushered into the consulate by another fresh-faced young Soviet in a somber suit and led to the consul general's office. Anisimov was waiting for him in the open doorway with a wide smile, his stainless-steel tooth gleaming in the light of the chandelier. Others were in the room.

"Come in, Inspector," Anisimov said, putting his hand on Bastide's shoulder. "I apologize for the late hour. You know Consul Popov and Comrade Zavorin. Allow me to introduce a new arrival to Marseille. This is Comrade Larissa Kedrov of our cultural services. She is here to help Comrade Zavorin with his exhibit."

Larissa Kedrov stepped forward. Bastide was visibly impressed. His reaction did not go unnoticed by Anisimov.

"Is she not beautiful, Inspector?" the consul general asked. "If all our official visitors were like her, I would meet them at the airport myself."

Anatole Zavorin had also monitored Bastide's reaction. He was privately savoring the inspector's difficulty in tearing his eyes away from Larissa Kedrov.

"I have heard of you, Inspector," she said in perfect French, meeting his gaze while she carried out her own cool appraisal. "I am told you are very professional."

"I'm pleased to hear that," Bastide replied, ill at ease with the social pleasantries.

"It is long after working hours," Anisimov said, "so we are having a little snack, a *casse-croûte* as you call it here. I hope you will join us? We can continue our business at the same time."

"I'd be glad to," Bastide replied truthfully, noticing the smoked fish, buttered black bread and varicolored cheeses arranged on a large platter.

"Pour the inspector some Georgian wine," Anisimov told Popov. "A policeman's work is thirsty business. Good. Now, Inspector, come sit on the couch with me. The only way to approach a serious matter is with a glass in your hand, am I not right?"

Bastide nodded in agreement and sat down, careful not to spill his wine. The woman sat across from him, folding her long legs carefully and rearranging her skirt. She's magnificent! Bastide thought. He'd never seen anyone quite like her. Bastide only half heard what the consul general was saying . . . something about new threats to the consulate and danger for his staff. He watched Larissa Kedrov bend over to select an open-faced sandwich from the tray. He noted the thick braid of black hair and the fine lines of her body.

"What do you think, Inspector?" Anisimov had just asked.

"Oh," Bastide stalled, trying to recover himself. "Ah, there is always a threat. It all depends on the degree."

"Of course," Anisimov agreed, "but I cannot shirk my responsibility. I have asked your préfet if you can help us. I know your job is homicide, but we know you and you know us. We need your suggestions."

Bastide felt he'd fallen into another pit. First it was de Coursin. Now the préfet had pushed him into an additional assignment that had nothing to do with his work. The consul general was sitting forward on the couch, expectantly awaiting his response. He was trapped.

"First of all," Bastide finally said, "you and your people must vary your daily routines. This applies to your families too. If, for instance, you drive the same routes on your official business, you must change them daily. If your wives shop in one area or *supermarché,* they should find others. You should double your vigilance at the consulate. Do not accept unexpected parcels or heavy envelopes without a thorough security examination. The identity papers of all visitors should be double-checked . . ."

Anatole Zavorin smiled inwardly as he listened to Bastide. It sounded like a beginners' course in security. Did the Frenchman think they were amateurs? But he remained silent. Things were working out as he'd planned. He decided it was time to focus attention on Larissa Kedrov.

"Excuse my interruption, Inspector," Zavorin said, "but I am particularly concerned about Mademoiselle Kedrov. As the consul general has mentioned, she is a new arrival. She has come here to help me with an exhibition at the Palais Longchamp. This means that, unlike most of our present staff, she will be spending much time away from the consulate on her way to and from the exhibition site, conferring with the museum's staff, having her meals in the city. Her safety must be assured."

"Yes," the consul general added, "I agree. Particularly as she is completely new here, particularly vulnerable."

Bastide had heard enough about Soviet security practices to find this sudden preoccupation with security out of character. A tiny warning bell sounded in the back of his mind. He decided to pose some questions of his own.

"Surely you have a staff member trained in security matters available to escort Mademoiselle Kedrov?" he asked.

"We could perhaps do that," Zavorin said smoothly, "but it would be most awkward . . . in a diplomatic and cultural sense. Why should our cultural representatives be protected by Soviet bodyguards in your country? It would be bad for our 'image,' as you say. The French press would surely accuse us of returning to the days of Stalin."

"I agree with Comrade Zavorin," Anisimov said. "Such a situation would be intolerable. Allow me to remind you, Monsieur l'Inspecteur, that diplomatic security is the responsibility of the host country."

"I am not a security specialist," Bastide reminded them. "Perhaps you would do better with an officer from the diplomatic protection unit."

"Oh no," the consul general interjected, "I have had experience with them in Paris. I mean no offense, but I believe they spent more time watching us than protecting us. We asked the préfet for your help because you are already on the case of the unknown corpse. As I've said, we know you."

"All we are asking," Zavorin added, "is that you assist us to tighten our security and make a special effort in the case of Mademoiselle Kedrov. If you could spare some time to accompany Mademoiselle Kedrov to and from the Palais Longchamp and on her professional business. A movement pattern would then develop . . ."

Zavorin stopped talking abruptly and made a show of clearing his throat. But Bastide had caught the significant phrase. Somehow "movement pattern" didn't seem to fit a cultural attaché's vocabulary. It was verbiage used by security officers.

"I'll be pleased to help Mademoiselle Kedrov," Bastide reassured them. In fact, he thought, I'd be overjoyed. He tried to draw Zavorin deeper into the security discussion by addressing him directly.

"What can you tell me about the threat you face?" he asked. "Who is behind it?"

"I believe the consul general knows more about that than I do," Zavorin sidestepped neatly.

"Inspector," Anisimov responded, "we cannot be sure, but we have internal reports that an anti-Soviet group has threatened our posts in France. Of course, these are lunatics and unreformed fascists, but it is just because they are so unstable, so unrepresentative of the French people, that they are dangerous."

Bastide took a sip of the Georgian wine. He found it too sweet to his taste. He put the glass down on the table and helped himself to a slice of black bread covered with a large hunk of smoked sturgeon. It was his first real experience in diplomacy and he was intrigued. He sensed something going on under the surface that he didn't understand. He felt uneasy. His job was to solve a murder. Not to baby-sit a foreign official, no matter how beautiful she was.

"Mademoiselle Kedrov begins her work tomorrow," Zavorin said. "Can you accompany her in the morning?"

"It would be a pleasure," Bastide said, turning to watch her reaction.

Once again, her dark eyes held his, direct, unembarrassed, and a slight smile appeared on her lips.

Léon Faubert had bought a small plastic suitcase. It was now packed with his old clothes. He'd left enough room for his toilet articles and a bottle of cognac. He was wearing a new, locally purchased wardrobe, including a khaki shirt, light slacks, a pair of blue espadrilles and a tan cotton jacket. The Beretta automatic was secure in the waistband of the trousers, hidden under the jacket. He planned to leave Sète early in the morning by bus. He'd decided to travel to Saint-Malo. It was a long trip, but he could get false papers there and he had an old friend, a fisherman, who would ask no questions. He also knew that some of the Saint-Malo fishing fleet worked the waters along the Irish coast. It would be easy to land there without hindrance and pass for a tourist. It would provide him with a safe haven for a period of months and enough time to decide on his final destination.

The hoot of a fishing boat passing under the drawbridge near the hotel made him start. He smiled at his own reaction. He hadn't realized how jumpy he was. A copper moon hung low in the night sky, competing with the colored lights strung along the canal. He'd sent the prostitute back to her trade that afternoon. He regretted her absence, but his planned voyage was strictly business. The scratchy loudspeaker music from a fun fair at the end of the canal carried to his hotel room as he leaned on the windowsill watching the strollers below and trying to decide where to have dinner.

At first he thought it was a trick of the light or that he'd drunk too much cognac in the past few days. He turned from the window and snapped off the light in his room. Flattening himself against the opened shutters, he peered more closely at the quai. Morel's bearlike walk gave him away. He moved his stocky frame with a heavy determination, a trait readily spotted by someone who'd lived and worked with him. Faubert stepped back into the darkness of his room.

"*Vieux salaud!*" he cursed, watching Morel pause to examine the hotel's entrance. Faubert scanned the quai for any sign of a backup. No, he told himself, Morel would have come alone. It was the only way he would operate in such a situation.

Morel had seen the light go off in the upper room. It told him something but he finished his examination of the hotel's ground-floor level. He'd taken in the brightly lit entranceway, the lace curtains of the office and the dull light and moving figures in the small lobby. He inspected the upper stories, moving his eyes from one window to the next. It was a small hotel and there were three double windows on each floor. Three rooms per floor. Lights were burning in each room except for the one room on the second floor. Morel took several steps to the right, removing himself from the line of vision of anyone on the upper floors. He stood for a moment sheltered by the overhang of a café awning, reversed his steps and turned into a small alley leading to the back street.

Faubert had lost sight of Morel. He'd vanished completely. "He's coming in from the rear," he murmured to himself, reaching for the Beretta. He hurried to the door of his room. He stood in silence for a moment, listening. Then he opened the door silently, stepped into the hall, leaving the door slightly ajar. He knew the path Morel would be taking. He'd already checked the entrances and exits the day he'd registered. Morel would enter a small service door at the rear, cross a storage area full of cased bottles and primagaz containers and come into the hotel through the narrow passage between the toilets and the owner's living quarters. The winding, steel-railed stairway would bring him up to the second floor directly opposite the door to Faubert's room. Faubert remembered the one creaky stair just below the second-floor landing that he'd stumbled over his first drunken night. It could serve as a warning signal.

Morel loosened the Colt in its holster and unsnapped the leather strap securing the haft of his knife. He'd moved across the empty courtyard, careful to avoid the empty bottles lying on the cobbles. He stood completely still before he opened the rear door to the hotel. Then he was inside the dark hall listening to the sound of a television in the owner's quarters and the dripping of a faulty spigot in a toilet. He drew the stubby Colt and moved toward the ground-floor lobby and the stairway.

Faubert stationed himself to the right of the stairs with his back pressed flat against the wall, the landing to his left. He took a deep breath and waited. Someone was climbing the stairs. Whoever it was had paused at the first-floor landing before continuing and had not used the stairway light switch. Faubert experienced a mental image of himself stepping out from cover to greet his old colleague only to be smashed back against the wall with two huge holes in his chest. The image made him angry. He shifted the Beretta and wiped his perspiring right hand on his trousers.

"Putain!" Morel cursed silently as one of the stairs creaked under his foot. He lifted his leg high to avoid the next two and put the weight of one foot on the last step before the landing. It was solid. He hoisted himself up, leaning on the wall for support. He could see the darkened room in front of him. He paused for a moment to listen. Then he gently released the cocked hammer of his Colt, slid it back into its holster and drew his knife. The room could be empty or it might be occupied by someone else. It would be easier to hide the knife than the Colt. If Faubert was there the silence of the knife would be preferable. Morel gripped the haft tightly, saw that the cutting edge of the blade was up and took a cautious step onto the second-floor landing.

Faubert launched his full weight at Morel, driving him forward through the half-open door, and brought the butt of his Beretta down hard, aiming just below Morel's right ear. They fell to the floor, Morel's knife gouging a hole in the carpet. Morel was surprised, but Faubert's blow had only stunned him, glancing off his skull. He lay still for several seconds and waited till Faubert reached under his jacket for the Colt. He twisted his body and struck Faubert across the bridge of his nose with a powerful, straight-handed karate blow. Bone cracked and Faubert gasped with pain, blinded by a rush of tears. Morel went for his Colt and drew back both legs for a double kick at Faubert's stomach. Faubert was faster. Despite his pain he threw himself on Morel, blocking his attempt to draw the automatic. He jammed the muzzle of his Beretta in Morel's right ear.

"One move," he warned, "and you're brainless!" He felt Morel's body relax under him. He snatched the Colt from its holster. "That's better," Faubert said, rising to his knees, holding the Beretta an inch from Morel's forehead. "Now, on your stomach!" He watched Morel roll over, alert for any trick or quick movement.

"I know you came here to kill me, Morel," Faubert said with a strange air of sadness in his voice, "but I don't want to kill you."

"Give it up and I'll take you in," Morel said, his words muffled by the rug.

Faubert laughed bitterly and shut the door to the room. "I knew this would happen," he said. "I'd hoped I might be wrong. I thought you'd want me to leave the country or surrender so you could put me away. What an illusion." He touched his damaged nose gingerly. The pain made him wince.

"We can still arrange something," Morel replied while he planned his next move. He wanted to keep Faubert talking. He was astounded that Faubert hadn't immobilized his hands and his feet. There was definitely something wrong with Faubert. Any first-year trainee would have been more cautious. From his prone position he couldn't tell if the Beretta was still aimed at his skull. But he had to take the risk that Faubert wouldn't fire because of the noise.

"Being betrayed by a friend," Faubert said, holding a handkerchief to his nose, "is worse than being betrayed by the system."

"Don't be a fool!" Morel replied. "No one betrayed you. You betrayed yourself. It was a stupid trick. Put away that *pétard!*"

"Oh certainly," Faubert said sarcastically. "We shall then have a drink together and I'll fly back to *la crémerie* for rehabilitation. *Mon oeil!*"

Morel knew the knife wasn't far from his right foot. If he could get to it . . . He heard Faubert blow his nose and he moved. Swinging himself in a flat arc, using all the power of his athletic body, he snatched at the knife and missed. Faubert's foot stamped on his wrist. The butt of Morel's Colt smashed down on his head.

Faubert stood mumbling over Morel's unconscious form. He felt betrayed for the second time. Faubert knew he'd have used the knife if he could have reached it. They wanted him dead. But it wouldn't be that easy. "Bastards," he said aloud, still staring at Morel. *"Bon Dieu,"* he told himself, "if they think they have problems with me now . . ." At that moment he put aside his plans for leaving France. A new idea had come to him. He'd already sent a message to the KGB resident in Marseille by dumping Drankov's corpse. Perhaps it was time to send a new message. This one would be for KGB headquarters. An impressive notification that their residents were no longer immune, despite diplomatic cover. He thought of the effect this would have on his DGSE superiors, the men who'd ordered his own execution. He allowed himself a brief smile before crouching over Morel to feel his throat for a pulse. Satisfied, he went to the bed and ripped some strips from the sheet. He bound Morel tightly.

"Voilà," he murmured, examining his handiwork. He thought for a moment before picking up Morel's knife. He crouched again to pull off Morel's shoes and socks. Then he deftly cut Morel's Achilles tendons with a detached, surgical precision.

"Next time," Faubert said, wiping the bloody knife on the rug, "I won't have you on my trail."

Bastide finished his telephoned description of the bizarre meeting at the Soviet Consulate and waited for de Coursin's reaction. It wasn't long in coming.

"I agree with the préfet," de Coursin told him. "Under the circumstances, cooperating with the Soviets is the best thing to do."

"Doesn't it seem strange to you that they'd want me involved in their security problems?"

"Not at all. After all, security is a police matter," de Coursin replied. "You say the cultural attaché was present at the meeting?"

"That's right; his name's Zavorin."

"The woman—what does she look like?"

"Larissa Kedrov is tall, *racée*, beautiful figure, speaks good French. Very attractive."

"I see," de Coursin said thoughtfully. "Well, I do appreciate your call, Inspector."

"This changes nothing?" Bastide asked.

"What do you mean?" de Coursin responded.

"I thought it might have some significance . . ."

"In regard to intelligence? Not at all. It's a simple request for police assistance. Inspector, you must stop searching for spies under every rock. I'd be the first to warn you of such goings-on."

"Monsieur de Coursin," Bastide said firmly, thinking of Drankov, "I don't like this arrangement. I don't think I'm being informed. I can accept the need for you to know about new developments—but my acting as a security adviser to the Russians?"

"I suggest you discuss all this with the préfet," de Coursin said, his tone cool and distant. *"Au revoir, Inspecteur."*

De Coursin immediately dialed another number. He canceled the official car waiting for him in the courtyard. He would have to miss the reception at the American embassy. He straightened his tie and left his office, walking purposefully along the corridor and up a flight of stairs to the archive center. Once inside, he sat at a metal desk and asked a female clerk to bring him the classified dossier on KGB swallows operating in Western Europe. Waiting for the file, he called Jean Canadel. Canadel kept track of Soviet seduction efforts. When he arrived, puffing from the climb upstairs, de Coursin had found Larissa Kedrov's listing. Her record was impressive: a British naval officer in Naples, a Dutch diplomat in Stockholm, an American nuclear scientist in Brussels. These were only a few of Larissa Kedrov's past targets. De Coursin had also read a typed annotation signed by Jean Canadel at the foot of the page:

> Field reports indicate that Kedrov, Larissa, is one of the top swallows in the business. She is beautiful, intelligent and good at her work. She holds an Order of Lenin for services to the Soviet state.

Some DGSE wag had added "I volunteer as a target" in blue ink under Canadel's note.

"*Bonjour*, Jean," de Coursin greeted Canadel, looking up over his half-lensed reading glasses. "I'd like to talk about Larissa Kedrov."

Canadel was plump and hairy. He had an unfortunate tendency to perspire heavily, and the area just below his tight shirt collar was already transparent with sweat. He wiped his brow with a soggy handkerchief and took a seat next to de Coursin, who recoiled from Canadel's pervasive dampness.

"Kedrov, Larissa," Canadel said slowly, rolling his small blue eyes. "Ah yes, I remember. The swallow from Uzbek. A magnificent creature by all accounts. It's a wonder she hasn't eliminated a whole generation of diplomats and military officials by screwing them to death." His laughter ripped across the file room like machine-gun fire.

De Coursin winced. "There isn't much detail here," he commented, tossing the file onto the desk. "What else can you tell me about her?"

Canadel tapped his forehead. "It's all in here," he said, "in my 'personal' file. Larissa has a special way of getting under the skin of a target. She is very subtle. She doesn't believe in 'heels in the air' on her first approach. She learns a lot about her man, dredging him for personal details, sympathizing with his problems, making him feel she really cares. When the time comes, he doesn't know what's hit him. She could rewrite the *Kama Sutra.*"

"Why isn't that all in the dossier?" de Coursin asked.

"If someone wants to know the details, he can come to my office," Canadel explained. "If we put everything we had in the swallow dossiers, it would shock the file clerks and half our officers would line up to read them during their lunch break."

De Coursin was intrigued. "Was she ever married?" he asked.

"We don't know. There was a rumor that she might have been married to a Soviet Air Force captain, but it's never been confirmed. According to one of her former colleagues, a defector from Berlin, she's had two abortions, but that information may be based on simple female jealousy."

"Does she . . . ?" De Coursin found himself hesitating.

"Really enjoy it?" Canadel prompted with a conspiratorial smile.

"Well?"

"I don't know. I wouldn't know that about any woman. You know the story. In the past the KGB recruited actresses, dancers and even women from the armed forces with tendencies toward nymphomania. This created a control problem. Things are much more professional now. Good swallows are hard to pinpoint. This Kedrov woman is a case in point. To put it crudely, you'd never take her for a whore."

"Do you have any pictures of her?"

"Yes. A street shot in Paris and a few reception shots from Vienna. I'll send some prints, but I'd like them back. I don't suppose you want to tell me exactly what she's up to?"

"Not for the moment, although I may call on you for further help."

"My aviary aims to please," Canadel said, loosing another burst of grating laughter.

"Thank you," de Coursin said. On his way back to the office he pondered the significance of Larissa Kedrov's sudden appearance in Marseille. Anatole Zavorin had obviously asked for her. From what Bastide had reported the target was obvious. It had to be Bastide himself. Why would Zavorin waste the talents of Kedrov on a simple *flic*? What could they possibly hope to gain by such a seduction? Marseille cops didn't defect with files of sensitive information or agree to lift documents simply because they were caught between the sheets with a beautiful woman. Most of them would be out on the street bragging about it the next morning.

De Coursin walked into his office and shut the door. He filled his onyx cigarette holder and struck a match. He lit the cigarette and inhaled. He was using Bastide and so was Zavorin. De Coursin wanted to know what the Soviets were up to and Zavorin wanted to be tipped on the activities of the French. Neither one of them wanted the messy Drankov murder to be linked with intelligence operations, but they both had to be prepared if it was. Once the story blew, it would be a race to cover their tracks and get to the international media with the proper disinformation. They also needed lead time to prepare their superiors to ride out the diplomatic shock waves.

It was entirely possible that the problem would not arise, that the Drankov affair would sink quietly into the dark trough of forgetfulness after a frustrated Marseille police inspector filed it away as an unsolved case. But de Coursin couldn't be sanguine about that prospect until Léon Faubert was out of the way. He checked the time. Morel was late calling in.

Bastide left the Préfecture in a vile mood. He paused in the Place Félix Baret to unwrap a cigar and managed to break it in two near the tip. Furious, he threw the debris into the gutter. He decided to walk to Le Haiphong before driving back to the Hôtel de Police. He'd gone to see Dinh Le Thong earlier in the week, but his old friend had been in Paris visiting a cousin.

He found Thong painting the façade of his restaurant. He'd spread a canvas drop cloth on the sidewalk and was applying gold paint to the outlines of a sampan cut into the red-lacquered door. A young Vietnamese boy with shoulder-length black hair was meticulously retouching the landscape of the Baie d'Along painted on the window.

"*Alors*, Van Gogh," Bastide called from a distance, "I've come to buy you a drink!"

Dinh Le Thong turned, wiped his hand and extended it in greeting. Thong's clipped brush of hair seemed to have turned a bit more gray since they'd last met. His eyes, though, were as bright and shrewd as they'd been when he'd taught Bastide the commando's trade during the dark days in Algiers.

"I'm pleased to see you, Roger," he said. "Come in, I'll let you buy me that drink."

The dark interior of Le Haiphong was cool, redolent of Asian herbs and *nuoc mâm*. Thong went to the bar and snapped on an orange-shaded lamp made from a large Scotch bottle.

"What will you have," he asked expectantly, "a whiskey?"

"Why not?" Bastide replied. "And pour one for yourself."

Thong laughed. "Oh no," he said, "I'll have an Orangina. You know what alcohol does to me. I turn red and start to giggle." He poured their drinks and put his muscular arms on the bar. "So," he asked, "how is the death business?"

"*Emmerdant!*" Bastide replied.

"Still no luck?" Thong asked.

"It's a real *foutoir*. I'm getting nowhere. Have you heard anything?"

"I only know Boniface is sticking his nose into it. My DST colleagues tell me he'd like to take over the case."

"I've hit a stone wall," Bastide remarked, sipping his whiskey.

Thong looked thoughtfully at the varnished surface of the bar. "You know," Thong said, "you ought to talk to Barbanov. He might be able to help."

Bastide frowned, trying to recall who went with the name. Then it came to him. "You must be joking. He's the maddest *moujik* in Marseille."

Michel *"le Russe"* Barbanov was an aged Russian refugee who played the balalaika in Le Sébastopol, a shoddy Russian nightclub near the Vieux Port. After several vodkas he always boasted of having served with the KGB under Khrushchev.

"He isn't as mad as all that," Thong said. "The DST taps him from time to time. Drunk or sober, he has a good memory. He maintains certain contacts. He sees many Soviets at Le Sébastopol, resident or transient, and he hears things. It might be worth your while."

"At this point I'd turn to the devil for help," Bastide replied. "And you, my friend, how goes it?"

"Not too bad," Thong replied. "The restaurant is doing well, my wife is pleasantly plump, my son is pursuing his medical studies and my niece is engaged to be married. But I am sick at heart."

"Why is that?"

"There is much bad news. More boat people are coming out under the most difficult conditions. The pirates in the Gulf of Siam wait for them, murdering, raping, robbing. Nothing is done. The world is bored with boat people. They are no longer newsworthy."

Bastide nodded. He'd read of the "pirates" Thong was referring to: Thai and Malay fishermen who'd found the gold, jewelry and money of Vietnamese refugees much more profitable than their normal catch.

"I'd like to be back there," Thong said grimly, "with thirty trained men and a well-armed, fast patrol boat. We'd soon see how brave the pirates are!"

Bastide downed his whiskey. "There is nothing you can do," he said. "Don't torture yourself."

A shiver ran through Thong's body. He managed a weak smile. "Go see Barbanov," he told Bastide; "it could be useful."

Janine picked Bastide up at the Hôtel de Police. They drove to La Ciotat to watch the sun set and eat *petite friture* at a seaside restaurant. He made a special effort to put the day's frustrations behind him. They had a long discussion about Théo Gautier. The old man was failing and Janine was worried. She knew he'd made arrangements to be put in a nursing home, leaving the instructions with his lawyer and a copy with Janine. But the decision would be in her hands if his condition deteriorated. The only family left was a sister even older than Gautier. She was in no condition to make decisions even if she'd been asked. Gautier had provided for Janine in his will. This made her position even more difficult. She knew Gautier's friends and business associates were likely to accuse her of influencing him in her own favor. Bastide promised to help when the time came for a decision. Janine's future wasn't mentioned, but it hung over them like an unanswered question. Bastide's mother had done her best to convince him they should marry but he'd countered her heavy hints with jocular responses and quickly changed the subject. Now, as Janine and Bastide lapsed into silence sipping the last of their white wine, he had little doubt that Janine was thinking along the same lines. He felt like a coward for not broaching the subject, but he wasn't ready yet. He wanted Janine close to him; he enjoyed her; he might even love her. But marriage? That was something he couldn't face.

Janine had to return to Gautier's apartment on the rue de Paradis. The cook was leaving at 10 P.M., and she didn't want to leave Théo alone. They talked about Mattei and his unruly children on the drive back to Marseille. The image of Babar trying to keep order among his madcap family soon had them both laughing. It helped lift the pall cast by their earlier discussion.

Janine dropped Bastide in front of his apartment. He waited till she'd turned up the rue de Chantier before striking out for Le Sébastopol. The nightclub was tucked away in a small alley. Bright red and blue lights formed an onion-shaped dome over the door and you had to descend two steps before you could enter the club. Cigarette smoke hung in layers over the red-clothed tables. Flickering candles were reflected in the burnished metal of the old samovar on the bar. There was an unaccountable odor of cloves in the narrow room. Bastide followed the gray-haired proprietor to a small table, ordered chilled vodka and surveyed the clientele. Four of the twelve tables were occupied by couples and a fifth by a noisy party of six. The three-man orchestra sat in a small alcove. The two balalaikas and a fiddle were completing a plaintive ode from the steppes. Bastide quickly identified Michel Barbanov. He was an angular man with a huge head. Tufts of gray hair poked out from under his beaded skullcap. He kept his eyes closed as his heavy fingers moved over the strings of the balalaika.

A small carafe of vodka was brought to Bastide's table in an ice bucket and the waiter filled a chilled glass. Bastide lit a cigar, sat back and tried to enjoy the music. When the piece ended, the people at the noisy table shouted their requests. Barbanov's flickering fingers led the trio into a rousing tune that soon had most of the clients clapping to its rhythm. Bastide sipped his vodka, smoked his cigar and waited patiently for the musicians to take their break.

When they finally left the small stage, Bastide motioned Barbanov over to his table. The Russian peered at Bastide through thick brows that hung like gray icicles over his eyes. "Do I know you?" he asked, sitting down heavily, eyeing the vodka.

"I don't think you do," Bastide replied before asking the waiter to bring another glass. "I'm Inspecteur Principal Roger Bastide of the P.J. I've been told you know a lot about your countrymen resident in Marseille."

Barbanov watched Bastide fill his glass with vodka. He tossed it down in one quick gesture. "I am a French citizen now, Inspector. Therefore, Russians are no longer my countrymen." This time Barbanov filled his own glass. "What do you think of Chagall?" he asked suddenly.

Bastide frowned. He was no art fancier, but he knew Chagall's work. He tried to make sense of Barbanov's question. "I suppose he was a great painter," Bastide replied.

"You suppose? Ha!" Barbanov exclaimed, banging his fist on the table. "Chagall was a charlatan. He couldn't paint an Easter egg!" Barbanov's arm rose like a piston and another glass was emptied. Bastide changed the subject.

"I'm told you once served in the KGB," he said. "Is that true?"

"Of course it's true," Barbanov told him. "It's no secret. The DST knows all about it. But I wasn't with the KGB long. I was too imaginative, too intelligent for them. They can't stand brilliance. It makes them nervous. Even Chagall had trouble with the KGB, and he wasn't even a good painter." Barbanov leaned across the table. "What's in your craw?" he asked in a semiwhisper. "I provide information to the DST from time to time," he said, "but I'm paid for it. Do you want to pay too?" Barbanov lifted the empty carafe and waved it at the waiter.

"Maybe," Bastide replied. "What do you know about the body that was found at the Soviet Consulate?"

"Oh, that." Barbanov shrugged. "Every Russian in the city has his own theory."

"What's yours?"

"I've already told the DST," Barbanov said, and a sly smile spread over his craggy face. "I suppose they haven't told you, eh?"

"What's your theory?" Bastide demanded, ignoring Barbanov's question.

The waiter pushed another carafe of vodka into the melting ice. Barbanov snatched it, poured himself a full glass and put the carafe on the table between them.

"It is simple. Child's play. Zavorin's work has come home to haunt him."

"Zavorin?"

"How much money do you have, Inspector?" Barbanov asked, tilting his head like an inquisitive bird.

"Enough," Bastide replied, irritated. He didn't want to play games. He was losing patience with Barbanov. "Listen, Barbanov," he said, "you may be able to charm the DST with your quaint antics, but they don't impress me. I might just pull you and your balalaika down to the Hôtel de Police for an uncomfortable night of questioning if you don't stop clowning! Now, what about Zavorin?"

"Any immigrant, any refugee, any refusenik knows Zavorin is KGB. You can smell it on him. His bad eye isn't a birth defect; it comes from looking over his shoulder." Barbanov laughed at his own joke and drank more vodka.

"What is the link between Zavorin and the corpse?" Bastide asked.

"That, policeman, I don't know. But I'll tell you one thing. The dead man, may God have mercy on his soul, is the product of some KGB operation. I can guarantee you that. I don't know who else is involved, but whoever is responsible doesn't like Zavorin at all."

Barbanov looked closely at Bastide. "You must be involved in the case," he said. "Is that it? You are investigating this 'murder'?"

Bastide nodded, resenting the question. The vodka was burning his stomach. He pushed his glass aside.

"I don't envy you," Barbanov said. "They should not waste your time. It is not a police matter. Has no one told you that?"

Bastide said nothing. Barbanov's insight was making him angry, rekindling the frustration he already felt.

"Inspector," Barbanov said, "I would like to help, but I've told you all I know. I think someone may be laughing at you."

Bastide removed some hundred-franc notes from his wallet, folded them and slid them across to Barbanov. The Russian pushed them into the pocket of his baggy jacket. He stood and inclined his head in a brief bow.

"I must rejoin my comrades," he said, indicating the two musicians waiting for him. "Will you be finishing the vodka?" Barbanov picked up the carafe when Bastide shook his head.

"I enjoyed our discussion," Barbanov said, "but I will tell you one important truth. Chagall couldn't paint a fly on Picasso's ass!" With that he turned to walk back to the alcove.

Bastide watched Barbanov take his seat, secure the carafe of vodka between his feet and strum a long, introductory chord on his instrument. The man is far from mad, Bastide thought. He's a clever survivor. When Bastide had paid the bill, tipped the waiter and stepped out onto the sidewalk, he found himself in basic agreement with Barbanov on one point. Someone must be laughing at him.

V

Léon Faubert climbed down from the high cab of the tanker-truck, waved goodbye to the driver and walked to a small café terrace shaded by plane trees. A young boy in running shorts came out to take his order. He asked for black coffee and a croissant.

There was heavy traffic in Martigues. A fine layer of powdery dust covered the Formica-topped table, but Faubert didn't notice. He was recalling his encounter with Morel. If he hadn't seen Morel on the quai, he would be dead now. He could imagine the scenario. Morel covering the incident with a blanket of official secrecy and escorting Faubert's body back to Paris for a quick, quiet cremation.

But he wasn't dead, and Morel was no longer stalking him. He knew they'd loose the pack once Morel was found. Faubert wasn't overly worried. What he had to do could be done quickly. He took his time, eating the croissant slowly, sipping his coffee and enjoying the sun. He thought of the chaos he'd soon create at *la crémerie*. He wouldn't be doing it only for himself. He'd be doing it for every Action agent who'd been abused and ignored in the past ten years: all the widows on reduced pensions who'd never know how or why their husbands had died in Chad, Bangkok or Budapest. It was time they all received the credit and respect due them. It would never happen if officials like de Coursin remained in command, playing games on the intelligence chessboard, sending dedicated men on fruitless missions and treating their agents like spoiled dogmeat.

Faubert's first reaction to the attempt on his life had been pure rage and a resolve to strike back at the DGSE. Once he'd left Morel in the hotel and steadied his nerves with a few cognacs, his plan had taken coherent shape. He'd seriously considered eliminating the KGB resident in Marseille, leaving no doubt that it was a DGSE operation. Hitchhiking from Sète to Martigues had given him further time to think. As the tanker-truck rolled through Fos-sur-Mer that morning, Faubert had developed another plan. He'd decided to take the KGB resident hostage. That would best accomplish what he wanted to do: confound the DGSE, embarrass the KGB and, thanks to the publicity, protect himself from *la crémerie*'s exterminating angels. He imagined the headlines, the news flashes interrupting normal TV and radio programming and the crush of journalists demanding information from the DGSE and the Ministry of the Interior. The thought of it made him smile.

He had never seen Anatole Zavorin in the flesh, but he knew him from his file. Action agents were privy to detailed information concerning the opposition on a need-to-know basis. When Faubert had been put in charge of the team sent after Grigori Drankov, he'd been required to study the Zavorin dossier. He'd been impressed. He'd learned that Zavorin's previous assignments in London, Oslo, Dublin and Paris had been marked by success. Faubert had been struck by Zavorin's obvious expertise at manipulation. He'd always maintained his cover and managed to emerge unscathed or untainted from the most lethal operations, sacrificing his subordinates if necessary. The parallel with de Coursin's operating methods had been obvious. Faubert put some change on the table and picked up his suitcase. He'd take the bus into Marseille. Truck drivers who picked up hitchhikers had long memories.

Larissa Kedrov was waiting for Bastide in front of the consulate when he arrived and parked the police Peugeot at the curb.

"Good morning, Inspector," she said. "If this is a sample of your weather, I might consider moving to Marseille."

"You'd be welcome," Bastide replied in a stunted attempt at gallantry.

She was wearing a white cotton dress with a stylish side vent that revealed her shapely legs. Her dark hair was no longer braided. It fell over her shoulders. Her gold-loop earrings shone in the sun. When they shook hands, Bastide noticed for the first time that her almond-shaped eyes were green. She was carrying a large portfolio under her arm.

"I am to discuss the placement of our exhibit with the museum director this morning," she told him. "Will you come with me in the consulate car? It would be wasteful to use two vehicles."

"No," Bastide replied. "Thank you, but I'd prefer to follow you. I might be called away."

"Oh? Very well. I am not used to being followed. This is like a Hollywood gangster film, is it not?"

"Not quite," Bastide said. He waited till the driver had helped her into the consulate sedan before returning to his vehicle. He followed them into the center of the city and up the Canebière toward the Palais Longchamp. The Russian chauffeur was a cautious driver, slowing for a stop long before the signal light changed and allowing pedestrians to pass in front of him even when they were crossing against the lights. Their snail-like progress gave Bastide time to ponder Larissa Kedrov's role.

If Barbanov was right and Zavorin was the KGB resident in Marseille, where did that put the Kedrov woman? Was she a legitimate cultural assistant or did she work for Zavorin in his *real* capacity? If she was KGB, why this charade about security and police protection?

By the time they'd pulled up before the tall iron gates of the Palais Longchamp, Bastide had made up his mind to demand more information from de Coursin. If it wasn't satisfactory, he'd go directly to the préfet. He couldn't work effectively in the present circumstances and was seriously considering a request to be relieved of the case.

He followed Larissa Kedrov up the wide stone stairway of the ornate Second Empire construction to the Musée des Beaux Arts. She moved with a controlled grace that emphasized her sensuality. He'd already noticed that she wasn't wearing a bra. Now he found it impossible to keep his eyes off her well-rounded bottom.

One of the curators met them at the museum's entrance: a short, bespectacled woman in a tailored brown suit. Larissa Kedrov introduced herself and presented Bastide, explaining that he was assisting the consulate with security for the exhibit. The two women moved off to the room set aside for hanging the icons. Bastide lagged behind, peering uneasily at the work of a seventeenth-century Marseille painter. He always felt ill at ease in museums. It wasn't his world. He didn't like the silence or the churchlike atmosphere. He was more used to the small exhibits hung on the wall of the Peano on the Cours d'Estienne d'Orves by contemporary Provençal artists. Paintings alive with vibrant colors depicting the Vieux Port, the fishing fleet, the narrow streets of le Panier and landscapes of the hot, sun-drenched fields of the Midi.

"*Monsieur l'Inspecteur!*" the curator was calling him. He joined them in the empty room. "I was just explaining to Mademoiselle Kedrov that our security system is very efficient. As you can see, these two windows are wired with an alarm and our watchmen are dependable. Is there anything you would like to know?"

"Ah, are the people who hang your pictures steady employees or part-time workers?" Bastide improvised.

"Oh, they're all on the city payroll," she explained. "Some of them have been with us for years."

"Are your storage areas secure?" Bastide asked.

"Oh my, yes," she replied. "Reinforced doors and heavy bar locks."

"Good," he said, bored with his own playacting.

"Is there anything else you'd like to know? Perhaps you'd like to inspect the storerooms?"

"No, that won't be necessary."

"Well, Mademoiselle Kedrov and I must check the inventory," she explained. "Would you like to join us?"

"No, thank you. I'll just look around." Bastide wandered into a section of the museum devoted to African art, examining the sculpture from Senegal and Zaire. The primitive pieces seemed out of place and lost in the high-ceilinged room. A small, uniformed man with thick glasses appeared, his shoes squeaking on the parquet floor.

"We're not open to the public yet," he told Bastide. "You'll have to wait till ten."

"Relax," Bastide said. "I'm from the police."

"You are?" the guard said, surprised. "Is there something wrong?"

"No, I'm just having a look around."

The man wasn't convinced, but he didn't follow Bastide as he moved to the next exhibit.

Bastide had taken in the French and Flemish painters of the

sixteenth and seventeenth centuries and was standing in front of a Rubens when the two women reappeared.

"Ah, Inspector," Larissa Kedrov said, "I hope you haven't been bored."

"Not at all," he lied.

"That isn't a great Rubens," the curator told him, "but we're proud of it."

They bid goodbye to the curator at the top of the stairway and walked out into the sunshine.

"I'm very pleased with the arrangements," Larissa Kedrov told him. "I am sure the icons will be hung well and with the proper lighting." She paused at the first landing and glanced at her watch.

"I hope you don't feel I'm being presumptuous, Inspector," she said, "but can I offer you a coffee? I would like to see a typical Marseille café, perhaps on the Vieux Port."

"Very well," he replied. "Your driver can follow me."

She appeared to trip on the next step, losing her balance with one firm breast pressed against him. He felt a surge of excitement and reached out to steady her at the same moment she grasped his arm.

"Oh, I'm sorry," she said, "how awkward of me."

Antoine Morel was propped up in a bed in a windowless room of the DGSE clinic in Neuilly. He was wearing a blue robe and there was a bouquet of red carnations on the bedside table. He put aside the file he'd been reading when de Coursin arrived. De Coursin hung his homburg on the door hook and they shook hands.

"How do you feel?"

"I'll survive," Morel replied.

"We've cleaned things up in Sète. As far as the hotel owner and his staff are concerned, you were the victim of a gangland feud. He is no more eager to talk about it than we are. What did the doctor say?"

"I'll have to put aside my rugby career," Morel joked, "but I'll walk again someday. The operation went well."

"Faubert's a bastard!"

"I don't see it that way," Morel corrected de Coursin. "He could have cut my throat just as easily."

"I suppose you're right," de Coursin sighed. "But where is he now? We're back where we started."

"I'm no psychiatrist," Morel said, "but I know my people—how they think, how they react. Faubert's going to punish us. He's no longer concerned about saving his own skin. If he has to go down, he wants to bring all of us down with him."

"What can he do? Jump off the Eiffel Tower trailing a sign proclaiming he's been betrayed?"

"I almost wish he would. It might make things simple. We'd just scrape him off the pavement and chalk it up to mental illness. No, he's far too clever for that. He's preparing a coup of some kind. What's going on in Marseille?"

"Zavorin's brought in a swallow. Larissa Kedrov. She's posing as his assistant in the cultural section. I think she's targeted on Bastide."

"What would they want from him, the latest homicide statistics?"

"I'm not sure. I think they'd like to use him as a sounding board, an insert into our side of the equation. They know we're involved. They know we're standing back. So are they. Neither side wants the intelligence aspect of the case to surface. But both have to be prepared if it does. I think Bastide's of more use to us than he will be to them. As long as he's on the job and it remains a police matter, the longer the DST will be kept at arm's length. I also have Bastide reporting to me regularly, but . . ."

"But what?"

"He's getting restless. He's not a dull *flic*. He resents taking orders he doesn't understand. He's suspicious. He may be a problem."

"Do you think he'll tumble to the swallow?"

"I'm not sure. It depends on how she makes her approach. He's beginning to see spies under the bed."

"I hope he knows what to do with one in the bed!"

"Perhaps we'd better put a wire on his apartment," de Coursin said thoughtfully.

"I can see it now," Morel said, smiling. "This whole clinic filled by snoops suffering broken eardrums from the creak of bed-springs."

"I'm glad to see you haven't lost your sense of humor," de Coursin remarked dryly. "Do you have any suggestions?"

Morel pushed himself up against the headboard before replying. "I'm worried about Zavorin," he said.

"What?"

"Faubert dumped Drankov's corpse at the consulate as a gesture of defiance to Zavorin. Now the stakes have risen for him. He's a hunted man, but Zavorin remains untouched. Faubert wants to get back at us. What better way than by hitting Zavorin? I'd suggest a twenty-four-hour watch on our old friend Anatole."

"That could be awkward," de Coursin said. "If he doesn't spot us, his people will. He might go to ground in the consulate. I wouldn't want that."

"Life can be complicated," Morel sighed.

"What are the odds of us stopping Faubert?"

"I'd say about sixty-forty. I've put our best men on it. I even pulled 'Lou-Lou' Martin out of Beirut to lead the team. If anyone will stop Faubert, he will."

"They know each other?" de Coursin asked.

"Old friends," Morel explained. "In this case, it's a particular advantage. Lou-Lou knows how Faubert operates. He can think like him."

"I hope they're not too alike. I wouldn't want two madmen on the loose."

"No," Morel reassured de Coursin, "we'll have no worries with Martin. He's cool as tempered steel and a stranger to any form of sentiment."

"Even with the best of men we'll get nowhere until we know where Faubert is. Do you really believe he may be going after Zavorin?"

Morel nodded, reached for a painkilling tablet, swallowed it and washed it down with some water. "You might consider informing Bastide of our problem," Morel suggested. "You wouldn't have to detail it for him, just the tip that someone is out to get Zavorin. After all, he'll be closer to the people in the consulate. He could be our trip wire."

"Out of the question. The director would never agree to that."

"If I happen to be right," Morel projected, "we might consider informing Zavorin. It would make me breathe a lot easier if he was called back to Moscow for a debriefing."

De Coursin made a gesture of rejection. "I've seen to it that our Marseille office is on full alert," he told Morel. "I've ordered total discretion."

The red light on the bedside telephone began to flash. Morel picked it up. "Yes, yes, just a minute." He put his hand over the mouthpiece. "It's for you. They've put it through from your office. Inspector Bastide wants to talk to you."

Bastide's voice was impersonal but determined. "I'd like to know what's going on," he told de Coursin. "This Kedrov woman's after something. She's unleashed all her charms. To be frank, I'd be between her legs at this moment if I'd played along. Monsieur de Coursin, I'm not trained for this game. I've had enough. I don't give a damn what the préfet might say, I don't like being used."

"Easy, Inspector," de Coursin said soothingly, raising his eyebrows in Morel's direction. "I understand your position. It's an awkward situation. At this point we do owe you more of an explanation. I prefer not to discuss it now, even though this is a secure line. I'll be in Marseille in two days' time. We can clear things up then, just the two of us."

De Coursin heard Bastide's sigh of resignation. "Very well," Bastide said, "but I ask you to remember . . . I'm completely serious."

"I understand," de Coursin replied gravely. "I'll call you when I arrive." De Coursin frowned as he put down the phone.

"What's our wayward *flic* want?" Morel asked.

"He is unhappy and he wants out. Larissa Kedrov seems to have frightened him."

"Frightened him!" Morel laughed. "It's his chance of a lifetime. Why doesn't he relax and enjoy it?"

"No," de Coursin said, deep in thought, "I think we'd better pull him. At this point I'm worried more about what Faubert might do than I am about Zavorin's maneuverings. Bastide is too independent. He's becoming an added hazard. Is that cover story about the diamond dealer ready?"

"It's ready, but it's thin. You're not going to use it now, are you?"

"We might have to. I think it's time to shift the case out of Marseille."

"You'll have to sell it to the director," Morel said.

"And the Minister of the Interior," de Coursin added, "but it has to be done." De Coursin reached for his homburg and glanced back over his shoulder at Morel. "You're fortunate being in bed, Morel," he said before closing the door.

Viktor Popov smiled at the barmaid and raised his glass to her in a silent toast. He'd dropped into the empty bar on the rue Vacon at 7 P.M. It was now almost 8 P.M. and he was well insulated from his worries and frustrations, thanks to three stiff whiskeys. He filled his hand with salted peanuts from a bowl and tossed them into his mouth. The bar was dark, its walls draped with green velvet. Color photos of the *patronne*'s prize poodle and two silver cups won in dog shows were displayed on a shelf over the bottles. The barmaid had put a recording of Juliette Greco on the pickup. Popov hummed in time to the music as he munched the nuts.

He'd spent most of the day with an official of the French Communist party. The man had been a complete bore. He'd spouted rusty dialectic in an effort to impress Popov and vented his anger on the Socialists as the prime cause of all France's problems. Popov had only wanted to know the details of a recent labor union vote, but the Frenchman had digressed so often that their meeting had dragged on and on. Popov was firmly convinced that there was no one quite so boring as a militant of the French Communist party. They intellectualized everything, from politics to sports, until the subject matter was as dry and sterile as a sun-bleached bone. A dark look passed over his handsome face as he remembered he had two more years to serve in his present assignment.

"Another whiskey?" the barmaid asked, pausing in front of Popov. She was a thin, blue-eyed woman with heavy makeup and a nervous habit of running a hand through her dyed blond hair as she watched the door for customers.

"Yes, if you please," Popov responded. "Will you have a drink yourself?"

"You're very kind," she told him, reaching under the counter for an already opened bottle of champagne and pouring herself a glass. She mixed his whiskey, pouring a generous shot into his glass, adding ice and soda.

Popov downed the remains of his third drink and picked up the fourth. The barmaid returned to the far end of the counter to sip her champagne and wait for new customers. Popov felt depressed. The whiskey wasn't helping. Ever since he'd been caught trying to move the body, he'd been surrounded by silent disapproval. The consul general had only reprimanded him once, but there was now a barrier between them. Even the communications technicians seemed ill at ease when he spoke with them. At one point, when Anisimov had failed to invite him to an official dinner, he'd been tempted to tell him he'd only acted on Zavorin's orders. But he hadn't said a word. There was something menacing about the KGB resident. Popov was afraid of him. He knew the power of the KGB. He had no desire to draw attention to himself as an enemy of the state's security forces. He tried to look on the brighter side of the situation. If Zavorin was pleased with his silence, it could eventually be useful. Perhaps Zavorin could help him obtain an interesting new assignment? He had a good record. He'd never been in trouble before. He'd been particularly careful to stay away from women in Marseille. He knew women were attracted to him, but he'd only taken advantage of his dark good looks once since his arrival. Even then, he hadn't ventured out of the consulate circle. She'd been a member of a visiting trade delegation. It had only lasted three days. When she'd left, she'd given him her address in Leningrad. But he hadn't written. He didn't intend to see her again.

The bar was suddenly filled with customers. A group of businessmen occupied the lounge chairs by the empty fireplace, and two young men in stylish, baggy sports clothes were settling in a few stools from Popov. Popov watched them as they joked with the barmaid. He felt a certain envy, wondering what it would be like to be a Frenchman. For a moment he imagined himself free of all commitments and living in Paris. After all, he had been born in Paris when his father was on post there. He'd once mentioned to his father that he considered France to be his second country. The old man had put his glass of tea down carefully, fixed Popov with his rheumy eyes and told him that Russians don't have a second country.

Popov decided to have one last drink. He caught the barmaid's eye and she dutifully filled his glass. Juliette Greco's husky voice was loping through "Jolie Môme." The volume of conversation had risen and he was beginning to feel better. The evening had taken on a cushioned glow. He didn't relish the thought of eating the solitary pork chop waiting in his refrigerator. He decided he'd have some pasta or a pizza on the Port before returning to his apartment.

"I see you're drinking Johnnie Walker," a man who'd taken the stool to his left said. "It's a good blend. I prefer Ballantine's, myself."

"Oh?" Popov replied, surprised at the stranger's approach. The man was heavyset and wore a Tyrolean hat that he'd pushed back on his head. "There's nothing like Scotch whiskey," he continued. "It took the French a long time to appreciate it. Don't you agree?"

"I don't know," Popov said. "I'm not French."

"But you speak our language perfectly."

"I was born in Paris," Popov told him hesitantly. He wasn't used to speaking with total strangers.

"I'm celebrating tonight," the man told him. "My wife's left for a week. I'm on my own and I intend to take advantage of my freedom."

He never stops smiling, Popov thought. He's been showing his teeth since he arrived.

"Are you English?" the man asked.

"No, I'm Russian."

"Really? That's interesting."

Boniface was enjoying himself. He'd decided that Popov was the consulate's weak link and that he'd go to work on him. He'd gauged his arrival perfectly. The Russian had obviously put away a large amount of whiskey. He had the delayed reactions of a man bordering on drunkenness. His eyes were at half-mast, and the alcohol seemed to have lowered his guard. "Listen, friend," Boniface said, "will you join me for dinner? I crave a good, juicy steak. What do you say to that?"

Popov peered unsteadily at the pink-faced Frenchman. The man seemed genuinely friendly and unpretentious. Some company might be enjoyable.

"After eating," Boniface said in a confidential tone, "I'll introduce you to some female companions. They're respectable women, but they like a good time. So, how about it?"

"Why not?" Popov replied thickly. "I would like that."

"Good." Boniface beamed, sensing his hook firmly planted. "Let's finish our drinks and be on our way."

They walked out into the warm evening air and Boniface paused for a moment, adjusting his hat, surveying the sidewalk in both directions. He had just taken Popov's arm to guide him toward his sedan when he saw one of his men approaching.

"Can I speak to you alone, Chief?" the DST officer asked quietly.

Boniface turned purple with suppressed anger. He forced a smile for Popov. "Excuse me for a moment," he said, taking a few steps to put some distance between himself and the Russian.

"You must be mad!" he growled. "You are *never* to interrupt me when I'm making a contact!"

"I know, Chief," the officer replied, "but this is an emergency."

"Emergency? Listen, you stupid bastard, I'm going to have your ass on this . . ."

"Orders from Paris," the officer cut in. "You're to cease all work on the Drankov affair."

"What? Who gave the order?"

"Delglade. The message came through about twenty-five minutes ago. He wants you to contact him immediately."

Boniface snorted with frustration and rammed his fist into an open palm. *"Fils de putain!"* he cursed, glaring at his subordinate. "You," he ordered, "get out of here!"

He forced another smile before he turned back to Popov, who had been examining a display in a philatelist's window. "My dear friend," he told Popov, shaking his head regretfully, "I'm afraid our *soirée* will have to wait. I've just been told one of my children is ill. I must leave you."

"I'm sorry," Popov said, swaying slightly. "Is it serious?"

"No, but with my wife away . . ." He shrugged his shoulders.

"Let me give you my card," Popov replied, fumbling for his wallet.

"No," Boniface said, "I'm afraid I don't have the time. Perhaps we'll meet again in the same bar. *Au revoir!*"

Boniface mumbled to himself all the way to his car. Bastide's name featured in his litany of curses. He didn't know how a lowly cop could exert influence on the upper levels of the DST but he already regretted having mentioned Drankov to the *saligaud.*

Bastide pushed his holstered Manurhin Magnum into a chest of drawers, took off his shirt and walked out onto the terrace of his apartment. The surface of the Vieux Port was calm, a seamless mirror, and the concrete of the balcony wall was still warm from the sun. A high-seas trawler was tied up not far from the Yacht Club. Some crewmen were dumping old bait off the stern and hosing down the afterdeck. Noisy seagulls were hovering and diving for fish scraps. A sleek, gray customs boat was easing into its berth on the Quai de Port, the throb of its powerful engines carrying across the still water. It was going to be a hot, stuffy night. He stood staring down at the moving patterns of light on the water. He was tired and frustrated. De Coursin hadn't been much help, but at least he'd soon be in Marseille and Bastide could deliver his ultimatum. Either he would be told everything about the Drankov business or he'd submit a formal request to be taken off the case. It wouldn't please the préfet or look good in his dossier, but he didn't give a damn.

He made his way to the kitchen, broke out some ice and mixed himself a strong *pastis.* He would have enjoyed Janine's presence, but she was still nursing the ailing Gautier. He went back to the balcony, stopping on the way to find a cigar, and sat down heavily on a canvas director's chair. He didn't feel like cooking his own dinner and he wasn't particularly hungry. He sipped his drink, closed his eyes and thought about Larissa Kedrov. He'd taken her to the terrace of the Samaritain after their visit to the museum. She'd asked him questions about Marseille and its history. When they'd ordered a second coffee, she'd quizzed him about his family and childhood. She had a direct way of posing her questions and he'd found her a good listener. She'd sat close enough for him to smell her perfume, and at one point, while they laughed over the classic tale of the sardine blocking the entrance to the Vieux Port, she'd momentarily put her hand on his thigh.

He opened his eyes and lit his cigar, remembering that moment. Bastide had known many women, but this Russian was an enigma. She had class, but she also had some mannerisms common to a high-class *pute*. Was she sexually attracted to him? It was possible, but he smiled at the thought. Was she a repressed sexpot eager to shed the tight jacket of government restrictions and have a fling while in the West? That, too, was possible, but it sounded like the scenario from a mediocre film. Was she after something else? He drew deeply on his cigar and blew some spinning smoke rings into the still air. That could be it. She worked for Zavorin. Barbanov claimed Zavorin was KGB. Was she one of Zavorin's flunkies? It was entirely possible.

"But why me?" Bastide asked aloud. "What would she want with Inspecteur Principal Bastide of the PJ?" That was one of the answers he'd have to get from de Coursin.

Three distinct knocks on his apartment door brought him to his feet. He walked quickly into the bedroom, pulled on his shirt and approached the door. "Who is it?" he demanded.

"Mademoiselle Kedrov," his caller replied.

He pulled the two heavy slide locks and opened the door. She was smiling at him, a shopping bag in her arms.

"I hope you will forgive me," she said. "I am disturbing you perhaps?"

"Not at all," he replied. "Come in."

"If you must go out, do not let me detain you," she said. "I told Consul General Anisimov of your assistance today. He insisted I drop off these few delicacies from our homeland as a gesture of our appreciation."

"Can I offer you a drink?" Bastide asked, pointing toward the terrace.

"You may. But first let me show you what I've brought." She began to unload the bag on the dining room table. "Iced Zubrovka vodka," she said, producing a frosted bottle. "It is straight from the consulate Frigidaire. Some Malossol caviar. Black bread—I noticed you liked it during your visit to the consulate. A jar of pickled herring and one of gooseberry jam. We

Russians are very proud of our jam." She put the jar of jam on the table. "There," she said. "I hope you enjoy them."

"I'm sure I will," Bastide replied, lifting the tin of caviar to examine the label. Her visit had caught him by surprise. He was trying to put his thoughts in order. Her sexuality filled the apartment like the promise of an electric storm. The questions he'd asked himself earlier were suddenly less important as he watched her move toward the terrace.

"It's beautiful," she commented, taking in the vista of the Vieux Port with its floodlit stone forts, moored yachts, fishing boats and busy cafés. "You are fortunate to live here."

"What would you like to drink?" Bastide asked from the door to the terrace.

"It would be a shame if the vodka became warm," she replied, turning toward him in a stance that accentuated the lines of her figure.

"I agree," he said, picking up the caviar and hurrying to the kitchen for some glasses. She followed him.

"Would you let me prepare our *zakuska*, our appetizer?" she asked. "Do you have bread I can toast?"

"Certainly," he said, reaching into his breadbox for a wrapped *pain de mie*. "Here," he said. "The toaster is on the sideboard." He left her to get the vodka. The bottle was still icy, but its surface was no longer frosted. Back in the kitchen he found two liqueur glasses, filled them to the brim and handed her one.

"*Tchin, tchin,*" he said, raising his glass.

"No," she replied, "you must learn the Russian toast. *Za vashe zdorove!* Your health!" She put the glass to her lips and drained it. He did the same. He felt the warmth in his throat and tasted the slight piquancy of herbs.

"The toast will be ready soon," she told him. "It is not wise to drink vodka on an empty stomach. The caviar will tame it, take away its mule kick." She opened the caviar tin, revealing the large-grained, glistening roe.

He was pouring more vodka into their glasses when a sudden thought erased his smile. Suppose Janine were to arrive at this moment? What could he possibly say? He reassured himself with the fact that she was busy with Théo Gautier; but there had been times when she'd arrived unexpectedly, using her own key to the apartment, to slip into bed beside him.

Larissa Kedrov had finished buttering and cutting two pieces of toast. She heaped a generous portion of caviar on them. "Now," she said, handing him one, "a protective layer of caviar and you can raise your glass to me."

He savored the delicate smoky salt taste. "Delicious," he murmured. He picked up his vodka. "What do I say?" he asked.

"*Za vashe!*" she told him. "Yours."

He followed her instructions and they emptied their glasses. Her eyes were like emeralds under the bright kitchen lights, and Bastide wondered what de Coursin would say if he knew about the unexpected visitor. He decided to put both de Coursin and Janine out of his mind. There was something happening that he didn't want to spoil with hesitations and second thoughts.

"Shall we move to the terrace?" he suggested. "It's much cooler out there."

She agreed and preceded him, carrying the toast and caviar while he brought the bottle of vodka and the glasses. She was almost enjoying herself. She didn't feel the usual pressure and tension. The Frenchman was obviously intrigued and the vodka had relaxed her. He was physically attractive compared to most of her targets. Stepping out onto the terrace, she decided to make the most of the evening.

Léon Faubert felt better after a full night's sleep. He'd taken a room in the Hôtel Surcouf off the rue Belsunce. It was a noisy district inhabited by North Africans who spent most of their time on the streets away from their small, crowded rooms and apartments. Faubert had awakened early and taken his coffee in a nearby café. He'd had his hair completely shaved in a dirty barbershop with mounds of shorn hair on the floor.

He stepped back now from the cracked wall mirror in his room. The shaved head and drooping mustache gave him the air of a tired Turkish wrestler. He examined his broken nose gingerly. The swelling and discoloration had diminished, but it was still sore and the bridge was disfigured. He cursed Morel. His next move was to determine where and when he could snatch Zavorin. He would have to choose the moment carefully. He went to the

sagging brass bed and opened his battered suitcase. He put aside
a map of Marseille, moved a set of handcuffs to one side and
shook Morel's Colt out of its wrapping of soiled clothes. He stood
looking at it for a moment. His Beretta was tucked into his belt
under his jacket. He'd dropped Morel's pig-sticker off a road
bridge into an irrigation canal while he was hitchhiking to Martigues. He half regretted not having jettisoned the Colt at the
same time, but he'd decided it might be useful. He rewrapped the
automatic, snapped the suitcase shut and put it on top of an old
armoire near the window. If an unwelcome visitor probed the
suitcase and found the Colt it might be stolen, but he wasn't
worried about someone rushing to report it to the police. It
wasn't that kind of a hotel. Faubert paused to look out the open
window. He scanned the street below, marking a vendor's cart
piled with oranges, three Senegalese men waving their arms and
laughing in animated conversation, and a lumpy prostitute with
hennaed hair leaning against a graffiti-spattered wall.

He remembered how they'd picked up Drankov. The Russkov
had been in Marseille to contact Zavorin. Faubert and his team
had tracked him to his dead-letter drop at one of the magazine
kiosks in the Gare Saint-Charles, surrounded him and duck-
walked him to their waiting car. The hydrocyanic acid had been
Faubert's idea. No blood, no wounds. He'd used it once before.
Its instant effectiveness had impressed him. He'd had no desire to
drag out Drankov's elimination. Drankov was dead by the time
they'd driven into the empty warehouse near the Quai d'Arenc
where they'd wrapped him in his canvas shroud. Grabbing
Zavorin would be more difficult. Faubert would be operating
alone.

He shut the window, picked up the map of Marseille, examined
himself once more in the mirror and prepared to leave the room.
He'd spent his time in the barber's chair deciding on his next
move. He would use a public telephone to call the Mairie, the
Chambre de Commerce and the Tourist Office on upcoming
cultural events in the city. By a process of elimination he'd select
which function Anatole Zavorin might attend in his official capacity as cultural attaché. He then intended to call Zavorin's office,
posing as one of the hosts, to inquire if the Russian had received
an invitation and if he planned to appear. If the reply was no,

Faubert planned to emphasize the importance of the function and plead for Zavorin's presence. It was a shaky procedure, but he didn't have much choice. He couldn't risk being spotted skulking around the consulate or Zavorin's living quarters.

He walked to the nearest post office, changed some money for the telephone and found an empty booth. A city employee he reached in the Mairie's cultural section told him of a Picasso exhibit at the Musée Cantini. An organ recital in the Basilique Saint-Victor was expected to draw a good crowd. Faubert was urged to make reservations quickly. The recital was two weeks distant. He crossed it off his list.

"Then," she said, "there is the exhibit of Russian icons at the Musée des Beaux Arts, Palais Longchamp. It's jointly sponsored by the Soviet Cultural Services and the city of Marseille."

"When's the *vernissage?*" Faubert asked.

"Let's see . . . it's in four days' time, the twenty-seventh of June," the woman told him. "But I'm afraid it's by official invitation only. Are you on our list, monsieur?"

"I don't believe so," he replied. "I am moving my business to Marseille. I arrived recently. I'm an art appraiser and dealer."

"Oh, really. Your name, please?"

"Max Cotta from Cotta et Frères," Faubert said after a moment's hesitation, inventing both the name and the firm.

"Monsieur Cotta, I can arrange to send you an invitation to the *vernissage* if you're interested. Can you give me your address?"

"I . . . I'm not yet settled into my apartment," he explained. "Is there some way I can pick it up?"

"Well, I could leave it at the *planton*'s desk on the first floor of the Mairie."

"That would be very kind," he said.

"I'll attach a form to it that you can fill out with more personal details and your permanent address. Once it's in our files, you'll receive notices and invitations to most of our cultural events."

"Thank you. Goodbye." He left the booth suppressing a grin. What a stroke of luck! The opening of the Soviet exhibit would be perfect. There was no need to call Zavorin's office now. Faubert knew he'd be there. The museum might be crawling with security men, but it would also be full of government and civic authorities, the Consular Corps and the media. The perfect setting for his little drama.

Once out of the post office, he paused to fold his map and stuff it into a jacket pocket. Feeling in need of a drink, he turned into a café and ordered a cognac at the zinc counter. He experienced a slight shock when he saw his shaven head in the bar mirror.

"Monsieur Cotta," he told himself, "I don't think we've ever met."

VI

The three men who arrived at Marseille-Marignane on the early morning flight from Paris were in their late twenties and early thirties. They were tanned and fit, and could pass as members of an athletic team. They didn't wait for bags; everything they needed was in their hand luggage. A silver-gray Citroën was waiting for them outside the terminal, its trunk open. They stowed their gear, climbed into the car, and the driver pulled away from the curb.

Lou-Lou Martin pushed his sunglasses up on his forehead and lit a fat Bastos cigarette. *"Alors,* Rousseau," he addressed the driver, "has anyone seen our friend yet?" Rousseau replied without taking his eyes from the road.

"Not a trace. We've been tooth-combing Marseille. No luck so far."

Martin nodded, the cigarette dangling from the corner of his mouth. He was dark with thick, black eyebrows. His hair was cut short as if he'd just walked out of a military casern. Since receiving the order to leave Beirut to join the search for Faubert, he'd been thinking of his old friend and colleague. Faubert had obviously cracked. Once flawed, an action agent was dangerous and had to be discarded like a piece of broken crockery. Martin approached his assignment with the application of a technician.

"And Beirut?" Rousseau asked. "How goes it out there?"

"A carnival," one of the men in the back seat replied.

"It was a good time to leave," Martin added. "We've been trying to trace hostages for three months from the slums of Beirut to the Bekka Valley. But we seldom know where they are. The bastards move them constantly. The Lebanese are no help, the Syrians are worse and Mossad does its best to muddy the waters. Breaking diplomatic relations with the Iranians hasn't helped."

They sped smoothly along the *autoroute* and passed through an ugly industrial zone where metal rooftops glinted in the sun and heavy farm equipment was on roadside display.

"Where are we going?" Martin asked.

"No hotels this time," Rousseau explained. "You're going to enjoy a safe home in La Madrague."

"Diable!" Martin cursed. "You might as well quarter us in Lyon!"

"It's not that far out. I clocked twenty-five minutes into the city, depending on the traffic. You'll have two cars. The villa's furnished with everything you'll need, but the toilets don't work very well. The telephone is secure. As we mentioned in the cable, you are commercial scuba divers on vacation from a job in the Middle East. You'll receive a cover briefing at the villa. Your hardware is there." Martin crushed his cigarette butt in the ashtray.

"We'll need a motorcycle," he said. "A fast one."

"A motorcycle?" Rousseau exclaimed. He glanced at Martin and saw he was serious. "So be it. My orders are to supply you with anything you need."

"How about a case of Dom Pérignon?" a voice from the rear chided him.

Rousseau chuckled. "I might just be able to do that," he replied.

The bright sunlight shafting in from the terrace crept onto Bastide's face. He murmured in his sleep, turning his head to escape the unwelcome warmth. He opened one eye and groaned as the heat intensified. His slow awakening accelerated. His eyes were now open, blinking at the ceiling. His head was pounding as if cinched in a vise.

He took a deep breath, knowing she was beside him before he turned his head to look. He told himself, "You are a fool." He rose on one elbow for a clear view of Larissa Kedrov. She was lying on her stomach, completely nude, her hair spread like a dark flower over the sheets. He closed his eyes once more, trying to ease the pain in his skull. He could taste the dregs of the herbed vodka at the back of his throat. Then the memories returned like guilty secrets.

They'd remained on the terrace, drinking, eating and talking till a yellow moon rose over the city. She'd spun out a travelogue description of her travels in Vienna, Bucharest and Budapest. He'd noted that she had always been careful to mention a cultural project or mission. He'd then recounted the instances of black humor in some of his cases, imitating the thick Provençal or Corsican accents of the protagonists, treating her to some authentic Marseille folklore. By 11 P.M. the vodka bottle was empty, the caviar finished.

"Monsieur Roger," she'd told him with mock seriousness. "I believe we are both drunk."

He'd agreed and offered to prepare some warm food or coffee. In response she'd left her chair to crouch beside him, one hand on his knee, the other caressing his neck. She'd said something then, but he couldn't remember what it was. He did remember her kiss: warm lips moving on his, her hand creeping along his thigh.

He sat up in bed, shook his head in an attempt to clear it and moaned at the pain caused by the sudden movement. He didn't want to remember any more. He tried not to look at her body, fighting a strong urge to recapture the night's pleasures. She murmured in her sleep and turned over, both arms thrown wide, one now resting on his leg. He groaned. This was temptation of the sort reserved for saints and martyrs. He didn't qualify on either count. He bent over, pressed his body to hers and gently kissed her awake.

Bastide was over an hour late getting to his office. Mattei was waiting for him, pacing the floor.

"*Enfin,*" he complained. "I thought you'd taken the day off!"

Bastide was in no mood to argue. He was drained of energy. A Soviet armored division seemed to be firing their cannon somewhere behind his eyeballs. He'd already resolved never to drink vodka again.

"Don't take your coat off," Mattei said. "The commissaire wants to see us. I told him you were checking something on the way to work. His secretary just called for the second time."

"All right, all right," Bastide grumbled, "let's go."

Commissaire Aynard was standing in front of his desk waiting for them. In the lexicon of Aynard's body language this meant the meeting would be short and there was no need for them to sit down. The commissaire was smiling as they entered. Bastide took this as a bad omen. Aynard smiled rarely, but when he did it usually meant something unpleasant was in the offing.

"Messieurs," Aynard told them with obvious relish, "your awkward and mysterious corpse is the result of a diamond scam. I've just had a call from the ministry. It seems the dead man was a Soviet citizen who'd been eased out of the U.S.S.R. by his employer, an international dealer in diamonds. The new employee became a true capitalist and tried to skim some of the profits. His boss didn't like it. Result—one dead Russian. Paris will be handling the case from now on with the help of Interpol."

"I don't understand," Bastide said, frowning. "Are they sending us the dossier?"

"Why should they?" Aynard replied. "It's their case now."

"But we've got to close the case here. We can't do it without more details."

"We don't need more details," Aynard snapped. "I told them we'd help to the extent we could, but I had the feeling they'd prefer us to stay out of it now."

"*Tant mieux,*" Mattei commented. "We were spinning our wheels anyway."

"*Monsieur le Commissaire,*" Bastide said, "did the ministry have an explanation for the corpse being dumped at the consulate?"

"Yes, and it was most logical. The diamond dealer in question is a ruthless man known for holding grudges . . ."

"Where is he?" Bastide interrupted.

"I understand he operates out of Ankara," Aynard replied, his face turning pink with anger. "Now don't interrupt me again. As I was saying, the body dumping at the consulate fits the pattern of this dealer's brutal operating methods . . . a symbolic repatriation of the man who'd betrayed him."

Bastide looked skeptical. "But it was done on French soil, in our territory. It was a local murder. Why should the ministry be handling it in Paris?"

"*Bon Dieu,* Inspector!" Aynard shouted. "This is unbelievable! You're acting like a spoiled child. There are aspects of this case that obviously require handling on a higher international level. I can't tell you what they are, nor do I intend to bother the ministry with questions. Considering what little progress you've made so far, I would think you'd be pleased to have the mess taken out of our hands."

Aynard's anger failed to impress Bastide. He glared at the commissaire while Mattei shifted uneasily. *"Monsieur le Commissaire,"* Bastide said, "do we know if the actual murderers are still here? The heavies who work for this diamond dealer?"

"Inspector," Aynard said, running his long fingers around the inside of his shirt collar, "I believe I've said all I need to say. You and your section will have nothing more to do with the consulate case, *unless* Paris asks you for assistance. Is that understood?"

"It is," Bastide replied.

"That's all, gentlemen," Aynard said. *"Au revoir."*

Bastide and Mattei returned to their office in silence. It smelled of stale tobacco and old coffee. Bastide hung up his jacket and walked to the window. He was angry. It was the first time a case had been snatched from him halfway through the investigation. He folded his arms, frowning at the cobblestones below, trying to make some sense of the situation. Mattei decided it was not the moment for conversation. He opened the drawer of his desk and withdrew a copy of *Paris Secret,* a magazine listing the erotic offerings of the nation's capital. He eased himself into his chair and relaxed, determined to let Bastide initiate any further conversation. Bastide knew he'd have to call de Coursin to report on Aynard's order. At that moment Pierre Lenoir burst into the office, out of breath.

"There's been a murder!" the young detective gasped. "An old woman in Capelette. Someone broke into her apartment and beat her to death early this morning. The motive was robbery according to the first officers on the scene."

Bastide rounded on him. "So?" he asked. "Why don't you get moving? You're acting as if this was something special. Old women are beaten to death every day. Get over there *now!* I want a full report by 6 P.M."

"Oui, Monsieur l'Inspecteur," Lenoir murmured, backing out the door.

Mattei finally broke the awkward silence. "That wasn't you, Roger," he said gravely. "It sounded more like Aynard."

"Ta gueule!" Bastide barked, grabbing his jacket. "I'm going out. I'll be back in an hour." He slammed the door after him.

Mattei dropped his magazine back into the desk drawer and pushed it shut. He took a comb from his pocket and began to run it through his thick hair. He was puzzled by Bastide's attitude. He'd never seen him like this before. He glanced at his watch and decided he'd go home for lunch. The children would be at school and he'd surprise his wife with a hot pizza and a good bottle of rosé. Perhaps, if she was in the right mood, they could make love before he returned to the office. The mere thought of it produced a *frisson* of anticipation.

Larissa Kedrov reported to Anatole Zavorin in his cramped office next to the code room. She was wearing stylish dark glasses and a white raw silk dress. An electronic hum penetrated the thin wall partition and she had to speak loudly to make herself heard.

"I had to push things a bit," she told Zavorin. "He is a puzzle. Not easy. I will have to be careful with my questions."

"We are over the first hurdle," Zavorin said. He thought she was being too pessimistic. He knew that once a man sampled Larissa's wares he'd be back for more. "Did you make another rendezvous?" Zavorin asked eagerly.

"No. He arranged for a police car to take me home, kissed me and left, asking that I lock the door on my departure. I took some time to inspect the apartment. Nothing of great interest. Did you know he fought in the colonial war in Algeria?"

"Yes," Zavorin replied. "He was a parachutist."

"I found some medals in a drawer, including the Croix de Guerre with palm."

Zavorin dismissed the information with a wave of his hand. "Nothing on the Drankov murder?"

"The only police documents I found were some old expense vouchers."

"The next time you see him bring up the murder. See what he has to say, what he thinks about it. Be alert to any mention of outside involvement: DST or DGSE. If you feel it appropriate, make a joke about the KGB. Anything to bring the conversation around to intelligence matters. If we're lucky he might comment on French intelligence, particularly if they are making his work difficult. Never discount the frustration factor."

Larissa Kedrov watched Zavorin's busy hands. They moved over the surface of his desk like two nervous spiders, lifting a pencil, shifting papers, flicking lint off a blotter. His walleye seemed to be fixed on the window. Her report had been direct and matter of fact. Zavorin had avoided mentioning the details of her night with Bastide. Other superior officers had often taken a prurient delight in the more intimate aspects of her work. One high-ranking veteran of the KGB had told her that a man's behavior in bed revealed more about his character than any amount of surveillance. Zavorin's reticence irritated her. She had a sudden desire to shock him.

"He is good in bed," she said huskily. "If all my targets were as attractive with their clothes off and as skilled, I would be a happy woman."

Zavorin frowned and turned his good eye toward the ceiling. "They will begin hanging the exhibition this afternoon," he said. "You should be there. I suggest you call Bastide and ask him to accompany you—at the consul general's request. Continued proximity is important."

"As you wish," she sighed, standing up. "Comrade Zavorin, what happens if he has nothing to tell me? If there is no DGSE involvement?"

"That is my worry," he told her. "Now go have some strong tea. You look tired."

"Inspector Bastide on the phone," de Coursin's secretary announced. De Coursin sat back in his chair, brought his hands together under his chin and allowed a few seconds to pass.

"Tell him I'm unavailable," he finally said. The secretary shut the door. De Coursin went back to his paperwork. He was drafting a secret cable that would restructure the DGSE presence in Beirut. With the Martin team gone they'd need to fill the gap. The Élysées didn't want any reduction of intelligence capabilities. De Coursin had decided the time was ripe to replace the one team with two . . . or three if he could get away with it. His stubby Mont Blanc pen moved smoothly over the surface of the paper without editorial hesitation.

"I'm sorry"—the secretary had appeared again—"the inspector said he'd call again in an hour. He said it was very important and asked that you call him if you returned before then. Am I to take it that you don't want to speak to him at all?"

"That's correct, Constance. When he calls again, tell him I've left on a voyage." De Coursin smiled as Constance left his office for the second time. She'd been with him for eight years. He could tell by the set of her shoulders that she resented not knowing why he was no longer accepting Bastide's calls. He was sure Bastide had called about losing the case to Paris. De Coursin felt slightly guilty, but the policeman was too inquisitive. Indications were that the Soviets were as eager to forget Drankov as he was. If Martin could find Faubert, their worries should be over. De Coursin decided to call the préfet in Marseille. He knew Bastide's commissaire had taken him off the case, but the man was turning into a pest. He would have to be sent back to his squalid murders and gangland killings.

The blue laundry van spun into the Square Monticelli and pulled to a stop at the rear entrance to a white villa with a red-tiled roof. Two men stepped down from the cab, opened the loading doors and swung full laundry bags over their shoulders. One of them rang the bell and the gray steel gate swung open. They shut the gate behind them and struggled up the villa's back steps. Jacques Boniface was waiting for them in the kitchen, frowning, his hands on his hips.

Lou-Lou Martin dropped his laundry bag on the floor and nodded a greeting.

"Well," Boniface said, "you managed to find us."

Martin ignored the sarcasm. "Show me the setup," he said shortly. It was almost an order.

The DST had occupied the villa for two years. It was a vantage point for recording the activities of the Soviet Consulate and eavesdropping electronically on its communications traffic. Boniface had been ordered to show the facility to Martin as part of his Marseille briefing. Faubert might avoid the scene of his previous dump entirely, but Martin had to be ready for anything.

Boniface led Martin and his assistant upstairs and into a large room packed with equipment. Martin whistled quietly, impressed with the technological display.

"That's a laser pickup," Boniface explained grudgingly. "It bounces a light beam off the Russkovs' windows, picks up the sound of conversations and returns it to that compact computer for analysis and reconstruction."

"Impressive," Martin murmured, moving past two DST technicians to get a clear view of the consulate from the half-closed shutters.

"It *was* impressive," Boniface told him, "until our friends over there decided on countermeasures. They've attached small vibration motors to the windows in key rooms that drive our computer crazy. It's been coming up with indecipherable gibberish lately."

"You need a spread-spectrum transmitter," Martin commented.

"Is that right?" Boniface snapped. "You know how much those cost? You people might have an unlimited budget. We don't."

Martin's assistant had unfolded a floor plan of the Soviet Consulate. Martin borrowed some high-powered binoculars from a nearby table and scanned the consulate, referring to the plan, locating the consul general's office, the communications center and Zavorin's hideaway. Satisfied, he turned to a recording device from which a coil of colored cables led to a nearby wall plug.

"I see you've got them wired," Martin said. "Any luck?"

"No. They've got good security discipline. They know they're bugged. You don't find them calling Moscow on the commercial lines . . . unless they want to order more caviar or talk to their Uncle Boris."

Martin smiled. He didn't mention that the DGSE had a parasitic transmitter tapped into the consulate's power line to pick up incoming and outgoing cable traffic. He checked his watch. They'd been in the villa too long.

"So, cowboy," Boniface asked, "what's your next move?"

"My next move is to leave you to your mud pies," Martin responded. "You have a full description of Faubert. You have our telephone numbers. I expect you to call immediately if he shows up here. I also want to know if you hear anything significant on the Drankov affair." Martin paused at the top of the stairs. "Thanks," he said, "for your *logistical* support."

As the DGSE men picked up their laundry bags, they could hear Boniface cursing upstairs.

"Monsieur Boniface," Martin commented, "takes his work much too seriously."

Larissa Kedrov knew something was wrong when Bastide met her at the Palais Longchamp. He hadn't been able to come to the consulate, but he'd agreed to join her at the museum.

"I'm sorry I'm late," he said, avoiding her eyes.

"Don't apologize," she said. "It was very short notice and I am feeling more secure in your city. I'm glad you could come."

He would have to tell her he was no longer on the case, but he hesitated. De Coursin might reverse Aynard's decision. He decided to say nothing. He found himself drawn to her once more, remembering their time together. They entered the museum, where she was soon busy supervising the unpacking of the icons. The paintings emerged from the straw-lined wooden cases in various sizes. Their colors seemed to glow in the light: deep blues, waxy greens and bright gold traceries of Cyrillic lettering.

Bastide examined the portraits of somber, bearded saints and pale-faced Virgins as they were placed against the wall, but his mind was not on art or religion. His thoughts had shifted to Janine and what he was going to tell her about Larissa Kedrov. He walked to the open balcony of the museum and lit a cigar. He sighed, exhaling the rich smoke, and tried to analyze his feelings. The Russian woman's sensuous magnetism had a profound effect on him. He found it hard to take his eyes off her. He turned away, conjuring up the image of Janine as an antidote. It was a ridiculous situation. The whole case was a disaster and he'd be well out of it. He made his decision and strode back into the museum.

"Excuse me," he said, "I'm sorry to interrupt, but I've been called back to my office."

Larissa Kedrov looked puzzled, her eyes searching his for an explanation.

"You leave me?" she asked.

"Yes," he replied. "Good luck with your *vernissage.*"

"But . . ." she protested, taking a step toward him. "What of the arrangement? The consul general was assured . . ."

"If he has any questions, tell him to call the préfet," Bastide told her.

"Will we see each other soon?" she asked.

"I'm not sure," he said.

"No smoking allowed in the museum, monsieur," the guard with the squeaky shoes warned.

"I'm just leaving," Bastide told him.

As he hurried down the stairway, he passed someone with a shaved head, a drooping mustache and a deeply tanned face.

Babar Mattei removed the Drankov file from its drawer and handed it to Commissaire Aynard's secretary.

"Here you are," he said ceremoniously, "and good riddance. Now perhaps we can get down to something serious." She thanked him and he closed the door behind her.

"Bastide won't be happy," Lenoir said nervously.

"You have a lot to learn," Mattei replied. He lifted another file out of the drawer and brandished it in the air. "I've kept a duplicate file, just in case."

"But that's against regulations!" the young detective protested.

"Mon cher collègue," Mattei said, "it is time you realized that regulations are made to be bent, twisted and sometimes ignored. What do you think would happen if Roger Bastide walked in that door and found I'd handed everything over to Aynard?"

Lenoir shrugged in response.

"He would have me hanging from the tower of Fort Saint-Jean by the only two olives I possess; that's what would happen! And he'd see you on the pavement handling parking violations."

"But the case is dead, as far as we're concerned."

"Lesson number two: no case that was in our jurisdiction is dead as far as we're concerned. Remember that. Murder cases have lives of their own. They often sprout like spring seeds when you least expect it. Now, tell me about the old woman in Capelette."

"It was disgusting," Lenoir explained. "The murderer used a hammer. Blood all over. I almost lost my breakfast."

"Very interesting," Mattei growled. "What about leads?"

"Her savings were missing. Her son showed me the coffee tin

she kept them in. It was empty. Someone had kicked in the door, ripped off the hinges."

"No one heard it?"

"No, there were no witnesses. One neighbor was out of town. The other says he was watching the television until sign-off time. He slept through the night till eight this morning."

"What's Colona say about time of death?"

"He puts it at 5 A.M."

"Where does her son live?"

"Three floors down in the same building with a wife and three kids. He's unemployed. I think he's on the bottle. He smelled like a distillery this morning."

"I see. I want you to go back there and lean on that neighbor. Our good doctor is seldom wrong. If the door was kicked in and a hammer used, I find it hard to believe that the deep sleeper heard nothing. Then pay a visit to the son. Send him in to see me with a couple of uniforms and stay there with his wife. Put her on the grill and don't worry about frightening her. A few tears might help. I haven't dipped my finger in the case, but my money's on the son at this point."

Lenoir prepared to leave, pushing a notebook into his jacket pocket. Mattei spread an old newspaper he'd retrieved from the wastbasket on his desk, drew his Manurhin Magnum from its holster and took his cleaning kit from a drawer.

"What do you think," Lenoir asked, one hand on the door-knob. "Is the consulate case really closed?"

"I hope so," Mattei replied. "I sincerely hope so."

Dinh Le Thong was waiting outside the Hôtel de Police in his vintage Citroën *traction-avant* when Bastide returned from the Palais Longchamp. He flicked the amber headlights as Bastide drove toward the garage entrance. Bastide parked with two wheels on the sidewalk, left the police sedan and joined Thong.

"What are you doing here?" he asked.

"Get in," Thong said. "I've got something to tell you."

Bastide climbed in and shut the door. "Well?"

"We'll go for a ride," Thong said, starting the engine. "My DST bosses would be very curious if they saw me parked in front of your *boîte.*"

Thong spun the Citroën around and drove up the Avenue de la Tourette till he came to a concrete plaza overlooking the Fort Saint-Jean and the entrance to the Vieux Port. He stopped in the parking area, well away from the group of tourists gathered near the coin-operated telescopes.

"There is something strange going on," Thong said, his voice flat. "I think your unidentified corpse may be more important than you suspect. There may be a link with the DGSE."

Bastide was tempted to tell Thong about the diamond smuggler, but the mention of the DGSE had brought him up short. "Why do you say that?" he asked.

"I was turning in a report yesterday. Boniface was in the office. I overheard him talking with one of his men. It appears he's been told to stay away from the case. He's furious."

"Good."

"That is of minor importance," Thong continued, "but he spoke of a certain Martin from the DGSE. I couldn't hear him that well, but I think this Martin is now in Marseille and involved with the consulate murder."

"Involved? How?"

"I am not sure but I made inquiries. Do you remember Lien, who worked for the DGSE in West Africa?"

"Your cousin?"

"Yes. He lost most of his right hand in an explosives accident, but he's still with *la crémerie.* He has a good memory. I casually dropped the name Martin and he recalled the man. He tells me Martin's one of the DGSE's best, specializing in liquidations."

"*Putain!* What's he doing here?"

"I'm not sure, but I thought you should know."

Bastide's mind was a jumble of tenuously connected thoughts. He was off the case. De Coursin wouldn't return his calls. The DST had been warned to stand aside. Larissa Kedrov had made her move and he'd cooperated. Now a DGSE killer was involved. He leaned back in the seat and took a deep breath.

Thong watched him. "Does any of this make sense to you?" he asked.

"No," Bastide replied, "it doesn't. But it should. Our time in Algiers looks simple now. We hunted them, they hunted us. Now I feel I'm trying to swim in molasses."

"I'll find out more," Thong said. "Boniface might open his big mouth again. If he does, I'll let you know."

"Did Lien give you a description of Martin?"

"Yes. He's dark and husky, with a military look about him. Thick black eyebrows. A thoroughly cold and professional operator."

"You know," Bastide said, "I'm fed up with these bastards using Marseille as a killing ground."

"Perhaps you shouldn't get involved," Thong suggested. "Let them play their games."

"And leave their debris on my streets?"

"But what can you do? The DGSE is always covered at the highest level. *Raisons d'état, mon ami.*"

"*Mon cul!* Is there any chance that your cousin can find Martin?"

"It's possible."

"Good," Bastide said, feeling a surge of adrenaline. "I'm going to trace the son of a bitch, find out what he's up to and warn him off."

Thong made a hissing sound, letting air out between his teeth. "I don't think that wise," he said. "It is not your affair."

"It *is* my business."

"Perhaps you should wait. You're tired."

"Take me back to the office," Bastide requested. "I've got a lot of work to do."

The director of the DGSE took a long time to fill his meerschaum. He was a retired admiral who'd spent many years afloat. He believed in thorough deliberation. The sea had taught him patience. He was a lanky man with large hands. A thick shock of gray hair hung over his forehead and he closed his blue eyes as he sucked at his pipe. Once he'd teased some smoke from the bowl, he settled into his chair and sighed with contentment.

De Coursin chewed on the stem of his cigarette holder, waiting for the director to speak. He hated these interludes of silence that always preceded important pronouncements.

"André," the director finally said, "the President has taken a personal interest in our Drankov problem. He called me to the Élysées for a talk. He is not pleased, not pleased at all."

De Coursin tried to speak, but the director stopped him, holding up his broad hand. "I know you've done all you can under the circumstances, but we look bad on this one. A rogue agent on the loose, a team of equalizers about to sow death in Marseille. The DST and the police raging on the sidelines. The Soviet Consulate a possible target for an attack." The director paused long enough to admire the sheen of the meerschaum in the afternoon sunlight.

"Have you located Faubert yet?" the director asked casually, as if Faubert had stepped out for a pack of cigarettes.

"No, sir, we haven't. But Martin and his team . . ."

"André," the director said, laughing, "don't be ridiculous. Three men in Marseille! What can they accomplish? If we called in the DST, the *gendarmerie* and the police, there might be a chance. Martin and his team might as well go fishing off the Château d'If for all the good they'll do us. The President says we're caught in our own web of secrecy. Poetic but apt. He's given me an order and I'm passing it on to you. We're to tell the Russkovs about Faubert and warn them he's on the loose."

"What?" de Coursin almost shouted. "You can't be serious."

"Oh, I am," the director said, "and so is the President. He's planning a meeting with Gorbachev in the near future. The Americans and the British don't know it yet, but he's got some important arms-control proposals to make. He can't afford to have the Drankov case explode into an international scandal at such a crucial moment."

"But . . ." de Coursin stammered, "you want to tell the Soviets everything?"

"The *President* wants . . . that means *I* want, that means *you* want—understand?"

"What about Faubert?" de Coursin asked, trying to regain his composure.

"Look, André, this is all fairly simple. Faubert is the prime threat, the main problem. It appears to all of us that Faubert has slipped his moorings and intends to wreak some kind of revenge on the Soviet Consulate in Marseille and the KGB resident in particular. Correct?"

De Coursin nodded.

"Good. Now, the President believes the least we can do under the circumstances is warn the Russians, put them on the alert so we don't have a minor massacre on our hands. This isn't our usual procedure, but it's a special case. The President reminded me that we weren't at war with the U.S.S.R. Who knows, we may benefit in the long run."

"What if they turn it into a propaganda campaign?"

"It's a risk we'll have to take. But we'll do it at a lower level."

"No presidential messages?"

"No. No ambassadorial-level meetings either. This is going to be between *la crémerie* and the Aquarium, DGSE to KGB. The Élysées will need the asset of plausible denial if things go wrong."

"I presume you'll be seeing the KGB resident at the Soviet embassy?"

"No, André," the admiral replied, smiling. "You are to meet with Zavorin in Marseille."

Léon Faubert had been pleased with his visit to the Musée des Beaux Arts. He'd arrived as the icons for the Soviet exhibit were being hung, so he knew exactly where the *vernissage* would take place. Posing as an artist interested in the paintings hanging in an adjoining room, he'd made some quick sketches of the entryway and surrounding corridors, complete with rough estimates of distances and notes on blind areas. He'd asked a museum employee for directions to the men's room. It was on the ground floor behind the stairwell. A thorough examination of the washroom and the toilet cubicles had proven profitable. The restroom might well play a role in his planned spectacle.

As he walked back toward the center of the city he felt an inner elation he could hardly contain. He chuckled to himself, imagining the director of the DGSE being called to the Élysées to explain what had gone wrong in Marseille and the KGB bosses in Moscow gritting their teeth after Zavorin's exposure and issuing orders for his speedy one-way return to Moscow. His glee was tempered by the thought that he would never be safe even in police custody. Some unofficial terminator might get to him eventually, but his whole life had been one continual risk. He would face the threat when the time came.

Faubert paused at the top of La Canebière and slipped into a café for a cognac. It was an old-fashioned establishment that had managed to avoid the plastic and stainless steel of the brash new cafés with their electronic games and noisy Muzak. There was sawdust on the tile floor, beveled mirrors behind the zinc bar and some old oil paintings of Marseille in circular insets on the wall. The stout patron was settled comfortably behind the counter reading a racing form. The aroma of simmering lamb stew seeped from the small kitchen. The only other customers, three men at a far table, were shaking dice for drinks. The atmosphere turned Faubert's mind toward the past, and that was not something he liked to dwell on. Over the years he'd built a mental wall around himself designed to keep nightmares at bay. He'd convinced himself that the killings he'd performed were not murders. He preferred to think of them as punishments . . . a form of revenge. He didn't really enjoy his work, but he was good at it and took a certain journeyman pride in his efficiency and technique. The human element had seldom entered his mind. To him, killing was like switching off light bulbs.

He ordered a second cognac and watched the patron leave his perch to refill the glass. A warm breeze blew in through the café's open front. Faubert recalled his visit to the museum. He thought about the dark-haired woman he'd seen there. Something special, he told himself. What I wouldn't give for a few hours with her! He hadn't entered the room where they were hanging the icons, but he'd watched her from a distance. He swallowed hard even now as he remembered. Faubert knew his own personal chemistry and recognized the warning signal. He needed a woman and the sooner the better. He would have to be particularly careful. No involvement in or near his hotel or with the *poules* working the Opéra district. He knew some of them were police informers, trading information on their clients for favorable treatment from the Brigade Mondaine. Others had links with the DST. He recalled a particularly well-educated prostitute who worked the George V and Prince de Galles hotels in Paris for the DGSE.

His erotic interlude would have to be in another *quartier*. He passed from thought to action. If this café seemed lost in a time warp, perhaps the same environment extended beyond its doors.

"Patron," he said, seeking the owner's attention, "will you have a drink with me?"

"*Volontiers,* " the man replied, pausing to light a cigarette before pouring himself a pastis. He brought the cognac bottle to the counter and topped Faubert's glass.

"Beautiful day," the patron commented, "but we'll have a mistral by tonight."

Faubert nodded in agreement before leaning over the counter. "Tell me," he murmured, "where can I find an honest, healthy *poule* in this neighborhood?"

VII

The safe house occupied by Martin and his team was not far from the Port de la Madrague. It was a low, one-floor bungalow surrounded by a white wall. The garden was bare and dry. The mistral wind picked up the sandy soil and threw it against the windowpanes with the force of shotgun pellets. Lou-Lou Martin was sitting cross-legged on the bare floor in the front room, reassembling a .223 Ruger Mini-14 rifle. He was stripped to the waist. He had the torso of a weight lifter and his muscles twitched and rippled as he worked over the weapon. One member of the team was preparing lunch in the kitchen. The other had gone to a neighboring villa, ostensibly to borrow some sugar. His real purpose was to reinforce the team's cover story. He was telling the curious housewife of his experiences working in the Middle East and how he and his two friends planned to enjoy themselves in Marseille during leave.

Martin picked up the laser-lock sight and fixed it to the reassembled rifle. He activated the sight and lifted the rifle to play the small luminous circle it projected onto the opposite wall. He swung the muzzle slowly and the pinpoint of light traveled steadily along the wall like a ghostly period. Satisfied, Martin removed the sight and put it and the rifle back into a long, felt-lined box. He closed the lid and gave the box a tap. The Ruger had accounted for two kills in Beirut. Martin had a certain affection for efficient weaponry.

He sprang from the floor, performed a few karate movements and drank from the bottle of mineral water on the nearby card table. He bent over the table to examine a large-scale map of Marseille. Using the Quai des Belges as a fulcrum, he'd used a red marker pen to draw pielike wedges from its center, covering the whole city. Each wedge was lettered and a number of blue dots recorded the placement of DGSE "correspondents," trusted part-time agents who'd been enlisted in the search for Faubert. Each correspondent had his own network of secondary informers to draw on. They would all remain in ignorance of the reasons behind the search. They only knew that a man was wanted and finding him would produce a bonus.

Martin scratched his chin and closed his eyes. Where would he go if he were Faubert? He would avoid the Vieux Port area, but he would not stray far from the city's center. Martin interrupted his reverie, picked up the pen, and drew a small ellipse, once again using the Quai des Belges as a central point. To the north it covered the rue de la République and the rue d'Aix, swung toward the east as far as the Boulevard Garibaldi and south over the rue de Rome and the rue de Paradis. He paused for a moment, thinking, before drawing a larger ellipse covering a bigger section of the city. He shook his head. If he were Faubert, he wouldn't want to be so far out. He would certainly stay clear of the residential area where the Soviet Consulate was located. The bourgeois who lived there cherished their dark apartments, their predictable lives, their heirlooms and possessions. Strangers and newcomers were noticed and considered possible threats. Faubert would be aware of this. Martin speculated that he would seek a highly populated zone where newcomers were anonymous and unnoticed. But where? The highest population density was in the Arab quarter near the Port d'Aix, but a non-Arab would be readily visible in that area. He'd be even more noticeable in the black African zone north of the Canebière. Martin moved his finger west to the Cours Belsunce. That area would be a compromise. Busy streets with a mixed population, cafés, restaurants, hotels and apartments shared by Europeans and immigrants; seamen, traders, barmen, pimps, laborers and hustlers. Martin decided that's where he would be if he was in Faubert's shoes.

The roar of a motor made Martin duck below window level. He moved across the floor in a crouch and took the 9-mm Walther automatic out of his jacket pocket. His colleague appeared at the kitchen door, a stubby Uzi in his hands. Martin signaled him to remain where he was and moved toward the door. The motor had subsided. They could hear someone walking toward the bungalow. The doorbell rang. Martin rose slowly, his automatic leveled.

"Who is it?" he demanded.

"A long-lost friend," the caller responded, using the password. Martin opened the door slowly, his weapon still extended. "Get in here," he ordered.

A thin Vietnamese stepped over the threshold. Martin slammed the door behind him, spun him around and pushed him against the wall. He held the Walther under the visitor's ear as he frisked him. Then he tapped the automatic on the man's shoulder. *"Ça va,"* he said. "Who are you?"

"My name is Lien," the Vietnamese explained. "I've brought your motorcycle."

"You're a day late," Martin snapped.

The Vietnamese shrugged. He was a man of forty with high cheekbones. Martin noticed the missing right hand and raised an eyebrow.

"A faulty blasting cap," Lien explained, brandishing his scarred stump. "It could have been worse."

"Tu parles!" Martin responded. "What did you bring us?"

"It's Japanese and it's fast," Lien told him. "It moves like the wind."

"You drove it . . . like that?" Martin asked.

"One hand is enough. Will you sign the receipt?"

"You stay here," Martin told him. "I'll give it a trial spin. *Then* I'll sign the receipt." Martin pulled on his jacket and pocketed the automatic. Lien handed him the keys.

"Have a drink," Martin suggested. "I'll be back in a minute." He slammed the door behind him.

"What'll it be?" Martin's assistant asked.

"Tea, please," the Vietnamese said, smiling. "I never touch alcohol."

De Coursin's people in Marseille had collared Sergei Yegerov, one of Zavorin's men, as he'd come out of a pastry shop on the rue de Paradis. They'd bundled him into a sedan and given him a quick course in attentive listening. By the time they'd reached the Prado, Yegerov had stopped mumbling about diplomatic immunity and was convinced he hadn't been kidnapped by fascist revisionists. When he was finally dumped in Montredon, he knew he was dealing with a rival intelligence service and he had memorized a key telephone number and the code name Carillon, the man who wanted to speak with his superior.

Thirty-six hours later, André de Coursin and Anatole Zavorin met above a deserted *calanque* near Cassis. The mistral was blowing itself out, but the waves were still breaking below, throwing an eerie phosphorescence over the dark rocks. Seabirds were calling like lost souls in the pine-scented darkness. As agreed, both men had brought two attendants, like seconds for a duel. Now they stood together alone, the four dark shadows at some distance. There was a moment of mutual silence.

De Coursin spoke first. *"Bonsoir,* Monsieur Zavorin," he said with a curt nod. "I am glad you could come. Please don't insult my intelligence by lecturing me on your interest in cultural affairs."

"I won't," Zavorin replied, "but I must ask you to get to the point. I have been told this is an urgent matter. What is the purpose of this meeting?"

"Your life is in danger," de Coursin said flatly. "I have come to Marseille to warn you."

"Unbelievable," Zavorin replied. "Has the DGSE come to this? You expect me to take what you say on face value, pack my bags and fly in a panic back to Moscow? *Voyons,* monsieur, be serious."

De Coursin sighed audibly. "I knew this wouldn't be easy," he said firmly. "Just listen to what I have to say. I promise you the truth. One of our Action agents has gone berserk. He killed Drankov and dumped him at your consulate. We were planning to discipline him, but he escaped. He is now at large. It is highly likely that he's returned to Marseille and is planning some action against you or other members of your consulate. He knows who you are. He is extremely dangerous."

Zavorin went a few paces closer to the cliff and looked down at the sea. His bodyguards moved a bit closer. De Coursin's escort did the same.

"This is ridiculous," Zavorin finally snorted. "What do you suggest I do?"

"It would be wise to leave Marseille for a time. At least until we find this person."

"I do not run," Zavorin said, swinging around. "Let the fool come. I shall be ready for him."

"Bravo," de Coursin said dryly. "A very pretty speech. But it's wasted on me. This isn't a question of you . . . or me. It's a question of our two countries, of foreign policy and of your famous *glasnost.* This man is out for revenge. We'll both lose if he wins."

Zavorin's brief laughter was muffled by the surf. "Tell me, monsieur," Zavorin asked. "As a professional intelligence officer, don't you detest this particular assignment?"

De Coursin took the time to light a cigarette, shielding his lighter from the wind. "Yes," he finally replied, "I do."

"Good," Zavorin said. "Now I know you are speaking the truth. I thank you and your superiors for your concern, but you can tell them I have no intention of leaving my post. I am sure you'll do your best to protect me. *Bonsoir,* Monsieur de Coursin."

De Coursin watched Zavorin walk back to his car, the two KGB heavies falling in behind him.

"Pigheaded fool," de Coursin muttered.

"Shall we stop him?" one of his men demanded.

"No," de Coursin told him. "I've had quite enough of Monsieur Zavorin for one night. Let's get to the airport. I must be back in Paris tonight."

Janine was on her way up to the apartment. Bastide had opened the door and was waiting for her. His mother had just called him from Arles to report the well pump at the *mas* was out of order, the pump repairman was hopeless and her garden would be a desert if something wasn't done quickly. He'd promised to call a friend in Fontvieille who knew something about pumps. Bastide was struggling with a major decision as Janine's footsteps echoed on the stairs. Should he tell her about Larissa Kedrov? They had never kept secrets from one another. At least, he didn't think they had. He still hadn't made up his mind when she came into sight, smiling broadly and laden with bags from the *supermarché.* They kissed. He helped her with her load and swung the door shut with his foot. Janine was wearing a light cotton sundress, sandals and a heavy gold bracelet.

"I'm glad to see you," she gasped, out of breath from her climb. "It took some doing to find a proper nurse for Théo, but I think this one will be fine. It's good to have some time to myself again."

Bastide put the bags of food on the kitchen counter, relieved Janine of hers and put his arms around her waist. "I've missed you," he said.

Janine drew back to look at him. "You're tired, Roger," she said, concern in her voice. "You've been working too hard."

He shrugged. "Show me a rested *flic* and I'll show you a *flic* not doing his job."

She came to him and put her hand on his shoulder. "Seriously, is there something wrong? Do you feel all right?"

"I'm fine." His reply was too vehement. "Where shall we go for dinner?"

She leaned back against the counter, folded her tanned arms and eyed him with suspicion. "Perhaps we should stay here," she suggested, "and make it an early night."

"No!" he insisted. "You've been stuck with an invalid for two weeks. We haven't seen each other and we're going to celebrate our reunion. You'll find a bottle of Bollinger and a terrine of *foie de canard* in the fridge. Here, let me get them."

They drank the champagne and sampled the *foie de canard* on the balcony as the last light faded over the port. Flights of star-lings swooped low over the tiled roofs of the *quartier* and a curious pigeon perched on the balcony railing, tilting his head to watch their movements. They fed it with pieces of cracker. Bastide told Janine what he could about the Drankov case and lapsed into silence when he finished. She was puzzled by his mood but de-cided it wasn't the time for questions.

"You *are* staying tonight?" he asked, as they prepared to leave the apartment.

"Of course I am," she reassured him with a smile. "Celibacy can be bad for you. Maybe that's your problem."

They dined on the terrace of Caruso on the Quai de Port. The night was warm, the wind had completely died and Bastide was suddenly hungry. He ordered a plate of gnocchi in rich, spicy tomato sauce and veal piccata. Janine chose paper-thin carpaccio glistening with virgin olive oil and studded with capers. They drank a bottle of Valpolicella and had Armagnac with their espresso. Bastide lit an Upmann corona and stared at Janine through the smoke.

"Why are you watching me?" Janine asked.

"Because you're beautiful," he told her, "and I love you."

Her dark eyes opened wide. She brushed some hair from her forehead. "You what?"

"You heard me."

"It's the first time you've ever said that," she said, avoiding his eyes. "You're acting strangely tonight."

"Perhaps I am," he replied, taking her hand. "I'm a strange person."

"Please don't joke," she said softly. "It's not the moment for jokes."

He reached out to raise her head and saw the tears in her eyes. He'd begun something he hadn't planned, but he couldn't help himself. It was as if he had lost his footing and couldn't prevent a fall. They sat silently while the waiter brought them a second cup of coffee. Bastide sipped his Armagnac and took a deep breath.

"I must tell you something," he said.

She waited expectantly.

"A woman spent the night at my place," he told her slowly and deliberately. "It was unplanned. It just happened."

He felt her wince. She looked out toward the passing traffic and the Vieux Port. Her chin was quivering. "Roger," she began in a choked voice, "I have no claim on you . . ."

"It meant nothing," he said. "She is nothing to me."

"Do I know her?" Janine asked, fumbling for her purse mirror.

"No. I hardly know her myself. I don't plan to see her again. I . . ."

"Tell me who she is."

"Her name's Larissa Kedrov. She's here to set up an exhibit for the Soviet Consulate."

"Bon Dieu," Janine whispered. "I don't believe it."

"Would I bother telling you if it wasn't true?" He'd suddenly lost the taste for his cigar. He crushed it into the ashtray. He knew a storm was gathering. He wasn't sure how to handle it.

"I think it's best if I go home now," she said, shifting in her chair.

"Please don't," he pleaded. "We'll go to my apartment and talk this out."

"Have you changed the sheets yet?" she demanded, her eyes flashing with anger.

He said nothing. Her anger seemed to subside. "I'm sorry," she said quietly. "I shouldn't have said that. But what do you expect? You hit me with a club without warning and . . . I just don't know . . ."

"I shouldn't have said I love you before telling you. That was stupid. But . . . I do. You see this case is . . . oh *merde!* It's hard to explain. Will you come with me?"

She thought for a minute, nodded, slung her purse and watched him count out the money for the bill. "Oh, Roger," she said, shaking her head, "I don't think I know you at all."

Anatole Zavorin had reported his meeting with de Coursin to Moscow. It was still too early for a response. He knew his coded cable must have caused a stir at KGB headquarters. Rival intelligence services rarely "cooperated" in such a manner. He could imagine the chiefs of the various sections in an emergency meeting at the long, felt-covered table in the offices of the First Chief Directorate. He had drafted the text with great care. He'd made it clear that no extra personnel were needed in Marseille. Such a move would have complicated an already difficult situation. He only wished he knew more about the DGSE renegade who was supposedly so dangerous.

Zavorin had shut himself in his office to think. He loosened the knot of his necktie and toyed with his desk pen. He first examined de Coursin's motives, seeking a trick or some deceptive move. Was it possible that the Frenchman was setting a trap of some kind? His analytical mind weighed the available evidence. Reluctantly, he decided the answer was no. He considered the possibility of neutralizing the threat posed by Faubert. If they could get to the man, he might be bought off, turned or eliminated. Such a move could be simple in an environment you controlled. In Marseille it was almost impossible. The fact that de Coursin had broken the traditional rules to warn him could mean the DGSE was serious in their concern. He had no illusions that they were really worried about saving his skin. He knew they were primarily protecting themselves. He was just a piece in the puzzle. One thing was certain: now that he'd refused to cooperate, they'd be watching him like a crown jewel, monitoring his movements and seeing to it that their own praetorian guards remained close enough to provide instant protection.

He had already briefed Yegerov and Boldin on the situation and issued them each a Makarov automatic with two clips. They were to work in shifts acting as his personal bodyguards. He had another Makarov in his safe, but he refused to carry a weapon. It would be of little use if someone was really after him and only an embarrassment if an attempt on his life was successful. He put the pen down and tightened his tie. It would have to be business as usual until the threat surfaced. Business as usual meant the *vernissage* of the icon exhibit. Zavorin frowned, contemplating the event. It would be a perfect opportunity for any gunman. The man would know about it. He would be assured of Zavorin's presence, and the crowd would make security difficult. He glanced at his calendar. The *vernissage* was in two days' time.

Zavorin picked up the telephone, buzzed Boldin and told him to send Larissa Kedrov to his office. He began editing a routine message on the departure of three French Navy minesweepers for the Persian Gulf. There was a light tapping at his door.

"Come in," he called.

Larissa Kedrov shut the door behind her and they exchanged greetings. He asked her to sit down. She was stunning as usual, her hair thickly braided, a necklace of gleaming freshwater pearls accentuating the lines of her fine throat.

"Comrade Kedrov," Zavorin began, "your work here is almost over."

"Almost?"

"Yes. The inspector is no longer of interest to us. If things had gone differently, I'm sure your mission would have been successful. As it is, you did the best you could with your usual skill. I said 'almost' because I would like you to remain till after the *vernissage*. It would be sloppy cover procedure to send you off earlier. Who knows, I may need your *cultural* services again." Zavorin permitted himself a fleeting smile.

"I understand," she replied. "I knew something was wrong. The inspector has avoided me since our last meeting at the museum. He seems to have qualms about the night we spent together. It's puzzling. It doesn't fit his character."

"It's just as well," Zavorin said. "If he was running after you at this point, we'd have additional problems. How are things going at the museum?"

"Everything has been hung. They are now working on the lighting. All will be ready in good time. I have enjoyed it. The icons are truly beautiful. Small masterpieces."

"Perhaps," Zavorin said disapprovingly, "but don't forget the superstition and ignorance they represent. Every inch of their gold leaf represented that much less bread on a workman's table."

She looked at him for several seconds, wondering if he really believed what he'd said. She could see his logic, but she resented being lectured to like a member of the Komsomol. He was indeed a strange man. "I shall go," she told him. "The curator is taking me to lunch."

He watched her leave, appreciating her beauty but unmoved by any desire. Zavorin was married to his work, and women had little place in his life. He had not told her of the threat and he'd warned Yegerov and Boldin to keep their mouths shut. Swallows were useful when needed, but they chattered among themselves like their namesakes. The fewer operational details they knew the better.

Zavorin left his desk, adjusted his suit jacket and prepared to visit the consul general. Anisimov had to be told of the need for increased security, but no more. Career diplomats could be as untrustworthy as the swallows.

Bastide and Mattei had parked by a public toilet not far from the entrance to a small yacht basin. They'd chosen the spot because there were many other cars parked there. The owners came and went, carrying boxes of food, tools, lines and sails to their boats in preparation for a weekend of racing or cruising. Mattei had positioned his Mercedes for a clear view of the walled bungalow about one hundred yards down the street to their right.

Mattei glanced at Bastide and smiled to himself. His boss seemed to be back to normal. He'd come into the office humming that morning and complimented Lenoir on a report he'd written.

When Thong had called to pass on some information, Bastide had slammed his fist into his palm with exuberance. He hadn't even complained when he'd seen the Mercedes. Mattei was having some dents removed and only half the work was done. There were irregular gray patches of filler on the blue chassis, giving the aging vehicle a unique camouflage effect. Mattei wasn't clear on exactly who they were looking for. First Bastide had mumbled about a warning, and later he'd said something about the DGSE being out of control. He hadn't asked any questions. Mattei didn't want to risk any change in Bastide's disposition.

It was particularly hot. The sun was boring in from an almost cloudless sky. Even with the windows down, the Mercedes was like an oven. Bastide lifted the small binoculars he'd borrowed from the narcotics section and scanned the wall, stopping for several seconds to examine the gate. He could only see the roof of the bungalow. It was frustrating not to have a clear view.

Bastide had indeed recovered from his black mood. He and Janine had returned to his apartment and talked till 2 A.M. It had not been easy. What had been said needed to be said. Once the Kedrov affair had been dissected and laid to rest, they'd even discussed the possibility of marriage, with both agreeing that such a decision could wait. The important result of their discussion was a complete understanding of how they felt about each other. For the first time since they'd met, they had admitted their mutual feelings for one another. When they'd finally gone to bed, their lovemaking had been tender and fulfilling.

Bastide put down the binoculars and frowned. What he was doing could earn him a reprimand or a suspension. But Bastide didn't really care. He'd been used as a cat's paw too long, and the mere thought that the DGSE had brought one of their own killers into his territory had infuriated him. He would have liked to walk into the villa and confront this Martin and his men directly, but he wasn't a fool. He had no desire to commit suicide.

"Ho!" Mattei said, sitting up in his seat and tapping Bastide on the arm. "Here comes something!"

Bastide put his binoculars on the gate. It was swinging open. A gray Land-Rover was rolling out onto the street. The driver was alone in the vehicle. Bastide could read the white lettering on the door: "Oceanic Diving Services." The Land-Rover turned right to pass in front of them. Bastide spun the focus knob to get a clear view of the driver. He didn't fit the description of Martin.

Mattei was watching Bastide, his hand on the ignition key. "Shall we follow him?" Mattei asked.

"No," Bastide replied, "it isn't the *type* we're after."

"He may never come out of there," Mattei commented, relaxing.

"Patience," Bastide said. "If he doesn't appear in an hour's time, you can go get a *pan bagnat* to munch on."

Bastide turned back to the gate. It hadn't closed. As he wondered about the delay, a motorcycle appeared. The rider hesitated in the driveway, gunning the motor as the gate shut behind him. He too turned to the right and roared down the street, leaving a trail of blue smoke. Bastide had a quick but clear view of the rider, the heavyset frame, the dark hair, the bushy eyebrows.

"Let's go," he told Mattei. "Don't lose the bastard."

Lou-Lou Martin's attention was focused on moving through the traffic as fast as he could. The telephoned tip on the possible sighting of Faubert had caught him off balance, but he and one of his men had left the bungalow within minutes. The call had come from a part-timer on the DGSE payroll, but the man had experience and a good reputation. After his drill with the map, Martin had directed his auxiliaries to concentrate on the *quartier* around the Cours Belsunce. The man who'd called had made a thorough check of the hotels—the new arrivals and their registry cards; the activities of their guests, what they may have told the desk clerks about their business or reasons for being in Marseille. He had come across a possible suspect at the Hôtel Surcouf. The clerk had noticed something strange about the newcomer. The Frenchman had arrived with unkempt hair. When the clerk had seen him the next day, his head had been completely shaved. When Martin had replaced the receiver, he was almost certain he'd located Faubert. The disguise of a shaved head would be a normal procedure for Faubert, but Martin was surprised his former colleague had been so careless in allowing someone to notice the sudden change. Martin had not wasted time pondering this seeming lapse. After all, Faubert was emotional and on the run. His procedures and thinking were bound to be muddled.

Martin increased his speed as he climbed onto the corniche. He could feel the weight of the Walther automatic in its shoulder holster under his jacket. The warm wind buffeted his face. He was pleased with the cycle. It had power and it handled easily. With luck, he thought, we might end this assignment quickly.

"Don't worry about the lights," Bastide told Mattei as the Mercedes squeaked through an intersection just before the red signal. "Don't lose him!"

"The idiot must think he's in a race," Mattei said through clenched teeth. He was pushing the Mercedes to its limit, spinning the wheel to swing around slower cars and watching the side streets.

Bastide drummed his fingers on the dashboard. This was a heaven-sent opportunity. It wouldn't be easy to reach Martin if he remained in the safe house, and he wouldn't always be traveling alone. Bastide made a quick decision.

"Stop him," he told Mattei. "Run him off the road!"

"What?"

"At the next curve!" Bastide shouted. "Get closer to him!"

Mattei pressed on the accelerator and leaned forward as if he was willing the tired sedan to go faster. They pulled alongside as the cycle slowed for the curve.

"Lead him a little," Bastide ordered, "then swing in." He drew his Magnum and put one hand on the door handle. Martin turned his head in their direction as Mattei cut him off. He tried to avoid a collision. The motorcycle's front wheel hit the raised concrete hard, but Martin retained control. The bike spun in a quick circle and came to rest against the sandstone cliff. The Mercedes' front wheels jarred onto the sidewalk. Martin jumped clear of the bike without falling, his hand moving toward his jacket.

"No!" Bastide's warning shout and the leveled Manurhin stopped Martin cold. "Both hands on your head," Bastide ordered. "See what he's carrying." Mattei patted Martin down, reached under his jacket and produced the Walther.

"You stupid *flic*," Martin growled, "you're making a major mistake!"

"Get in the car," Bastide snapped. "There, in the front seat."

Traffic was slowing, drivers and passengers gawking at the armed men. Bastide shut the front door after Martin and climbed into the back seat. "Cuff him!" he told Mattei. Mattei pulled

Martin's two hands behind his back and secured them with handcuffs.

"Now to the Parc de Pharos for a quiet talk," Bastide said.

"Someone's going to steal that bike," Martin said over his
shoulder.

"That's your worry," Bastide remarked. "Let's go."

"I hope you're ready for an early retirement," Martin said as
they bumped back onto the roadway. "I'm on official business. I'll
give you a number to call."

"Keep your lips together and enjoy the scenery," Bastide ordered. He slid the clip out of Martin's automatic and pushed it
under the back seat. It took them seven minutes to reach the Parc
de Pharos. Mattei followed Bastide's directions, drove across the
empty parking area and swung to a halt on the deserted far side of
the Palais overlooking the wide blue sweep of the outer harbor.

"Martin," Bastide said, speaking close to his captive's left ear,
"listen carefully and don't interrupt. I know you're in Marseille to
do a job. I want you to take what I say back to your bosses. Tell
them we don't like their methods. We don't want people like you
operating in our territory, and we'll have your ass in court if there
are any illegal killings here. Do you understand?"

Martin craned his neck, his cold eyes boring into Bastide as if
he was making a careful mental portrait. "You're in over your
head," he murmured. "You're either incredibly naive or stupid
. . . or both."

Mattei's beefy hand shot out, grabbed Martin's chin and
pushed his head back against the seat. "Watch it," Mattei warned.
"We eat tough guys like you for breakfast."

"Does the name de Coursin mean anything to you?" Bastide
asked. Martin's reaction was instantaneous. He blinked in surprise and shook his head several seconds too late. Mattei loosened his grip. He was puzzled by Bastide's line of questioning.

"You know," Bastide said, "I have a friend down at the Palais
de Justice, a young, ambitious *juge d'instruction* who would love to
chat with you about your mission here. He's one of those idealists
with precise ideas about the law and the role of government.
He'd be shocked to hear that your people were stepping outside
your charter, planning dirty tricks on French soil."

Martin remained outwardly calm, but his mind was racing.

He'd thought he was dealing with a dumb policeman. Now he wasn't sure. The mention of de Coursin's name had convinced him the *flic* knew more than he should. Martin had never been threatened with the law before.

"I'll tell you what I want you to do," Bastide said. "I want you to tell your superiors exactly what happened. Tell them we want you and your boys out of town. Tell them it will be very embarrassing for them if they bring in any replacements or attempt to go on with the hit. Do you understand?"

Martin nodded.

"As far as you're concerned," Bastide continued, "we don't want to see you in Marseille again. If you don't leave quietly in the next twenty-four hours, I'll take you in, your photo will be on the front page and the judge will make mincemeat of you." Bastide turned to Mattei.

"Take off the cuffs," he said, resting the cold muzzle of the Manurhin against Martin's neck as a caution against any heroics.

"Now," Bastide said, "take off your pants and your shorts."

"What the hell?" Martin blustered.

"Do it!"

Martin removed his trousers and his shorts. Bastide reached over and put them into the back seat.

"Is this a joke?" Martin demanded.

"I suppose it is," Bastide replied. "We've heard that you DGSE heroes are experts at survival. I'd just like to see how you make it back to your *planque* in Madrague. Who knows, you could meet one of our uniforms on the way and have some explaining to do. We'd like to trail along and watch your progress, but we've got more important things to do. Get out!"

"My weapon?" Martin asked as the door was slammed.

"We'll put it in our trophy case," Bastide told him. "Unlabeled, of course."

They left Martin standing in the sunshine like a misplaced seminude statue. Mattei glanced in the rearview mirror before they turned the corner.

"The bastard's tying his shirttails under his crotch," he chuckled.

"Good for him." Bastide smiled. He lit a cigar as they waited for a traffic light to change on the Quai de Rive Neuve.

"I don't understand what that was all about," Mattei said, "and I'm not sure it was the right thing to do."

"Neither am I," Bastide said thoughtfully, "but I meant what I said and I do feel much better." He paused for a moment. "If things go wrong," he told Mattei, "you're out of it. You were only along for the ride and under my orders—understood?"

"If you say so," Mattei agreed, shaking his head in puzzlement.

"Good," Bastide said. "Let's stop for a quick *pastis* before we go back to the office." Bastide lifted the mouthpiece of the car radio and called in for someone to pick up the abandoned motorcycle.

"He did what?" de Coursin demanded. "It's not possible!" he muttered into the telephone. The call had come in as he prepared to leave his office. DGSE Marseille was relaying the news of Lou-Lou Martin's encounter with Bastide.

"He told Martin to leave the city in twenty-four hours," the DGSE officer reported.

"And if he doesn't?" de Coursin asked.

"He's threatened to have him up before a judge and he mentioned something about the media."

De Coursin winced. "Why didn't you report this to me sooner?" he demanded.

"Martin had trouble getting back to Madrague. They . . . ah, took his trousers."

De Coursin raised his eyes to the ceiling. "I don't believe it," he murmured.

"What instructions do you have for Martin?" the officer asked.

"Tell him to sit tight," de Coursin replied, making a special effort to remain calm. "I'll get back to you soon." He put the receiver down and took a deep breath. He leaned against his desk and reviewed the hasty notes he'd taken during the telephone conversation. Martin had finally made some progress in the search for Faubert. He'd been on his way to Faubert's possible hiding place when Bastide intervened. Now Bastide was threatening to blow the DGSE operation sky-high! If de Coursin hadn't been standing in his office in broad daylight, he would have thought it was all a nightmare. Something had to be done quickly. The director had left for a weekend at his summer home in

Brittany. De Coursin would have to take full responsibility. He picked up the phone and asked his secretary to put through a *priorité d'état* message to the préfet in Marseille.

"Took his trousers," he murmured as he waited for the call to come through. It had begun to sound like a script from a Louis de Funès film.

Viktor Popov double-checked the locks on the consulate's main door, made a hasty inspection of the consul general's desk to make sure all classified documents had been locked in the safe and made his way to the kitchen area in the rear of the building. It had been a trying day and he was looking forward to some vodka before returning to his apartment. He was on call as duty officer again . . . a task he detested. His name seemed to be on the roster at suspiciously frequent intervals. He had decided Zavorin was responsible. The KGB resident and his staff never shared the duty burden. He pushed open the kitchen door and found Sergeant Sheshin had beaten him to the vodka.

The husky sergeant got up from the table when Popov appeared and took another glass out of a high cabinet. He looked ill at ease in his civilian clothes. "Will you join me, Comrade Consul?" Sheshin asked.

"With pleasure," Popov replied. He accepted a full glass and sat down across from Sheshin. There was a plate of cheese, pickled onions and sliced black bread between them. Popov helped himself.

"It is not good for a man to drink alone," Sheshin said, slurring his words.

Popov noted the level of the vodka bottle and guessed Sheshin had been at it for some time. He downed his drink and refilled both their glasses. He liked Sheshin. He saw the wounded special forces veteran as a man of character. Someone who had lived dangerously, someone immune to the triviality and compromises of the consular corps.

"Comrade Sheshin," Popov said, "you never speak of your time in Afghanistan. You have never told me how you received your wound."

Sheshin shrugged. "There is not much to tell," he replied. "We of Spetsnaz were on an operation in the mountains. We located a suspected terrorist camp, and went in with helicopters. My section had just jumped to the ground when they hit us with automatic fire. The helicopter went up in flames. The ammunition exploded. I was hit by Russian bullets. An irony, no?"

"Was it a bad wound?"

"Yes." Sheshin slugged back the vodka and smacked his lips. "Yes, a bullet under the shoulder blade, one in the thigh. But the petrol burns were the worst. The scarring was bad. My left arm here"—he tapped his bicep—"looks like it belongs to a mummy."

"I am sorry."

"Oh, don't be sorry, Comrade," Sheshin laughed. "It is all part of the profession. It's a man's game and you take what comes. I miss it, though."

"You'd rather be in Afghanistan than here?" Popov asked.

"Of course. This is a charade. Diplomacy! What a laugh. Here, have some more vodka. No, I tell you, Comrade, this is no life for a man. Look at Zavorin and his people. They play at games . . ."

Popov glanced uneasily at the kitchen door and Sheshin laughed.

"Don't worry. They have left. I think they have gone home to lock themselves in. They are pissing their pants."

"Why do you say that?" Popov demanded.

"I know what is going on. Did you know that Zavorin has issued pistols to Yegerov and Boldin? No, I don't suppose you would know that. It appears someone is after them. It may be the same man who dumped the corpse outside. What do you say to that?"

Popov drank his vodka but said nothing.

"They don't like to share their secrets with the GRU," Sheshin continued, "but I've snooped around the message center. Zavorin thinks something might happen at the opening of the icon exhibit."

"Something?"

"This killer might hit again."

"But why? I don't understand."

Sheshin leaned across the table and put his hand on Popov's shoulder. "Because the cold one you tried to move was one of theirs."

Popov's eyes widened. "I don't believe it," he said. "How do you know?"

"Believe me, it's true. It's a worm's nest, Comrade, a real worm's nest."

"Does the consul general know about this?" Popov asked.

"Of course not. He is the last to know about anything. No, that's not correct. You are the last to know. I suppose I've told you too much as it is. Look, the bottle's almost empty."

"But shouldn't the consul general be warned?" Popov asked. "His life may be in danger."

Sheshin rose unsteadily and rummaged in the refrigerator for another bottle of vodka. "Of course he's in danger. So are you. So is that beautiful 'assistant' of Zavorin's and all of us for that matter." Sheshin returned to the table, sat down heavily and opened the bottle. He filled his mouth with pickled onions and chewed on them. Once he'd swallowed, he waved his finger at Popov.

"Take my advice, young man," he intoned seriously. "Don't become involved. Let them play their games. You continue stamping visas. Keep your nose clean. Nothing at all may happen. If you step into their world, they'll slice you up like a sausage. Come, one last drink before I go off for my dinner."

Sheshin poured out the crystal-clear liquor and glanced at Popov with a fatherly smile. "I am almost drunk, Comrade," he said in a mock whisper. "Consider what I have told you as rubbish."

VIII

Léon Faubert awakened at 9 A.M. He lay quietly in bed and stared at the dirty gray ceiling of his hotel room. He could tell from the rays of sunlight seeping through the openings in the sagging curtains that it was going to be a hot day. He watched a large, long-legged spider make its way cautiously up the wall and listened to the noises from the street. He had slept under a single sheet, the Beretta under the pillow. He felt a contained excitement. In eight hours he was due to begin his own operation. No one would be giving him orders or telling him how to proceed. He had planned everything himself and when he'd finished he should have achieved all his objectives.

He knew that something could go wrong. There were always the intangibles, those details you could never anticipate. Zavorin might remain at home with a sudden attack of the flu. Some old DGSE hand might recognize him when he passed through the reception line at the museum. An eager policeman or a GIPN marksman might drop him as he made his move. He'd weighed all these negative possibilities and decided that the odds were in his favor. If things did go badly, he'd take some people with him. Zavorin was first on his list. He was also determined to punish any DGSE men who might be on his trail. Since Morel's attempt on his life, he'd developed a fixation, a psychosis centered on revenge. In his troubled mind the DGSE's attitude was extremely unfair. He didn't know who might have taken up the chase after Morel, but he intended to make them pay if he possibly could.

A knock on the door signaled the arrival of his *petit déjeuner*. The Tunisian girl who delivered it mumbled a timid good morning and hurried out of the room. He lifted the morning paper off the tray and glanced at the headlines. Fighting in Chad, more trouble in the Persian Gulf and a racial killing in Toulon. He tossed the paper aside and poured himself some black coffee. He hadn't had a drink for twenty-four hours and he lifted the cup with a steady hand. He climbed out of bed, ran some cold water into the wash-basin and splashed it over his neck. His day was carefully planned. He'd have a bath in the communal tub at the end of the hall, a leisurely lunch, and a half bottle of wine at a cheap restaurant on the rue de Baignoir, followed by a nap. Then he'd dress for the *vernissage* and take a cab to the Palais Longchamp.

He walked to the window to pull back the curtains. As he stood blinking in the bright light, it occurred to him that his planning was incomplete. For the first time in his life he hadn't prepared a fallback position or an escape route. It took him a few seconds to remember that his plan didn't call for either.

Bastide had decided to walk to the Hôtel de Police. He'd risen early; it was a beautiful morning and he wanted to think without Mattei making small talk. He crossed the street to the quai and paused to admire a luxurious ketch berthed near the Yacht Club. A tanned young man with sun-bleached hair was swabbing the teak decks with a mop. The bright work sparkled in the sun and a yellow inflatable dinghy was bottom-up on the foredeck. He wondered what it would be like to own such a yacht, to sail on the tide according to your whim, far from the noise and dirt of the city. He didn't waste much time thinking about it. The dream was too far removed from everyday reality. He had turned to walk on when someone called his name. He recognized Consul Popov hurrying toward him, waving his arm.

"Bizarre," Bastide said under his breath, waiting for the Russian to reach him.

"Ah, Inspector, I was at your apartment, but I missed you. I thought I would not catch you, but I saw you looking at this boat . . ."

"Slow down," Bastide said. "Is there something wrong?"

"No. Well, yes," Popov said nervously. He needed a shave. He looked as he had the morning they'd found him trying to move the body. "Can we go somewhere to talk?"

"Certainly," Bastide said, gesturing toward a café. "Let's have some coffee." They crossed the street and Bastide paused on the café terrace.

"No, please," Popov said quickly, "let us go inside." Popov led

Bastide to a small table in the far corner of the bar. They sat down and ordered two espressos. Bastide watched Popov carefully. The consul kept his head down, began to pop his knuckles, caught himself and put his hands flat on the table as if trying to immobilize them. This is a Russian with a problem, Bastide told himself. He waited till the coffee was served before speaking.

"Well, *Monsieur le Consul,* what can I do for you?" he finally asked.

"I . . . I've come to you, Inspector, because you have been assigned to protect us," Popov told him, the words rattling out. "I cannot tell you everything but something dangerous is happening and the consul general knows nothing about it. I didn't myself until last night. It has to do . . . with the murder. You know, the dead man at the consulate. I shouldn't be here but you are providing security . . ."

Bastide held up his hand. "Drink some coffee," he suggested. "Would you like a cognac to go with it?"

"Yes," Popov said, nodding, "perhaps that would be a good idea."

Bastide shouted to the waiter, ordering two cognacs.

"Now think of what you want to tell me and speak slowly and calmly."

"It is difficult for me. You are a foreigner, a police officer. But I believe I am doing right."

Bastide nodded sympathetically, hiding his mounting impatience. The arrival of the cognac delayed Popov further while he finished off half the snifter.

"They expect the killer to return tonight . . . during the *vernissage* at the Palais Longchamp . . ."

"Who is 'they'?" Bastide interrupted.

"Zavorin . . ."

"Your KGB resident?"

Popov recoiled as if someone had hit him. "You know?" he asked.

"I think every third person in Marseille does by now," Bastide told him. "Why would this 'killer' be targeting your people?" he asked Popov.

"I do not know." Popov shook his head. "But I do know that the corpse was working for the KGB."

"Who killed him?"

"I don't know. But I have heard that Zavorin expects an attempt on his own life or on others attached to the consulate. He has said nothing to the consul general. He has warned no one."

"Are you sure of your information?" Bastide demanded, frowning.

"I . . . I think I am."

Bastide sipped his coffee and tried to make sense out of Popov's revelations. Martin flashed into his mind immediately. But why would the DGSE suddenly launch a lethal, semiofficial extermination of the Soviet Consulate staff? Even if he took into account the strange machinations of the intelligence agencies, it didn't stand up.

"Zavorin has issued automatics to his staff," Popov blurted. "They will act as his bodyguards this evening."

"Does Mademoiselle Kedrov know of all this?"

"I can't say."

"She's KGB too, isn't she?" Bastide asked.

Popov avoided Bastide's eyes and said nothing.

"What do you want me to do?" Bastide asked.

"Can you be there? Can you protect the consul general? He is a good man. He has served his country well. He deserves better . . ."

"Monsieur Popov," Bastide said, "take my cognac. Drink it and listen to what I have to say. I suggest you go back to the consulate and tell your consul general what you've told me. Perhaps you're unduly alarmed and the situation isn't as serious as you think. If it is, he'll be grateful. If it isn't, he may know something you don't know . . ."

"You don't understand," Popov cut in, "things work differently with us."

"I'm sure they do. It's only a suggestion. If it will make you feel better, I promise to be at the *vernissage* with two of my men. It's only a question of a few hours' time and we'd be glad to provide this service."

"Thank you," Popov said, pumping Bastide's hand. "Thank you very much."

"Does anyone know you planned to talk with me?" Bastide asked.

"No one."

"You weren't followed?"

"No."

"Well, I hope not. I wouldn't mention our meeting to anyone."

"I won't," Popov promised. He glanced at his watch. "I must return to the consulate," he said, popping up like a marionette. "Oh, allow me to pay for the drinks."

"No," Bastide motioned him toward the door, "I'll take care of it." He watched Popov till he was out of sight. "Diamond dealer crime, *mon cul!*" he said under his breath. Like it or not, the case of the consular corpse had returned to Marseille.

Commissaire Aynard had not been so agitated since his ulcer operation. He'd come storming through the door of the Homicide office, thin lips set in a downward curve. The points of russet color on his pale cheeks made him look like an unhappy clown. "Where is he?" Aynard demanded, his voice abnormally high.

"He's on a case," Mattei had replied. "Is there a problem?"

"A problem! Of course there's a problem," Aynard replied. "I don't normally spend the most important part of my morning visiting you down here, do I?"

"No, you don't," Mattei agreed, shaking his head for emphasis.

"The préfet wants to see Bastide immediately. Find him. It's important."

"Sir, may I ask what this is about?"

"Oh yes, you can ask. But I can't tell you. I can't tell you because I don't know myself! The préfet did not tell me. Once again, thanks to Bastide, I look like a fool. I not only don't know what this emergency is about, but I can't find my Inspecteur Principal of Homicide when I need him!"

Mattei pulled on his blazer.

"When you find Bastide and deliver him to the Préfecture," Aynard said, "tell him I'll be waiting in my office. I'll expect a full explanation." The commissaire preceded Mattei out the door and paused on the landing. "Take my car and driver if it will save time," he said.

"No, thank you, sir," Mattei replied. "I have transport."

Aynard turned his back and began climbing the stairs to his office. Mattei hurried toward the ground floor, two steps at a time. "Catastrophe, catastrophe!" he murmured. "Where the hell could he be?"

The answer to his question came quickly. Mattei had just driven past Fort Saint-Jean when he spotted Bastide walking toward him on the Quai du Port. He flashed his lights and pulled over to the curb.

"*Salut,* Babar," Bastide said, "what's up? You look like you're in trouble."

"Not me," Mattei told him. "You're in trouble, or you will be soon."

Bastide climbed in beside Mattei and shut the door. "What's the problem?"

"I don't know, but the préfet wants to see you. Aynard is having a fit. He wants me to drive you there."

"*Merde!*" Bastide cursed.

"No doubt," Mattei commented sarcastically, "but that's the way of the world."

He started to put the Mercedes in gear, but Bastide stopped him.

"Wait," he said. There was no doubt in Bastide's mind about the préfet's summons. Martin had undoubtedly reported to de Coursin on their meeting; de Coursin had contacted the préfet and the préfet was going to roast him for interfering with a DGSE operation.

"Babar," Bastide said, "I'm not going to see the préfet."

"*Bonne Mère!* Are you mad?"

"Maybe I am. But the timing's all wrong."

"I don't know about the timing," Mattei argued, "but it sounds like you're determined to commit professional suicide. *Allons,* don't be foolish."

"No," Bastide said firmly. "Listen, I want you to spend an hour or more looking for me before you go back to the office. Tell Aynard an informer passed on a tip on this murder Lenoir's investigating. You know, the old woman. Explain that I may have things cleared up by this evening. You don't know where I am in the city or how to reach me. Grab Lenoir and tell him to keep his mouth shut. In fact, get him out of the building before you talk to Aynard."

"*Putain!*" Mattei exclaimed. "I'm going to catch all the shit!"

"Try standing sideways," Bastide quipped.

"The least you can do is tell me what the hell is going on!"

Bastide was silent for a moment. "You're right," he said, "but it won't make much sense to you. This whole mystery corpse business is a soup cooked by the DGSE and the KGB. I've been on the fringe of it, and now I'm in it up to my neck. That biker we snatched yesterday was a DGSE heavy."

"I guessed as much," Mattei said.

"I don't have time for details," Bastide continued, "but the Soviets expect trouble at their Palais Longchamp exhibit."

"They told you this?"

"One of them did—unofficially."

"We're supposed to be off the case," Mattei reminded Bastide.

"As far as I'm concerned, the case is still ours. I want you and Lenoir to go with me to the museum. We must be as inconspicuous as possible. Don't take your Mercedes. We'll draw an unmarked sedan from the motor pool and park at least a half block from the Palais."

"What are we supposed to be doing there?"

"Protecting the Russkov."

"That must be a joke."

"It isn't, but that's only part of it. If I'm wrong, it will be a disaster . . . for me. If I'm right, we could collar the bastard who dumped that *macchabée* at the consulate. Our first job is to look for obvious security plants, our own and the Russkovs', and the arrival of any suspicious types. Remember, we're looking for a pro. He used hydrocyanic acid on his victim, but he's probably an accomplished shooter. It looks like Zavorin will be his prime target, but he could pop anyone. We also have to watch for the DGSE heavy we left trouserless."

"I could bring some uniforms along for backup," Mattei suggested.

"No, not on this one. I hope to have official invitations for you and Lenoir when I arrive, so none of us will have to use our police identity cards. For one night in your life you're going to be a full-fledged art lover. Now, let's move before Aynard comes looking for me."

"Where to?" Mattei asked.

"Head up the rue de Paradis. I'll tell you where to stop."

The two cognacs he'd drunk with Bastide, coupled with a bad case of nerves, had launched Popov on a binge. He sat behind his desk in the consulate. He'd hidden a pint bottle of Hennessy in a handy drawer. It was already half empty. He'd told his secretary to postpone any appointments till Monday and to take messages from all callers. It was already noon, but he had no appetite. Popov was having second thoughts about his meeting with Bastide. The seriousness of what he'd done settled on him like a heavy weight. He knew even a lenient Soviet court would consider his action treasonable. Not only did it involve passing state secrets to a foreign police official, it also concerned sensitive information on the KGB. *They* wouldn't even bother about the façade of a trial.

He opened the drawer, uncapped the cognac and took a deep swallow. Popov, he told himself, you are an idiot. He sagged in his chair, the bottle still in his hand, and shut his eyes. The telephone rang. He sat bolt upright and hid the bottle in the drawer. The phone rang again.

He snatched the receiver. "Consul Popov," he replied, striving for a normal delivery. It was his secretary. A man insisted on speaking with him. He would not give his name, but he said he'd spoken with the consul that very morning. It was something about the *vernissage*.

"Oh," Popov said, "put him on."

"Monsieur le Consul?" a familiar voice asked.

"Yes," Popov replied cautiously, "who is this?"

"We had coffee together this morning," Bastide explained.

"What is it you want?"

"I have two friends who are in desperate need of invitations for tonight's *vernissage*. Could you get them for me?"

Popov's brow furrowed as he tried to understand the significance of Bastide's request. His alcohol-dulled brain finally functioned. The Frenchman had said he would bring two other policemen with him.

"Yes," Popov said, "I can get them for you. Ah . . . will you pick them up?"

"No," Bastide said, "I don't want to bother you at your office.

Can you meet me at the Café Monaco at the corner of rue de Paradis and the Prado?"

"Well . . ." Popov hesitated. "I don't know . . ."

"I suggest you come," Bastide said authoritatively. "The sooner the better."

"Yes, I understand," Popov replied, his voice fading to a whisper. "I'll be there within an hour."

"Alone?"

"Yes, yes, of course."

Popov put down the phone. He felt sick. His stomach was churning and there seemed to be a fire deep in his chest. A succession of troubling questions and dire possibilities crossed his mind. Would his efficient secretary consider the telephone call unusual? She might already wonder why he'd canceled his appointments. She might feel it her duty to mention his strange behavior to someone. Had she noticed the cognac on his breath? What would he tell her on leaving the office? He would have to get the invitations from Zavorin's office. What if Zavorin or the Kedrov woman questioned him about them? He thought of a solution. He would send his secretary for the invitations. He'd have her tell Zavorin they were needed to fill a last-minute request from some French party members he'd forgotten to put on the list. He sat straight in his chair, called his secretary in and gave her the necessary instructions.

André de Coursin blew his nose as unobtrusively as possible and slipped his handkerchief back in his pocket. The director's study was blue with acrid pipe smoke. It irritated de Coursin's sinuses and made his eyes water. It was enough to make him forgo his usual cigarette.

"So, this inspector has threatened to expose our operation?" the director asked.

"That's correct, sir," de Coursin replied. "He mentioned picking up our team leader and turning him over to a judge. He also hinted that the media would be interested in what we are doing. That is why I took the initiative in your absence of contacting the préfet in Marseille."

"You did what should have been done," the director said. He was wearing a heavy wool turtleneck sweater, rough trousers and heavy walking shoes. A wide picture window behind him provided a view of the Brittany coast, a panorama of wild seas, rugged gray rocks and foaming surf. De Coursin had been summoned to give a verbal report on the situation in Marseille. He'd flown to Saint-Brieuc in the DGSE executive jet and been driven to the director's summer home near Binic. He watched the director tap out his pipe in an ashtray made from a naval shell casing and select a cool briar from the stand on his desk.

"Do you think the inspector has been disciplined?" the director asked.

"The préfet promised we'd have no further trouble."

"Has he spoken to the inspector yet?"

"He promised to call as soon as he does. My office will patch the call in here."

The director turned to look at a ship's clock on the wall. "Perhaps the préfet is having trouble finding his wayward *flic.*"

"I have told our people not to move until we hear from the préfet," de Coursin explained.

"Meanwhile, you are protecting Zavorin?" the director asked.

"Yes, sir. I warned him of the threat and, as you know, offered protection. He refused. Our Marseille office has him under surveillance."

"Tell me more about this *vernissage* you mentioned."

"The Soviets are opening an exhibit of icons at the museum of the Palais Longchamp. It promises to be quite an affair: champagne, caviar, speeches and the cream of Marseille society. Zavorin will be present in his role as cultural attaché. I'm sure the swallow, Larissa Kedrov, will be there too. With Faubert at large it's quite worrying. But we have taken precautions."

"You probably have nothing to worry about," the director said. "If Faubert moves, he'll hit when we least expect it. What do you suppose got into that inspector? Why is he causing all this trouble?"

"I'm not sure. He's a good police officer with an outstanding record. I don't think he likes intelligence operations."

"He's not alone," the director said, smiling. "When I was in the Navy, I thought intelligence officers were useless leeches." He chuckled. "Now look at me." The director filled his pipe from an oaken humidor and lit it, adding new body to the fading smoke pall in the room.

"I'll tell you what I want done," he told de Coursin. "Order our team in Marseille to sit tight for the moment. If this thing isn't settled quickly, we may have to unleash Martin."

De Coursin nodded. "Good," the director said. "Tell me this, how many of our Marseille staff will be at this famous *vernissage?*"

"Three, sir. The two officers I've assigned to watch over Zavorin and a Vietnamese who works for us on a part-time basis."

"How many of them would recognize Faubert on sight?"

"None. Martin is the only one who's worked with Faubert in the past."

"Damn!" the director cursed. "That stupid inspector is complicating our lives."

Popov entered the Café Monaco like a fugitive. He saw Bastide at the counter and hurried to him, digging deep into his breast pocket to produce the sealed invitations.

"*Bon Dieu,*" Bastide told him, "relax. No one here will recognize you. Act natural. Have a drink."

"No. I must return to the consulate." Popov's hands were shaking and he still hadn't found the time to shave.

"Have you heard anything more about the *vernissage?*" Bastide asked.

"No. I've avoided Zavorin," Popov replied. "If they ever discover I've talked to you . . ." He glanced quickly over his shoulder at the street outside.

Bastide realized that Popov was close to a breakdown. He felt a certain sympathy for the young Russian, but he didn't want anything to disrupt the *vernissage* or ruin their chance of collaring the killer. He decided Popov needed calming.

"Have you eaten?" Bastide asked.

"No, no, I'm not hungry."

"Well, it's late and I was about to have a *casse-croûte.* I insist that you join me. Come, let's take a table." Bastide ordered the food and a bottle of Côtes du Rhône before he left the counter. He brought his half-finished glass of *pastis* to the table. "I insist you have some wine with me," Bastide said. "The *pâté de campagne* they serve here is special."

"I should go back," Popov whispered. "They'll be suspicious."

"I'm sure you exaggerate. They probably don't even realize you're gone."

"My secretary senses something. I can tell. I don't trust her. She might work for Zavorin too, for all I know."

The barman brought a wide plate filled with *pâté, saucisson, rillettes, gruyère* and a thick slab of butter. He put a basket of freshly sliced, crusty bread beside it and opened the wine. Bastide filled their glasses, sipped the wine and nodded his approval. "Not great," he commented, "but solid." He buttered a piece of bread and spread the chunky *pâté* over it. "Eat," he recommended. "You'll feel much better."

Popov gulped some wine and made a halfhearted attempt at the food.

"Tell me more about Monsieur Zavorin," Bastide said. "How long have you known him?"

"I won't be able to go back," Popov murmured. It was obvious he hadn't been listening to Bastide.

"What did you say?" Bastide asked.

"My career is finished," Popov said mournfully. "I am compromised."

"Certainly not. I'm the only one you've talked to. I won't say a word."

"I will have to remain in France," Popov continued. "Can you arrange it?"

"Stay in France!" Bastide said, surprised. "You're not serious?"

"It's the only solution. If you can't help, introduce me to someone who can."

Bastide put down his glass and examined Popov attentively. He had no doubt the Russian was serious. He would have to handle his request carefully. "I'm not sure you realize what you've said," Bastide stalled. "Give yourself a few days; think about it some more. You need rest. Things aren't as bad as they may seem."

"I want you to introduce me to the senior French intelligence representative in Marseille," Popov said, tossing off the rest of his wine. The cognac he'd absorbed earlier had caught up with him. His red-rimmed eyes were barely open. It was hard for Bastide to

take his request seriously. But a nervous drunk could be dangerous, particularly if he thought someone was patronizing him.

"*Monsieur le Consul,*" Bastide said, "I'll be glad to, but I'm
worried about the *vernissage.* I'm sure you'll agree it's important
that nothing goes wrong this evening?"

Popov poured himself a full glass of wine. His reasoning had
become even more disconnected. "I could teach Russian at a
university," he said, ignoring Bastide's question. "But I'd need
protection, perhaps a new name." He raised his glass abruptly
and slopped some wine onto the table. One drop left a spreading
purple stain on his shirt sleeve.

Bastide decided Popov had become a liability. There was no
way of predicting what he might do next. "Are you planning to
attend the *vernissage?*" Bastide asked.

"Of course," Popov replied, fighting to keep his eyes open. "I
must be there. I owe it to Comrade Anisimov. The consul general
is a kind man."

"Have some more *pâté,*" Bastide insisted. "I have to make a
phone call."

Mattei answered on the third ring. He began rattling off a tale
of woe the moment Bastide identified himself. "You wouldn't
believe what I've gone through," he said. "Aynard launched himself like a rocket when I told him I couldn't find you. He was
almost incomprehensible. He concentrated his venom on me.
Told me Corsicans were not to be trusted. Can you imagine that?
He insulted my ancestors and hinted that my underworld connections had contributed to my income over the years! I almost
attacked the little rat turd. I am seriously thinking of bringing
official charges. I could have strangled him with pleasure. Where
the hell are you now?"

"Babar," Bastide said, "I'm sorry you had to take all that. I'll
see you get an apology. Now, listen carefully, we have an added
problem. Consul Popov is with me at the Café Monaco. He's *ivre
mort.* We can't risk his appearing at the *vernissage.* God knows what
he'd say or do. He needs to be put away safely until tomorrow
morning. Any ideas?"

"Magali could handle him," Mattei finally suggested after a
long pause. "She could put him in one of her upstairs rooms for
the night."

Bastide nodded in silent agreement. Magali, *"les gros tétons,"* ran a small bordello near the Cours Julien. She had always been cooperative with the police. Bastide knew Mattei had been there more than once for at least a drink when his wife and family were away for the August holidays. He'd never pried further, but he'd been told the fading Magali had a special place in her heart for Mattei.

"Sounds perfect," Bastide agreed. "Give me another half hour with him before you come by. That should give you time to call Magali about her visitor."

"Do you realize what we're doing?" Mattei asked. "It's a kidnapping."

"Be here in half an hour," Bastide said, ringing off.

Popov had sunk closer to the tabletop. He tilted his head, looked up and blinked at Bastide. "Protection," he said, enunciating unnaturally, "I will need protection."

"I've just arranged things," Bastide told him. "Someone will come for you soon. You have nothing to worry about."

Popov smiled and closed his eyes. Bastide sat down and cut himself a piece of cheese. He motioned for the barman and ordered a double cognac. It would be the *estocade* for Popov, the final blow. He wanted the Russian to be completely pliable by the time Mattei arrived.

Consul General Anisimov grunted with the effort of pulling on his black Oxfords. It would not be long before all official functions would be a thing of the past. He had an optimistic view of his imminent retirement, picturing himself devoting his time to reading, fishing and playing cards with his old friends. At least he wouldn't have to wear stiff shoes that were too small for his tender feet. He would spend his housebound days in felt boots and the hell with protocol.

His wife was in the next room preparing herself for the *vernissage.* He could hear the clink of glass as she shifted the perfume bottles on her dressing table. Anisimov smiled indulgently. His Natalie was not an attractive woman, but he did give her credit for working at it. Unfortunately, she had never learned how to treat his subordinates, and he knew that it would be hard to find someone in the consulate who liked her. But it had been the same in Lagos, Algiers and Barcelona.

He finished tying his shoes and straightened up, red-faced from the effort. Perhaps he could lose some weight in retirement when there was no need to attend consular lunches and dinners. He moved to the mirror and began to brush the thin strands of gray hair still covering his balding head. His thoughts turned to the *vernissage* and he speculated on how many of the Consular Corps members would attend. He knew the Swiss consul general would be there in his role as doyen of the corps. The Americans and the British would certainly make their appearance. He knew he could count on the Dutch, the Italians, the Germans, the Spaniards, the Turks and the Portuguese. The rest? You could never be sure. The bulk of them would be honorary consuls representing smaller nations. They, at least, seemed to take their appointments seriously.

He opened his closet and stared at the array of neckties hanging from the door rack. He selected a silk tie of silver-gray and returned to the mirror. As he tied the knot, he recalled his last conversation with Zavorin. The KGB resident was concerned about security . . . again! The man must be paranoid, Anisimov decided. The breed were all alike. They thrived on unseen threats and hidden plots. Anisimov would be glad to see Zavorin for the last time. It was an added bonus that retirement would bring.

Léon Faubert examined the dark suit he'd bought off the rack at Dames de France. He'd had the house tailor take a bit off the sleeves and trousers on the spot, but it wasn't a bad fit. He'd put on his one remaining clean shirt and an old blue necktie with white polka dots. The total effect was not exactly what he'd had in mind. The array of clothing didn't quite jibe with the shaven-headed, mustached character in the mirror. He hadn't achieved the anonymity he'd been seeking. There wasn't much he could do now. He didn't have the time. He decided not to worry about it. He wasn't going to a Chamber of Commerce meeting. It was an art exhibit. Strange clothing combinations would be the rule.

Faubert sat on the bed and reached under the pillow for his Beretta. It was a 92SB Compact with wood grips and a capacity of thirteen rounds, an efficient little killing machine. He checked the mechanism, the safety and the full clip. He stood up and shoved the pistol into the waistband of his trousers at the small of his back.

He walked to the open window and took a deep breath. He ignored the din from the street, fixed his eyes on a distant church tower and thought about Zavorin and de Coursin. In a few hours they would both be embarrassed and discredited. He didn't know what the immediate reaction would be in Moscow, but he could imagine the scene at *la crémerie*. There would be calls from the Élysées and the Prime Minister's office, consternation at the Quai d'Orsay, tongue-tied government spokesmen trying to answer an avalanche of calls from the media.

A brief smile crossed his face and disappeared. The important thing was to remain alive. That would be his victory. He wasn't seeking fame . . . only revenge. But publicity would provide his only protection; the media would serve as his shield.

He checked the hour. It was almost time to go. He was leaving his suitcase standing in a corner. An unfinished bottle of cognac sat on the table, and he'd remade the bed after his short nap. He slid his right hand into his pocket to make sure he was carrying the invitation.

"Come along, Monsieur Cotta," he told himself, "you have work to do."

The waltz of the "minders" had begun. Anatole Zavorin's protectors had gathered in his cubbyhole office for a final briefing. Yegerov and Boldin stood before Zavorin's desk in their best suits, their black shoes polished to mirror brightness, their trousers creased.

"Did you read about the icons?" Zavorin demanded.

"Yes, Comrade," Boldin replied. "We studied the brochure at lunch. We did not memorize the text. It was too . . ."

"Yes, yes," Zavorin said impatiently, "I didn't expect you to. I only want you to know something about the exhibit if some guest asks you a question." Yegerov glanced uneasily at his partner. The evening promised to be difficult. Protecting Zavorin was simple enough, but responding to questions about icons? That would be beyond his normal experience. "You have your weapons?"

The two men nodded affirmatively.

"Now listen carefully," Zavorin said. "You are to remain close to me, but try not to be obvious. Keep your eyes open for any suspicious person, any sudden move. Do not draw your weapons unless I am directly threatened. Do not fire them unless we are under attack. If I detect a threat and you don't, I will say the word 'TpeBóra,' alert. You will do the same to warn me."

"What of the consul general," Yegerov asked, "are we to protect him too?"

"I am your primary responsibility," Zavorin told them, "but if you see a move against him you will act."

"What of the French police?" Boldin asked. "Have they been informed that we will be armed?"

"No. But I would not worry about them. Personally I don't think anything will happen this evening. You will undoubtedly return here after the *vernissage* to lock up your Makarovs unfired. I don't know exactly what security the French are planning for the exhibit, but on no account are you to submit to a search of your person. Remember, you are protected by diplomatic immunity."

"Will Comrade Kedrov be at the museum?"

"Yes. She is there now helping with the last-minute preparations."

"Will she be armed too?" Boldin asked.

"I certainly hope not," Zavorin snapped, irritated that he hadn't thought of the possibility. Swallows were only authorized to carry a weapon in very special circumstances. Boldin's question had planted a nagging doubt in Zavorin's mind. *She is too intelligent for that,* he reassured himself. *She would not dare to do such a thing without a direct order.*

"Yegerov will drive," Boldin said. "Shall I ride in the back with you?"

"No," Zavorin said, "you'll remain in the front seat. Yegerov, remember to go through the gate when we arrive and turn the car so we are facing toward the street. I think we have covered everything. Oh, one more point. There will be plentiful food and drink. You are to have one glass . . . and make it last. Eat what you wish. Try to look like you're enjoying yourselves."

"Yes, Comrade Zavorin," Boldin answered for both of them.

"Good. I will see you at the car shortly," Zavorin said. "Warm the engine and check the tires."

Zavorin closed his eyes when they'd left his office and rested his head on the back of his desk chair. He felt no fear, but he was irritated. His whole routine had been upset simply because the French couldn't control their own people. He was angered when he thought of all the work he'd neglected in the past few days. His detailed report on security at the French nuclear center at Cadarache had been delayed. He knew the KGB's Scientific and Technical Directorate had a submission to make to the State Scientific and Technical Committee in three weeks. It would be incomplete without his contribution. He was also troubled by Popov's absence. The consul's strange behavior had been reported by Popov's secretary. It might only be the unpredictable conduct of a man on the verge of total alcoholism, but Zavorin was concerned. As soon as the *vernissage* was out of the way and things calmed down, he would find a way to recommend Popov's transfer. His Marseille operation was too important to tolerate undependable weak reeds under the same roof.

Vo Quoc Lien examined the photos of Léon Faubert with great care. He knew his life might depend on a speedy recognition. The thin Vietnamese was sitting in the DGSE office with the two full-time agents assigned to cover the *vernissage*. A senior officer had briefed them on their duties before passing the photos around. Lien had the uneasy feeling that his two colleagues were not taking the matter seriously.

"Faubert would never take such a chance," one of the agents commented as Lien finished his perusal and put the photos back on the desk. "He is far too clever. He'd be more likely to put a bullet through Zavorin's head . . . from a great distance."

"I can't say that would bring tears to my eyes," the other agent said. "One less Russkov won't affect the world power balance."

"You have said we are to protect this man?" Lien asked.

"That's correct," the senior officer confirmed. "Paris doesn't want one hair of his head disturbed. They also insist on complete discretion. You, Navarre, will be wearing the uniform of a museum guard; Parent, you'll be an interested patron of the arts. Lien will be in a white jacket behind the refreshment table."

"Naturally," Lien said softly.

"What's that?"

"Nothing," Lien replied.

"I want you all to keep a mental note of who is there and who doesn't seem to fit in. Your report is to include mention of any plainclothes DST or police officers you see. I had a last-minute urgent message from the director's office. It instructs us to report immediately if Inspecteur Principal Roger Bastide appears at the museum. I'm not quite sure what it's all about, but I do know that Bastide has been in contact with de Coursin via our secure line. Would any of you recognize Bastide if you saw him?"

The two agents shook their heads. "We move in different circles," Navarre volunteered. "Contacts with *flics* are counter-productive."

"How about you?" the senior officer asked Lien.

"I only know he is charged with homicide investigation in the city. I would not recognize him," Lien lied.

"Well, I would," the officer continued. "He's about five foot eight, husky build, graying dark hair, black mustache. I don't remember the eyes. I've only seen him twice. If you spot him, call me. As to Faubert . . . he is to be taken alive, if possible. That's it. I suggest you get moving. You can change into your *costumes* in the utility room."

They all stood to leave, but the senior officer motioned for Lien to remain. "Can you still handle a *pétard?*" the officer asked, nodding toward the stump of Lien's right wrist.

"Of course," Lien said, smiling. "I'm left-handed."

Jacques Boniface of the DST had left his office early to hurry back to his apartment in the Parc Talabot. He had told his wife he was going to an official function, but she resented the fact that she hadn't been invited. He could tell the extent of her latent anger by the way pots and utensils were being banged on the kitchen counters. He hadn't received an invitation to the Soviets' *vernissage*, but he'd decided to attend without one. He knew his identity card would get him through the door. He was still under orders to stay clear of the Drankov case, but he'd decided his overall responsibility for keeping track of Soviet activities in the region justified his presence.

"I'm sure the préfet's wife will be there," his wife shouted from the kitchen.

"This is business," he responded. "Another boring function. I'm sparing you an ordeal."

He was putting on one of his best suits, a dark blue material with thin pinstripes. He buttoned the vest tightly, pulling it down over his paunch to remove the wrinkles, and threw the strap of his holster over his shoulder. He buckled it, secured the holster to his belt with a leather thong and slid his .38-caliber Smith & Wesson Airweight into place.

"No use my trying to preserve this roast," his wife complained. "It'll be dry by the time you get home, the beans will be over-cooked and the salad wilted."

"I'll probably have to stop at the office on the way home," he told her. "What's on television tonight?"

"Look yourself," she snapped.

He directed a violent *bras d'honneur* in the general direction of the kitchen and pulled on his suit jacket, leaving it unbuttoned. Satisfied that the shoulder holster wasn't apparent, he reached into the closet for his Tyrolean hat. He squared it carefully on his head and walked toward the door.

"You're not wearing that hat?" his wife demanded. She'd come to the kitchen door, a stout woman in a frilled apron, dyed red hair framing a tired, resentful face. "It looks ridiculous," she told him. "Particularly with that suit. You look like a sausage sales-man."

He slammed the door behind him and muttered curses as he rode to the ground level in the deserted elevator. He walked to the parking lot, unlocked his car door, paused for a moment and tossed his hat into the back seat.

IX

The long, hot day had faded into a warm, pleasant evening. A flight of starlings swooped and banked over the elaborate stonework of the Palais Longchamp. The small birds flashed as they climbed toward the sun and plunged toward the ground like black darts. A spectacular sunset streaked the sky, its shades of amber interlaced with the feathery trails of high-flying jets. Two delivery trucks and a caterer's van were parked inside the grounds at the base of the stone stairway. City employees and caterer's assistants were unloading boxes of food and cases of champagne. A long trestle table had been set up in the gallery. A member of the Soviet Consulate's administrative staff was supervising the stocking of the bars. He had brought two cases of vodka and three cases of Georgian wine from the consulate's duty-free reserves as a special treat for the invited guests. A microphone pedestal had been set up in the center of the room, where an electrician was installing the sound system.

Larissa Kedrov stood in the far corner of the gallery, looking out one of the windows onto the well-kept grounds. Her black, braided hair was secured with a broad silver clip. She was wearing silver crescent earrings, a single pearl on a silver necklace chain, and the same dress she'd worn on arrival in Marseille. She watched six uniformed policemen climb out of a van. They were assigned their stations by a busy *brigadier* who'd been waiting for them at the gate. She guessed their role was largely ceremonial. Two were placed on each side of the stairway, two more at the door to the museum. The remaining two hovered near the *brigadier,* ready to assist with parking chores.

She wondered if Bastide would appear. She was taking the morning flight out of Marseille. For some perverse reason she had hoped to see him before she left. She was still puzzled by his behavior. Few men had walked away from her of their own free will. It had crossed her mind that her failure with Bastide might be the first sign that her allure was fading, a reality all swallows had to face sooner or later. But the simple act of preparing herself for the *vernissage* had calmed her fears. She was a very good judge of her own appeal. She had examined herself carefully and objectively, unclothed and clothed. It had been a reassuring exercise. The admiring glances she'd received from the male museum workers had substantiated her findings.

It wouldn't be too long before the consul general and Zavorin arrived to establish the reception line. Larissa Kedrov decided to renew her makeup. She walked down the wide stairway and entered the ladies' restroom. She was alone. She applied new lipstick, retouched her eye shadow and dabbed some Arpège perfume behind her ears. She wasn't sure what might happen at the *vernissage,* but Zavorin's atypical nervousness during the last twenty-four hours bothered her.

They rushed Popov into Magali's place. He hung between Bastide and Mattei, rubber-legged and mumbling, as they pulled him up the stairs. Magali slammed the door behind them, shaking her head.

"I don't like the looks of this," she said. "I smell trouble."

"He's just a friend in difficulty," Mattei reassured her, turning on the charm. "You're looking particularly desirable today."

Magali was pushing sixty. She wore a yellowing wig that sat on her head like an abandoned bird's nest. Her huge breasts—the source of her nickname—were supported by a foolproof brassiere reinforced by a visible network of metal stays. Her wide, myopic eyes retained a certain innocence despite their rimming of tarlike mascara.

They stumbled into an open room on the ground floor and dropped Popov onto the bed. "Protection," Popov murmured before closing his eyes.

"Babar Mattei," Magali warned, "if I get into trouble over this . . ."

"Not at all," Mattei reassured her. "It's serious business. We'll have him out of here by midnight."

A brunette prostitute, clad in a frilly, cheap camisole tied loosely at the waist, peered into the room. "What's up?" she asked, inspecting the two policemen quizzically.

"A short-time guest," Magali told her. "He's going to have a nap. I want you to keep your eye on him. Make sure he stays in the room." She escorted Bastide and Mattei into the hall, shutting and locking the door.

"We haven't met," Magali said, smiling at Bastide.

"He's another old friend," Mattei interjected. "We've got to rush. I promise you, we'll come back and collect him soon."

"Very well. Listen carefully, my little *figatelli*. I will not have him here overnight, *tu piges?*"

"Understood. No problem whatsoever."

Bastide was already out the front door when Mattei caught up with him. "We've got to get over to the museum," Bastide said. "Where's Lenoir?"

"He's waiting on the Canebière."

They climbed in the car. "Babar," Bastide said, "you do surprise me. Does your wife know about your friend Magali?"

"No," Mattei said flatly, starting the engine, "but a good *flic* should have contacts everywhere, *n'est ce pas?*"

"I can't argue with that," Bastide agreed. "Now, let's see if you can move this thing quickly."

Zavorin's sedan was waved into the grounds of the Palais Longchamp by one of the uniformed policemen. Yegerov swung it around and parked facing the gate. The *brigadier* opened the rear door for Zavorin, snapping a quick salute. Zavorin acknowledged the greeting with a nod and waited for Yegerov and Boldin to join him at the foot of the broad stone stairway. He climbed the stairs flanked by his two bodyguards.

Larissa Kedrov was waiting. "Good evening, Comrades," she greeted them. "All is in order. Would you like to preview the exhibit?"

"No guests yet?" Zavorin asked.

"No. The consul general has not arrived."

They entered the reception area and walked through it to the exhibit gallery. Zavorin greeted the curator, said hello to the consulate employee who'd just finished his supervisory chores and glanced at the microphone.

"You will be introduced by the curator," Larissa Kedrov told him. "Do you intend to speak at any length?"

"No. Five minutes at the most. The consul general may wish to say something. Ask him when he arrives." Zavorin walked the length of the serving table, inspecting the buffet. There were finger sandwiches of caviar, smoked salmon, cucumber and ham, silver serving dishes of meat, anchovy piroshki on warming plates and bits of herring on toothpicks to be dipped in a mustard sauce. He could see that the vodka and champagne were iced and the serving glasses were sparkling clean. Satisfied, he turned to inspect the microphone in the center of the gallery. He tapped it with his finger, eliciting a reverberating thump.

Larissa Kedrov was amused by Zavorin's inspection. It was almost military in its precision. Yegerov and Boldin reminded her of comedians in a silent movie. They were obviously not used to their bodyguard role. Their attempts to cover Zavorin at all times had them breaking step awkwardly and changing direction to remain at his side.

"The consul general is here," the staff member called from his vantage point at the window.

"Come," Zavorin said, "we must greet him."

The guests had begun to arrive. Most had parked in the surrounding streets. There was limited space inside the gate, but it was reserved for officials including the préfet and the député-maire. Mattei parked in a narrow space a block away from the museum. They'd picked up Lenoir on the way and he'd told them that Commissaire Aynard had sent his assistant out looking for Bastide. The Préfet of Police had roasted Aynard for Bastide's nonappearance. There would clearly be all hell to pay.

"I think the Préfet of Police may attend the *vernissage*," Lenoir said as they walked toward the Palais. "What will you do then?"

Bastide dug in his pocket and handed out the invitation. "I'll apologize for the delay," Bastide replied. He was concerned, but he was doing his best to hide it. An inspecteur principal doesn't defy the direct orders of a préfet and a commissaire with impunity.

The call from Paris caught Lou-Lou Martin in the shower. He went to the telephone, barefoot and dripping, a towel wrapped around his waist. *"Allo?"* he snapped. The inactivity and isolation in the safe house had made him tense.

"Martin?"

"Yes."

"It's Carillon." De Coursin used his code name. He had no faith in secure lines. "Proceed with your project," he ordered. "Begin now . . . at the event. I suggest you get there in a hurry."

"Cinq sur cinq," Martin replied. "Nothing more?"

"Just move!"

Martin replaced the receiver and sprinted for the bedroom. He decided to go to the *vernissage* alone. A three-man DGSE team in an art gallery was out of the question.

De Coursin knew he was taking a serious gamble but he had waited long enough for the préfet to find Bastide. The director had told him to use his own judgment. He'd decided that Martin's place was at the *vernissage,* particularly since he was the only person on the spot who could recognize Faubert.

De Coursin tapped his cigarette holder on his desk. Two hours ago he had been tempted to fly to Marseille himself, but his fine sense of bureaucratic self-preservation had canceled the move. No matter what happened at the *vernissage,* he would be better off in his office. If things went well, there would be no problem. If they went badly, he could pull things together more efficiently from Paris.

"Hurry up," Bastide said, striding off toward the Palais Longchamp while Mattei locked the car. "We'll go in separately," he told them. "Keep your eyes open. If you see the préfet or Aynard, I'll expect a warning. Remember, we're here to see that no one gets hurt."

Bastide and Mattei stood by a stone planter full of geraniums and watched Lenoir climb the stairway. Mattei then took the same route. Bastide followed them. The reception line had slowed. Some guests had paused to chat with the official hosts, delaying the entry of the others. Bastide advanced step by step. A young consulate officer was asking approaching guests for their invita-

tions before passing them on to Anatole Zavorin, who then introduced them to Consul General Anisimov. The line moved another five feet. Bastide gave his name and stepped in front of
Zavorin. The KGB resident turned toward him. Bastide noticed
his look of surprise, but the Russian recovered and quickly extended his hand. Bastide also noticed the two blank-faced heavies
standing just behind Zavorin.

"Welcome, Inspector," he said. "I did not know you were interested in the arts?"

"All Marseillais are artists at heart," Bastide replied. Zavorin
propelled him toward the consul general with a gentle, practiced
movement of his wrist.

"You remember Inspector Bastide?" Zavorin asked.

"I most certainly do," Anisimov answered, beaming. "I am
glad you could come. We shall have a drink together later, no?"

"I look forward to it," Bastide said. He moved on past the
consul general and saw Larissa Kedrov. She was standing at some
distance from the reception line, watching him. He hesitated and
she moved toward him.

"Good evening," she said, smiling. "I had hoped to see you
again."

In his preoccupation with Popov and worries about the threat,
he'd forgotten she would be there.

"You're looking beautiful, as usual," he said uneasily, noting
that Mattei was waiting for him at the gallery entrance.

"I am leaving tomorrow," she told him. "Perhaps we can talk a
bit later, after the speeches."

"Yes," Bastide said. "That would be nice."

"I must look after the other guests," she said, leaving him. He
watched her walk across the parquet floor, hips swinging, and felt
a deep pang of desire.

"I just saw Boniface," Mattei hissed as they entered the gallery.
"I think he's alone."

Bastide nodded imperceptibly. "How about the préfet?" Bastide asked.

"No sign of him."

"Did you see the two *flingueurs* guarding Zavorin?"

"Yes. He's taking no chances," Mattei replied.

It was clear to Bastide that Zavorin had ensured his own protection. The consul general was obviously without minders.

The gallery was a babble of voices. The bad acoustics magnified the din of conversation as guests gathered near the microphone or made their way from one icon to the next with programs of the exhibit in their hands. Lenoir was at the far end of the room, craning his neck for a better view of the reception line. Bastide indicated Lenoir with a toss of his head.

"Tell that idiot not to be so obvious," he muttered. Mattei moved slowly through the crowd to Lenoir's side. Bastide surveyed the buffet. He glanced at the group of waiters and bartenders. He was about to turn away when he saw Lien. The Vietnamese was opening bottles of Perrier. Their eyes met for two seconds before he turned back to his work.

If Lien is here, other DGSE agents are here, Bastide reasoned. The Vietnamese wouldn't be operating alone. Bastide examined the crowd with particular care, seeking any sign or hint of something unusual or suspicious. The bourgeois of Marseille were well represented: women fresh from the hairdressers showing their best jewelry and paunchy men in three-piece suits more interested in what the buffet offered than the sacred paintings. They spoke in low voices, greeting acquaintances with discreet acknowledgments and edging closer to the microphone in order to be part of the opening ceremony. The city's bohemia was also there. Painters, writers, poets and sculptors in corduroy jackets and jeans; women in earth-mother dresses of rough wool wearing head scarves. The men were long-haired and bearded. Many of the women were unkempt and bereft of makeup . . . determined to prove there were more important things in life than sex appeal.

Bastide wondered how Drankov's killer might look in this crowd. Would he have the aura of a businessman or a banker? Would he be disguised as an artist? Could he be dressed as a barman or a museum attendant? Was he far away and uninvolved? Bastide moved back toward the reception line. He'd decided to stay as close to the consul general as he could.

Boniface had seen Mattei at the same moment Mattei spotted him. He'd been surprised to find Mattei at the *vernissage*. He'd made up his mind to talk to him when he saw Bastide standing not far from the reception line. This new development convinced him it would be best to watch and wait. It promised to be an interesting evening.

Léon Faubert paid his cab driver, glanced at his watch and walked through the gate of the Palais Longchamp. The reception line was sparse and moving quickly now. As soon as the mayor arrived, the officials would go into the gallery for the introductory remarks. Faubert handed over his invitation and passed through the line. It was hard to keep his eyes neutral when he shook hands with Zavorin. He hoped the Russian wasn't prescient. He duly noted Zavorin's guardian angels before he exchanged a ritual handshake with Consul General Anisimov and moved on to the gallery.

Lou-Lou Martin approached the reception line. Bastide saw him and turned his back, taking a sudden interest in a piece of standing sculpture. He glanced toward the gallery. Mattei was at the entrance. Mattei nodded, confirming that he too had spotted Martin.

"Putain," Bastide cursed to himself. He had ten seconds to decide if he wanted Martin to enter the gallery. Mattei had edged closer, ready to step in when needed. There was a roar of motorcycle engines and the sound of car doors slamming just outside the Palais. The député-maire had arrived. Martin finished shaking hands with Anisimov, turned toward the gallery and stopped as Bastide stepped in front of him. Bastide took his right hand in a firm grip.

"Bonsoir, ami!" Bastide said in a loud voice. "I was afraid you couldn't come." Mattei immobilized Martin's left arm. They hustled him off to the right and pushed him into an alcove behind a potted palm. Mattei spun Martin around and pushed him against the wall. Bastide ran a practiced hand inside his jacket, removed a replacement Walther automatic from its shoulder holster and stuck it into his own belt.

"Your watch must have stopped," Bastide said. "Your twenty-four hours expired long ago. You obviously need a hearing aid."

"I'm under official orders," Martin growled. "You're out of line!"

"Ferme ton micro," Mattei snapped.

The mayor was being led into the gallery by the consul general. "Go get Lenoir and a uniform," Bastide told Mattei. "I want this *zigouiller* locked up. *Grouille-toi!*" Bastide drew the Walther automatic and pushed it into Martin's back. "Just relax," he ordered, "and turn toward me slowly, so people will think we're having a nice conversation. No comedy or you'll take on some sudden weight."

"Listen, *flic,*" Martin murmured through clenched teeth, "there may be a killer here!"

"I know," Bastide replied. "He's right in front of me."

"De Coursin gave me my orders," Martin blurted. "That should mean something to you."

A waiter carrying a bucket of ice walked past them. "You'll miss the speeches," he warned.

"We'll be there soon," Bastide said.

"I don't believe how stupid you are," Martin said.

"A matter of opinion."

The sound of applause reached them from the gallery. The speeches had started. Mattei reappeared with Lenoir and a uniformed policeman.

"Take him in and lock him up," Bastide told Lenoir. "Don't let him talk to anyone. Here, take this." Bastide handed Lenoir the Walther automatic. "Get back here as soon as you can."

"What's the charge?" Lenoir asked.

"Expected assault with a deadly weapon."

"The permit's in my wallet," Martin said.

"Come on," Bastide told Mattei, "let's go."

"Art is a truly international treasure," Consul General Anisimov said, his hands clasped over his vest. "It touches all of us in a personal way. These may not be world masterpieces, but they were produced by great craftsmen with native talent . . ."

A flashbulb froze the scene. The photographer moved quickly to a new position for a better camera angle. A three-man television crew was filming the ceremony. The cameraman had found a small wooden platform to stand on. His assistant was flicking bright lights on and off at the cameraman's command, much to the député-maire's obvious annoyance. The sound technician was crouched over his portable recorder. Bastide's eyes moved slowly over the crowd. He edged closer to the speakers. He sensed someone staring at him. The police préfet's deputy was standing in the official group, glaring at Bastide. At least the préfet himself hadn't come.

". . . dedicated to the enduring friendship of the French and Soviet peoples," Anisimov concluded and ceded his place to the député-maire.

"It is not often we have the opportunity of seeing at first hand the *religious* treasures of Russia," the député-maire began, inserting a political needle with his very first sentence.

Bastide was thinking of what Martin had said about the presence of a killer. Should he have asked more questions? Things did appear to be going well. The député-maire finished and Zavorin resumed his role as master of ceremonies.

"Now, ladies and gentlemen," he announced, "I invite you to enjoy the exhibition at your leisure and I recommend the buffet." There was a ripple of polite applause as the grouping of people near the microphone began to fragment.

The two shots froze everyone in their tracks, reverberating in the gallery like hammer blows. Bits of white plaster fell from the high ceiling. A man had grabbed Zavorin. He was holding him in a tight throat lock. The assailant was brandishing an automatic in his right hand. The crowd drew away from the two men, like protoplasm in contact with an irritant. There were whimpers, gasps and murmurs of disapproval from the frightened guests. Zavorin was manhandled close to the wall and dragged toward the exit. Mattei had drawn his weapon in a reflex action. He held the Manurhin muzzle up as he watched the gunman intently. Bastide had almost done the same. Fortunately, he'd resisted the impulse. Boniface had palmed his Smith & Wesson and was moving slowly through the frozen spectators. Lien had come quickly around the bar. Now he was motionless, his hand gripping the 9-mm Browning in the pocket of his serving jacket. Neither of Zavorin's bodyguards had drawn their Makarovs. Yegerov took a hesitant step and Faubert's arm swung in his direction, the blue-black muzzle of the Beretta aimed at Yegerov's chest.

"Stay where you are," Faubert ordered in a calm, authoritative voice, "all of you." He brought the muzzle of the automatic to Zavorin's ear. "I want all those weapons on the floor," he said, "and step away from them. Immediately!"

Mattei put his Magnum down slowly and backed off. Boniface was next.

"*Allez! les Russkovs,*" Faubert addressed Yegerov and Boldin. "That means you too." The two Russians produced their Makarovs and put them down carefully. Lien had withdrawn his hand from his pocket. He now stood with both arms folded, hoping the gunman hadn't noticed him.

"*Hé,* Chintok!" Faubert shouted, still dragging Zavorin to the exit. "Produce your piece. *Mau len!*" Lien drew the Browning from his pocket and deposited it on the parquet.

"All of you flat on your gut," Faubert ordered. "I don't want anyone hurt, but the slightest move and we'll have an abstract pattern of a KGB resident's brains on the gallery walls!"

The DGSE agent, disguised as a museum attendant, made eye contact with his partner. They exchanged surreptitious signals indicating it was not the time to try anything.

Faubert reached the exit leading to the stairway. Two late arrivals, a middle-aged man and his wife, appeared just outside the gallery and stopped, their mouths dropping open in horror.

"Come in," Faubert commanded. "Join the others." He motioned for them to cross the gallery floor. "Everyone turn their backs and move to the far wall." There was a shuffling and a murmur of protest.

"Silence!" Faubert shouted with instantaneous effect. "Listen carefully. You are to remain as you are for ten minutes. The first person to turn this way before that time will cause the death of a Soviet intelligence officer." Faubert laughed. His misplaced humor had a chilling effect on everyone.

What the hell is he playing at? Bastide asked himself. The gunman couldn't hope to get far. He'd apparently made no provision for a getaway car and there were uniforms outside. The man was surely mad and particularly dangerous. If only one of those uniforms would come in! At least the gunman hadn't picked him out of the crowd . . . and he still had his weapon, though using it in these circumstances was out of the question.

Faubert moved swiftly after giving his orders to the frightened guests. He manhandled Zavorin down the stairway. Reaching the ground floor, they came face to face with the *brigadier* of police, who was on his way upstairs to see how soon the député-maire would be leaving.

"Stop right there!" Faubert told the shocked policeman. "Lift that peashooter out of its holster by the trigger guard and slide it over here." The *brigadier* did as he was told. Faubert kicked the weapon well out of reach. It skittered over the smooth marble floor. He ordered the policeman to lie down.

"Come along, Comrade," Faubert said, dragging Zavorin around the stairwell toward the men's restroom.

Zavorin was struggling to breathe and stay on his feet. His knees felt weak. Earlier he'd almost blacked out. He was trying to think, to reason, but his mind wasn't working properly. He knew his captor was Drankov's killer. He wondered how long he had to live.

Bastide could tell that curiosity was dominating the fear in the gallery. There were only a few minutes to go. "Don't move," he said to everyone, hoping to avoid a tragedy.

"I think he's gone," a young woman whispered.

"One more minute," Bastide warned.

The second hand of his watch reached its apogee. He was the first out of the gallery. He drew his Magnum, paused at the landing and ran to the balcony's edge. Nothing. All seemed quiet. The policemen by the main entrance were chatting, oblivious to what was going on inside.

"Block the stairs," Bastide shouted to them, "and shut the gates!"

Mattei joined him. "Did you see him?" he demanded.

"No, come on." Bastide started down the stairs, keeping against the wall. Rounding a bend, they saw the *brigadier* getting cautiously to his feet. "Where is he?" Bastide asked.

"In the men's room!" he told them.

"The men's room?" Mattei said. "Where is it?"

"Behind the stairs. Be careful," the *brigadier* warned. "He might shoot through the door."

"Don't let anyone leave the building," Bastide said. "Get someone up to the gallery. See that no one steps outside." An array of curious faces had appeared on the upper balustrade.

"Get back in the gallery!" the *brigadier* shouted. The faces faded from sight. He ran outside for help. The préfet's deputy hurried down the stairs.

"What's going on?" he demanded.

"He's in the restroom with his hostage," Bastide explained. "We'll try to talk with him."

The deputy hesitated. He knew Bastide would be facing disciplinary action by nightfall, but he couldn't risk reprimanding him now. "I'll radio for a GIPN team," he said, eager to do something positive. Bastide was cool to the idea. The elite SWAT team based in Fort Saint-Nicolas was a last resort as far as he was concerned.

"We may not need them," he suggested.

"Not need them? You think you can settle this?" The deputy's voice became shrill. "Inspector, you're in enough trouble already. In fact, what makes you think you're in charge here?"

"The man in there is a murderer," Bastide said. "As long as I'm running Homicide, he belongs to me."

Bastide's logic made some sense to the deputy and it was no time to argue. "Very well," he said, "but I'm still calling in the GIPN."

"As you wish," Bastide replied. He took off his jacket and put a reload for his Magnum into a trouser pocket. The deputy rushed off to use his car radio. Bastide motioned Mattei closer. "Start talking to him," Bastide said. "I'm going to see if the door to the men's room is visible from the curve in the stairs."

Mattei nodded and began to inch his way forward along the stone balustrade. "You in there!" he shouted. "You're going nowhere. Throw out your weapon!"

Faubert had just handcuffed Zavorin to the water pipe under a washbasin. The Russian was forced to sit on the floor. Mattei's voice carried to them the second time. Faubert was outwardly calm. He walked closer to the door, careful to stay out of the line of fire, and waited for another summons.

"Send out your hostage," Mattei bellowed. "You're making things worse." Faubert smiled. Whoever was doing the shouting, he thought, had never taken a course in the psychological approach to life-threatening situations.

Zavorin's heart had stopped thumping like a defective pump. He had taken several deep breaths, leaning his head against the cold wall. He was struggling to regain his composure. He couldn't understand why his captor had sought asylum in the men's room. It was an obvious cul-de-sac. He couldn't possibly escape.

"Listen, *flic,*" Faubert shouted, "and listen carefully. This man is dead if you don't do what I say. Understand?"

Bastide came back down the stairs in a crouch. He indicated Mattei should answer positively.

"Understood," Mattei replied. "What is it you want?"

"Bring the TV camera crew down here and one member of the written press."

"What?" Mattei demanded, surprised.

"You heard me. I want to talk to them. Send them in here!"

Bastide nodded affirmatively.

"*Très bien,*" Mattei said. "It will take some time."

"Make it fast."

Mattei edged back until he was close to Bastide. "What do you think?" he asked.

"Go get the TV people and the writer," Bastide told him. "I don't know what the hell he's up to, but we've got to play for time. Hurry." Mattei sprinted up the stairway. Bastide sat on his haunches and tried to think. There was no way he could get a clear shot or see the men's room door from the stairs without becoming a target. He blamed himself for not noting the exact placement of the restroom windows during his previous visits to the Palais.

Lenoir rushed in from the terrace and crouched beside him. "*Ça y est,*" he said, out of breath. "Martin's locked up. What happened?"

"We've got a gunman in the *pissoir* with a hostage," Bastide explained. "Don't ask any more questions. Just be ready to do as I tell you."

A clatter of footsteps announced the return of Mattei with the journalists. "Stay away from the balustrade!" Bastide ordered, motioning them to keep low. The long-haired cameraman was wide-eyed. He crouched beside Bastide, steadying the camera brace on his shoulder. "What does he want?" he asked.

"He wants to talk to you."

"Let's go then," the cameraman said with enthusiasm, recognizing what might be the chance of his career.

Bastide grabbed him by the shoulder. "Don't be an idiot!" he warned. "He could drop you like cold mutton if we're not careful."

The middle-aged newsman from the *Provençal* sat down heavily on the stairs and lit a cigarette. "I'm in no hurry to become a hostage," he said.

"Tell him the journalists are here," Bastide said to Mattei. "Ask him why he wants to see them."

Mattei shouted the questions. They waited. "I'm giving a press conference," Faubert finally replied. "They are to come in one by one, a minute apart. No one else."

"You're looking for more hostages!" Mattei shouted. "How do we know they won't be harmed?"

"Don't be an idiot," Faubert said disdainfully. "I've got something important to say. Send them in!"

The cameraman struggled to get to his feet but Bastide restrained him. "Hold it," he ordered. "Do you know what you're getting into? He's *dingue*. If you go in there, it's on your own responsibility."

"I know," the cameraman said. He turned to the other members of his crew. "You ready?" he asked. They both nodded.

"And you?" Bastide asked the writer.

"Oh," he shrugged, "I'd lose my job if I didn't."

Bastide knew he was taking a risk. The three men would be his responsibility if anything went wrong, but four more men to watch would make things difficult for the gunman. The GIPN team would be arriving at any minute burdened with heavy firepower and eager to employ it. He examined the TV crew's tape recorder. It was a standard utility model. He knew how to use it.

"How much time left on your tape?" he asked the sound technician.

"About fifteen minutes."

Bastide handed his Magnum to Mattei. "You carrying your derringer?" Bastide asked.

"Yes, but . . ."

"Let me have it."

Mattei took the small, two-shot .38 from an inner pocket and handed it over. Bastide slid the derringer between the recorder and its leather carrying case and stuffed some excess mike cable over it.

"I'm going in with you," Bastide told the cameraman.

"Wait a minute," the cameraman protested. "You can't do that!"

"If I don't," Bastide warned, "you don't either."

"If he sees you, he'll shoot all of us!"

"He doesn't know me," Bastide said, passing his wallet and all his identity papers to Mattei. "Here," he said to the sound technician, "let me have your wallet." The technician complied. Bastide examined the contents and handed an identifying photo back to him.

"*Allez,*" Faubert shouted to them. "Time is running out!"

"*Ça va, ça va,*" Mattei responded. "They're on their way."

"You go in first," Bastide told the cameraman. "I'll follow. Then the rest of you. Babar, you and Lenoir be ready to move. Tell the GIPN to keep their distance. Warn them five of us are in there, including the hostage. Go!" he said, pushing the cameraman toward the men's room. Bastide slung the recorder over his shoulder and watched the cameraman move hesitantly toward the door, his camera steadied with one hand, the other raised above his head. They could hear the swinging door open and close. Bastide kept his eyes on his watch. He'd only dealt with hostage takers twice. This one was different. The old procedures were unlikely to work.

"I'm going now," he told Mattei. "You're in charge!"

"Be careful," Mattei warned, slapping him on the shoulder. "You've only got two shots in that *pétard.*"

Bastide tapped the door with his knuckles before pushing it open. It was exactly one minute since the cameraman had entered the men's room. Faubert held the cocked automatic at arm's length, aimed directly at Bastide. The cameraman was sitting on the floor, his back against the wall, his equipment on his lap. Zavorin recognized Bastide but didn't react.

"Welcome," Faubert said. "Go sit on the floor next to your friend." Bastide did as he was told. They waited in silence, the only sound in the room the automatic flushing of the urinals. The lighting technician was next. Another minute passed and the journalist pushed the door open. He was pale-faced, a cigarette hanging from the corner of his mouth.

"Sit down," Faubert ordered. "All of you listen carefully. There is no need for anyone to be hurt. If you obey me, you'll be out of here in an hour. I am going to feed you some sensational information. I want it to be filmed, recorded and written down. Are you ready?"

"We can't film anything if we don't stand up," the cameraman told him.

"Eh bien," Faubert said, taking a few steps backward. "Get up slowly, but stay where you are."

"We need an outlet for the lights," the cameraman said.

Faubert scanned the room. "Over there," he said, indicating a plug in the floorboard. The technician inserted the extension. The bright light made them all look like invalids. Bastide checked the battery power of the recorder and held the mike away from his body. He watched Faubert closely.

"I have a statement. Then you can ask questions," Faubert told them. "Are you ready?"

The cameraman was focusing his lens. "Go ahead," he said.

"My name is Léon Faubert," he began, enunciating his words carefully and looking directly into the camera. "I work for the DGSE . . ."

Mattei met the GIPN team as they rushed into the Palais. They wore blue zipper jackets stamped with their insignia. They were carrying canvas bags loaded with weapons, ammunition, CS gas cannisters and stun grenades. The team leader recognized Mattei. *"Alors,* Babar," he said, out of breath. "What do we have here?"

"We've got Bastide and four others under the gun in there," Mattei explained. "The gunman may be crazy. Bastide's got a hidden derringer. We take it nice and easy, understood?"

Weapons clicked and snapped as they were assembled. "Who's in charge?" the team leader asked.

"I am," Mattei replied forcefully. *"Nothing* happens without my approval."

"Doucement, ami," the team leader told him. "I'll just put my men in place. What's the layout?"

"One door entry, behind the stairwell. I don't know about the side of the building. There must be windows."

"What's our bad boy carrying?"

"I've only seen an automatic."

"What's your plan?"

"I'll keep vocal contact with them every three minutes. You see what we can do on the other side. You might be able to put gas through the windows. I don't know how long we can wait. The gunman wants to give a press conference."

"A press conference? He *must* be crazy."

"Let's hope he keeps talking."

". . . I was then ordered to eliminate Drankov," Faubert said, continuing his monologue.

Bastide, wearing the sound man's earphones, glanced down at the slowly revolving disc of tape and readjusted the volume. Faubert's voice seemed electronically unreal. The newsman from *Le Provençal* was scribbling in his notebook, eyebrows raised in constant surprise. The derringer was within easy reach, but Bastide couldn't take the risk. He might get off a snap shot, but if he missed the gunman would drop them all. The cameraman waved his hand and Faubert stopped talking.

"I need to reload," the cameraman explained. "If you keep this up, I'll run out of film. We won't have any for the questions."

"Reload," Faubert ordered. "I'll finish soon. Then I'll tell you what questions to ask. The first one will be 'who ordered the elimination of Drankov'?"

"Hey, you in there!" Mattei shouted. "Is everything all right?"

"Everyone's fine," Faubert replied. "Don't bother us!" He turned back to the cameraman, who'd just snapped the film in place. "Put your camera on that *salaud* there," he demanded, swinging the Colt in Zavorin's direction. "I'm going to tell you all about Anatole Zavorin of the KGB."

More uniformed policemen arrived. They slipped upstairs to control the guests. The two DGSE agents were arguing with the *brigadier*. Lien had remained behind.

"No one leaves," the *brigadier* told them, his arms spread wide. "Those are my orders."

"Stick your nose in this!" The DGSE agent in the museum guard's uniform pushed his identity card at the *brigadier*. "We've got to get out of here," he said. "Let us through!"

The *brigadier* examined each card carefully before returning them. "Go ahead," he finally said, dropping his arms. They rushed down the stairs. One of them hurried in search of a telephone. The other approached Mattei, brandishing his identity. "DGSE," he said.

Mattei turned to him, distracted and irritated. "So! This is a police matter. Can't you see I'm busy?"

The agent leaned closer. "The shooter in there may be one of ours."

"Bon sang!" Mattei exploded. "It's not possible!"

De Coursin had just returned to his apartment when he'd heard the special bulletin on the radio. He'd driven to his office and telephoned Marseille before returning a call from the director. The Marseille office confirmed his worst fears. Faubert had taken five hostages, including Zavorin and four journalists. Zavorin's capture was bad enough, but four journalists! That was a disaster. He chewed on his cigarette holder, listening to the meager facts from Marseille. He finally put down the receiver and tried to think. He wasn't allowed that luxury. His phone buzzed and flashed.

The director spoke as if he were biting off each word and spitting it out. "We must do something immediately," he said. "Put a blanket over this and smother it. Use all the personnel you need. I've spoken to the Élysées. You have *carte blanche.* No one who comes out of this alive is to talk. I'm counting on you."

"We're thin on the ground down there," de Coursin replied. "It will take time to organize . . ."

"I don't want to hear excuses!" the director shouted. "I want results!"

"Yes, sir," de Coursin said. "I'll keep you informed."

The director slammed down the receiver.

De Coursin dialed a number. He requisitioned the director's executive jet and ordered it to be ready for takeoff in an hour. He then dialed the Service Action duty officer, proclaimed a red alert and demanded that six of their best men meet him at the aircraft within the hour. He put down the phone and looked at his watch. The calls had given him a temporary sense of accomplishment. Now, alone in the silence of his office, he was forced to face the truth. No matter how fast he moved they'd probably be too late.

"I'm almost out of film," the cameraman said.

"Then save it," Faubert ordered. "Go on with your question," he told the reporter from the *Provençal.*

"Have you ever regretted the 'eliminations' you've carried out?" the reporter asked.

"No," Faubert replied. "I have just followed orders from my superiors."

"You say that this de Coursin makes such decisions?"

"He does, but up to now he's always been in the shadows."

"The tape's about finished," Bastide said.

"Stop it," Faubert snapped. "We now come to the *pièce de résistance.*" He had not planned or premeditated what he was about to do. The idea had just occurred to him. He was mesmerized by the sound of his own voice. It was as if his true self had been sitting in on the drama as an observer and had found the proceedings dull.

"You are going to witness something historic," Faubert said. The timbre of his voice had become ethereal. The change in its pitch alerted Bastide. Something bad was about to happen.

"Anatole Zavorin," Faubert said, "consider yourself privileged. You're about to die on television." There was a murmur of shock and protest from the cameraman and the light technician. The journalist pocketed his notebook and moved closer to the wall. Bastide's eyes narrowed. He raised the mike slowly, disengaging the cable that covered the derringer.

"I won't do it," the cameraman murmured.

"Then you'll die with him. I'm sure one of your friends would be more than willing to handle the camera then." Faubert approached Zavorin and crouched beside him.

"So, Anatole," he said mockingly, "you should be happy. You'll be a martyr of the Soviet Union . . . and a warning to other KGB scum that get in our way!" Faubert stood up. "Are you shooting in color?" he asked.

"Yes," the cameraman gulped, his hands shaking.

"Good. Steady your camera! Let's have the lights and the sound." Faubert looked directly into the lens. His eyes seemed vacant and he spoke in a monotone.

"You are about to witness the execution of a spy," he said, raising the Beretta. Zavorin winced and closed his eyes, trying to push himself under the washbasin.

Bastide's right hand flashed into the carrying case and came out holding the derringer. His first shot punched a scarlet hole in Faubert's lower throat. Faubert lurched, his free hand trying to staunch the spurting blood. Bastide's second and last shot caught Faubert in the right eye. His legs gave way, his head struck a washbasin with a hollow thump and he fell to the floor.

"*Jésus!*" the cameraman exclaimed, backing away from the carnage. Bastide retrieved Faubert's weapon and knelt over him. There was nothing to be done. The .38 slug had opened the back of his skull. The light technician slumped against the wall in shock. The journalist was retching in a toilet cubicle.

Mattei came through the door with Lenoir and two heavily armed GIPN marksmen. "*Bordel!*" he said. "You got him."

"Yes," Bastide replied quietly, "I got him." He bent over one of the basins to splash cold water on his face. The thick pool of blood from Faubert's wounds had spread across the floor. Mattei moved out of its path.

"See to Zavorin," Bastide told him. "I think he's passed out."

The two DGSE agents appeared, the préfet's deputy behind them.

"Good work," he said, after surveying the scene. "The préfet is on his way over."

Bastide handed the derringer back to Mattei. "Let's get out of here," he said. The DGSE agents moved to block their exit.

"Sorry, Bastide," the préfet's deputy said. "No one leaves here for the moment. *Raison d'état.*"

Bastide was only half listening to Commissaire Aynard. He was exhausted. They had remained in the restroom with Faubert's body for an hour until de Coursin arrived from Paris. Then they'd had to wait another forty minutes until the director of the TV channel and the publisher of the newspaper appeared. De Coursin had held a whispered conversation with the executives. An agreement had finally been reached, the film and tapes confiscated and the TV crew and journalists left in the Palais in the custody of the DGSE. The préfet had not spoken to Bastide. De Coursin had only addressed him once. "Good shooting," he'd said as he'd left. Bastide had been driven back to the Hôtel de Police by the préfet's deputy, where Commissaire Aynard was waiting to speak to him.

"You are fortunate things turned out as they did," Aynard was saying. "You have a knack for hanging on by your toes. Not too many hours ago you were practically a fugitive. The préfet was ready to fire you and I could only agree with him. Now, luck or fate has been kind. You were involved in something very messy. I still don't know exactly what it was. I do know that you and those journalists heard something you shouldn't have. The DGSE and the newsmen's employers are working out that problem. You, Bastide, are my responsibility." Aynard paused, expecting a reaction. There was none. Bastide stared at the commissaire, waiting for him to finish. He felt numb, but he knew a reaction would come in time. In days, a week, a month, his ability to blot out the horror would weaken and it would be there, particularly at night when he was alone. He knew he would relive the shooting when he closed his eyes. He was already having second thoughts about what he'd done. He'd asked himself if he couldn't have overpowered the gunman without using the derringer.

"I've discussed the situation with the préfet," Aynard said, clasping his thin hands together on the desktop. "We're sending you to the ministry for a while. The préfet's put your name at the top of the list for the next exchange slot . . ."

"Exchange slot?" Bastide blurted, puzzled.

"Consider yourself lucky," Aynard said with a cautionary wave of his finger. "You're to retain your rank. It's not a demotion."

"What exchange?"

"Our international program of cooperation with other police organizations," Aynard explained. "Surely you've heard of it?"

"It's never interested me."

"I suggest you get interested. You're allowed three choices in order of preference. You pick your country, as it were. Your eventual assignment, of course, will depend on what's available. Do you speak English?"

"Very little," Bastide replied.

"Well, language qualification isn't essential."

"I prefer to stay in Marseille," Bastide said. "This is my city."

"Not for the moment, it isn't," Aynard replied. "The farther away you are the better. Be sensible, *Bon Dieu!* You've defied the Préfet of Police; you've disobeyed my orders and you know too much about a very sensitive subject. The press would hound you if you remained here. Count your blessings, Bastide. We're only protecting you for your own good. You're to report at the ministry in forty-eight hours!"

"Forty-eight hours! I have things to take care of before I go anywhere. My apartment, my mother in Arles . . ."

"Inspector," Aynard said, obviously irritated, "I know about your mother. We'll watch over her. She can always visit you. It is now close to midnight. It's been a tiring day for all of us. I bid you goodnight!"

"There is one thing," Bastide said.

"Well?"

"I understand you insulted Inspector Mattei and made some inexcusable remarks about his integrity and Corsican origins. If he doesn't receive an apology, I'll be forced to make a full official report of the incident." Bastide turned and walked out of Aynard's office without waiting for his response.

Mattei was waiting in the corridor. He fell into step beside him. "So," he asked, "what's the verdict?"

"I'm still on the payroll and you'll get your apology," Bastide replied, heading for the stairs. His mind was a blur and he definitely needed a drink. He knew Mattei could handle the apartment and his mother could fend for herself. For the moment he was more concerned with Janine.

As they reached the ground floor, Mattei stopped in his tracks and clapped his hand to his forehead. *"Bonne Mère!"* he cursed, "we've forgotten Popov! Magali will never forgive me."

Bastide couldn't help laughing despite all his troubles.

About the Author

Howard R. Simpson, a former U.S. Foreign Service Officer, is now a defense writer and newspaper columnist. One of his last Foreign Service assignments was as American Consul General, Marseille, in 1976. He now lives in Europe. *A Very Large Consulate* is Mr. Simpson's fourth novel to feature Inspector Bastide, and his fifth novel for the Crime Club.